THE CUCKOO SISTER

ALISON STOCKHAM

Boldwood

First published in Great Britain in 2023 by Boldwood Books Ltd.

I

A CIP catalogue record for this book is available from the British Library.

Paperback ISBN 978-1-83518-812-5

Large Print ISBN 978-1-80415-989-7

Hardback ISBN 978-1-80415-988-0

Ebook ISBN 978-1-80415-986-6

Kindle ISBN 978-1-80415-987-3

Audio CD ISBN 978-1-80415-994-1

MP3 CD ISBN 978-1-80415-991-0

Digital audio download ISBN 978-1-80415-985-9

MIX
Paper | Supporting responsible forestry
FSC® C171272

Boldwood Books Ltd

23 Bowerdean Street, London SW6 3TN

www.boldwoodbooks.com

For my parents, Lynn & Fred, who never tried to talk me out of my dreams.

1

The darkness of the evening deepened, draping itself over Maggie as she sat immobile outside the hospital. It was busy as people rushed in, rushed out, rushed home. Time slowed. Maggie felt like she was in one of those photographs where the headlights from passing cars blur into lines, the light still there long after the movement has gone. She felt sharply in focus, with the world around her blurring into a messy tangle.

How did I get here? What happened? It didn't seem so long ago that she was doing a job that she loved, enjoying her freedom, with no ties and with every possibility still at her feet. Now? Her days blurred into a non-stop carousel of chores, only ever interrupted by the seemingly endless stream of arguments between her and Stephen. It was the only focus on which she could hang her days.

An image of Stephen came to her mind, him trying to get out the door and being delayed when he sat down to put on his shoes, only to find the empty banana skin that Maggie had not been able to locate earlier after Emily had eaten its contents.

'Where is it, poppet? It needs to go into the compost bin so the worms can have their tea too,' Maggie had tried to encourage her.

Emily loved worms and was always digging them up to show her mother, like a proud, tiny David Attenborough. It was to no avail and the offending item had gone undetected, until Stephen sat on it in his immaculate work suit.

'What the – for goodness' sake! Maggie! I'm going to have to change, I'm going to be late! I didn't need this today of all days.' He softened his voice a little as he turned to his daughter. 'Emily – the sofa is not a bin.'

Emily had burst into tears at the still sharp tone of her father's voice. Her baby brother, Elliot, also started crying, scared by the sudden shouting. Maggie, exhausted and holding two sobbing children, had succumbed to tears as well. Stephen had apologised but the atmosphere had taken days to recover. The sharp feeling of failure had sat with Maggie as she tried to do better, tried to keep everyone happy, tried to be good enough.

Maggie snapped her head up, aware suddenly of what she was meant to be doing. She should go back. How long had she sat in the dark, muddle headed, on this bench? She didn't know. Only by using the cold that had moved into her fingers, her toes and had reached her core, as a marker did she guess that she had been sitting there far longer than she would have imagined. She got up, tried to encourage the bite in the air on her face to wake her up, get her to focus, but she couldn't do it. The events of the day were playing over and over in her mind.

It had been an awful day, full of tantrums and tears. Everyone was tired. Everyone needed it to be bedtime. Trying to make a decent dinner and being distracted by the children, Maggie had brought two bouncy balls into the kitchen, a way of keeping the children close and entertained while she got their tea ready. Now, with hindsight, crystal clear in the blackness of the evening, Maggie scoffed at herself, remembering feeling a rare success.

She'd solved the need to be in two places at once dilemma. Clever her.

If she had been able to look at this scene from the outside, then maybe she would have seen it coming. She might have been able to visualise just what might go wrong. But, in the middle of it all, it didn't even cross her mind. This is what would haunt her, all her days from this one forward: she hadn't even considered it.

Maggie walked, with no real direction. Just wanting to move, to know that she could. Her feet felt heavy, her legs as though she was wading through thick mud. Her body pushing her onwards, her mind pulling her back. She felt utterly conflicted – what to do, where to go. Images were coming at her, thick and fast now that she was alone with no distraction for her brain. It was busy outside A&E, the hustle and bustle of people coming and going, ambulances arriving. A revolving door of life-changing moments going on around her. She had to get away, to get some peace so that she could think straight. She walked into the darkness of the hospital site, towards the office buildings in front of her and away along the road.

Now she was alone, her shadow from the streetlight her only companion. She leant on its lamp post for balance as she saw herself picking up the pan of pasta and taking it to the sink. One of the balls that the children had been playing with had been abandoned, and it sat, unnoticed, until the exact moment Maggie stood on it. It rolled away, she lost her footing and in trying to right herself, she dropped the pan.

Everything slowed down. But only enough for Maggie to be able to see the horrific thing that was going to happen. Not enough time to do anything to stop it.

The starchy-sweet smell of the pasta came back to her and Maggie turned and vomited onto the grass. She was shaking.

Screams ricocheted in her head. Emily and Elliot howling in pained terror as the scalding water landed on them.

'Mummy! Mummmyyyyy!'

The water splashed over Emily, like a slap in the face; landed on Elliot's back like shards of glass cutting into his baby soft skin.

Maggie spat out the bile from her mouth, its sourness clinging to her taste buds like poison. She gulped down the cold air and stood up. She was resolute. She knew that she had to keep on walking. She couldn't go back.

She had done the one thing she feared most. She had hurt her children. She was disgusting, she was neglectful and the best thing she could do for anyone was to keep on walking. Just get away. She put one foot in front of the other until she had no idea where she was.

Suddenly, her pocket buzzed, making her jump. Maggie reached in and took out her phone. She held it up, her screen photo of all of them together and smiling. Happy families. They say the camera never lies. *Everything lies.* Trying hard to concentrate on the letters in front of her, Maggie looked at the screen again. Rose.

Her sister was calling her, most likely wondering where she had got to. She'd just popped out for a breath of fresh air. The yellow strip lighting and low ceilings of the hospital had been making her eyes hurt and her head pound. She'd left the children with Rose and Stephen, hadn't noted the time, so now she had no idea how long she'd been gone. Maggie couldn't seem to focus for more than a few seconds at a time. Her mind was distorting her thoughts and replaying the scenes from the afternoon, constantly interrupting any clear or rational thinking.

The phone jumped impatiently in her hand as it continued to ring and ring and ring. Eventually, it fell silent as it went to voicemail. Maggie waited until a notification beeped. Then it rang again.

She dropped her hand to her side, dropped the phone to the grass verge and kept on walking. Rose would be all right. She always was.

Rose had been the one to save the day. Maggie had been in a state of hysteria arriving at the hospital. The A&E staff had been so kind, gentle with both her and the children, reassuring them at every stage. It had shown Maggie that she had not at any point explained to the children what was happening. She had been so on autopilot, calling 999, getting them under a cooling shower to stop their skin cooking, to stop the burn seeping into their flesh, that she hadn't thought of how scared they must have been. It was yet another failure – stacking up on all the others.

Leaving Emily and Elliot in the clearly more capable hands of the doctors, Maggie had trembled as she brought her phone to her ear, not really knowing how she would begin to explain this to Stephen. He would be angry. Over the years, his affectionate understanding of her flaws had turned into thinly veiled annoyance. She was making his life harder. She was supposed to make it easier. He had his job. The kids were hers, and clearly, he felt that she wasn't up to scratch. No matter what she tried, somehow since the children, they'd been out of sync. She often felt a million miles away from him, despite being in the same room.

His phone rang and rang then cut off. Pulled up short, Maggie brought the phone down to look at the screen. He had rejected her call. Angry at his persistent keeping of family at arm's length when it came to work, she dialled his number again and stood, tense, while the tone rang. A shorter time now before it was cut off once more.

'Are you kidding me?' Maggie shouted and the sound echoed down the empty corridor. Dialling a third time, Maggie closed her eyes. She knew it wouldn't help her cause if he could not be got hold of. Defective mother, absent father. She was in the middle of working out what she was going to say to the safeguarding people who were on their way when suddenly Stephen's voice was in her ear, urgent and whispered.

'What is it, Maggie? I'm in the middle of an important meeting. Can't this wait?' he asked through clenched teeth, talking to her but clearly performing for the benefit of the others in the room with him.

'We're in A&E. The children. There was an accident, a pan of boiling water got dropped.' Maggie noted that she had moved into the passive, not placing the blame where she felt it sat. With her.

'What?' he asked, suddenly switching his focus, work forgotten as panic rose in his voice. 'What happened? Are they okay?' he asked, and she heard the sounds of him rising from his chair and leaving the room for the confidentiality of the corridor. Maggie waited until he was where he could talk.

'I don't know yet. They've been burnt. They were splashed with the boiling water, but I don't know how badly. I got them into the shower and called the ambulance. The doctor is looking over them now. I have to get back to them.' Maggie's eyes brimmed with un-spilt tears as she glanced back towards where they were. She was grateful that he was at the end of the phone. He would understand how she was feeling. He was silent for a long time as he processed the information.

'So, the doctor is with them now. They're being looked after, they're okay?' He was working something out in his head, but Maggie couldn't decipher what. She heard a door opening, the noise of his office flooding into the background.

Maggie opened her mouth to speak but paused.

'I just have to finish this meeting first.' He sounded strained. 'It won't be long. Then I'll be right there... I can get the... yes, I can make the quarter-to train. I'll miss the earlier one even if I leave now. I'll finish up here, then head straight to you. I'll be there as soon as I can... Pardon? Yes, yes, I'm done now...' he said, to whoever in the room held his attention, to whoever was more important to him than his family.

'I've got to go. I'll be there as soon as I can,' he said, his attention already turned back to the meeting. It was clear in his voice. Maggie could tell she was alone. Not wanting to ask for fear of his answer and the sinking disappointment she knew she was about to feel in the very core of her, she stalled...

'The social worker is coming to talk with me, you know. Routine. Do you think you'll manage to be here for that?' She was guarded. Her anger at him rising.

'I'll do my best, okay? Give them a kiss from me, I'll be there as soon as I can. I'll leave as soon as I can.'

And with that, the line went dead. He had hung up. Immediately she noticed that although he had been scared for the children, he had not once asked her how *she* was. The kids mattered to him. She did not. Not any more.

Maggie stood, shaking, in the whitewashed corridor. She needed someone who loved the children as she did, who could support her as she was falling apart. She had thought that Stephen would be that person. Obviously not. After a fleeting moment to acknowledge the trouble that her marriage appeared to be in, Maggie had lifted the phone and dialled again. Rose...

Maggie felt guilty as she walked away from the ringing phone on the verge, but also felt her shoulders relax as the insistent beeping of the ring tone faded into the distance. Distance was what she needed. Distance was what everyone needed. She was toxic, and the only way that she could improve the mess she had made was to walk away. To remove herself from the equation. Maggie shuddered at her own euphemism.

Rose would be furious. Rose, her beloved younger sister who had immediately dropped everything the moment Maggie had told her where she and the children were. She had not hesitated to see if it was more important than what she was doing because they were *always* the most important thing to her. Maggie had only had to hold herself together until Rose had arrived, walking into the department as fast as she could in her heels, tucking her phone away into her camel-coloured coat as she did so. Rose was the polar opposite to her tall, dark-haired sister: petite, with an hourglass figure and blonde hair that fell down her back in waves. She had intense green eyes and a quality that made people turn back to look at her as they walked past. She was clearly *someone*. It was only because Rose had been there that Maggie had managed to keep it together once they got to the children's bedsides.

The doctors were still tending to Emily and Elliot when Maggie and Rose had walked back in. Standing by their beds, talking to a medical student, was a lady who had not been there before. On one hand, she looked like the other nurses in the department, but there was something... different about her. Her body language was distinct, less open. She caught Maggie's eye and smiled, tucking a strand of her straight brown hair behind her ear as she did so. She looked nervous, like she hadn't been doing this job too long and still wasn't sure how best to get started. Maggie's stomach felt like it had dropped through the floor, as though she were on a fairground ride that she desperately wanted to get off.

'Mummy's back, Auntie Rose too,' Maggie called over to the children, not feeling that she could make her way to them, not feeling they were hers. They were being treated and she needed to give the doctors space.

'How are they?' Maggie asked, not entirely sure who she was directing the question to. She just needed to know that they were okay.

'You must be Mummy.' The woman glanced down at her notes. 'Maggie,' she said, looking up at her again. 'The doctors are liaising with the burns unit at the moment. It's borderline and they want to be sure,' she said matter-of-factly.

Maggie couldn't hold the words in her mind long enough to decode them. 'Borderline' – what did she mean by that? Just how bad was it? What had she done?

'Maggie?' the lady repeated at her, bending her head slightly to try to catch her eye. The lady looked at her in a way Maggie felt was half pity, half suspicion.

'I'm Rose, the children's aunt,' Rose said, moving herself forward and offering her hand. 'And you are...' she smiled.

Rose had all of the charm. People generally fell at her feet and she had to do very little other than be herself. It was wonderful to watch. People melted in front of her as though they were butter and Rose a warmed knife. She rarely had to be sharp. No one needed her to be.

'I'm Ms Watson,' the lady replied, looking a little shy. She coughed, embarrassed, as Rose continued to smile at her. 'Ms Watson. Penelope. Um. People call me Penny,' she faltered and started checking her notes again as a blush rose up from her chest, peppering her collarbone with a pinkish rash. This continued slowly up her face until she was practically glowing before she looked up again.

'Penny,' Rose repeated. 'How lovely.' She smiled at her. Penny looked as though she couldn't quite work out if Rose was being kind or gently teasing her, which was also a fairly common reaction to Rose, Maggie noted. She had this effortlessness that could be misconstrued as false, but it was from a lifetime of getting her own way. Things *were* effortless if you were Rose. You got what you wanted.

Chairs appeared for them, a gesture clearly for Rose. She glanced at the medical student who had brought them and threw him enough sunshine to get him through the rest of his shift with a smile on his face. Once he had gone though, she stood next to Elliot's bed and started chatting to the children. She nodded at Maggie, indicating that she and Penny could start their own conversation now that the children were distracted.

Penny shifted in her seat, cleared her throat, and began. Maggie sat, holding her hands in each other to stop them shaking and tried to look Penny in the eye. It wasn't fair, Maggie thought, how the body language of fear was so close to that of guilt. She had spent the children's entire lives petrified that someone was going to catch her out, to tell her that she was a bad mother, that she shouldn't be a parent at all. After all, it's not like she planned them, was it? She didn't choose to become a mother, other than deciding not to have the abortions she had actively considered. How many times in their short lives had she questioned whether she'd made the right choice? The resentment at her own needs being pushed to the back of the queue overwhelmed her at times. Good mothers didn't feel like that, did they? Maggie was terrified that she wasn't worthy, and now, finally, someone was here to tell her that.

'So, Maggie,' Penny finally said, looking up to smile at her. It made Maggie feel as though she were on trial all the same. 'As I believe the doctor told you earlier, I'm from the safeguarding liaison team. We just like to check in with families who may be having a difficult time of things, to see if we can offer any support. So...' She paused again to look at her notes. 'Tell me what happened. How did we all get here?'

Maggie said nothing. Penny looked at her expectantly and then gestured her arm at her in a 'you next' manner. Maggie stared at her, worrying that Penny would think her stupid for staying silent, but what could she say?

'Maggie?' Penny tried again.

Maggie cleared her throat and looked up at the ceiling, aware she was behaving oddly, yet unable to stop herself.

She turned to Penny and said blankly, 'I was cooking dinner. Pasta. There was a toy on the floor of the kitchen I hadn't seen. I turned to the sink to drain the pasta water and I trod on it. I slipped, I lost my hold on the pan and I dropped it. The children were in the kitchen with me, playing. The pan bounced, and the water jumped out and splashed them. I took them upstairs to put the cool shower on them and called 999.' She stopped. If she just stuck to the facts, then any further questions would give her a steer on what they were trying to get her to say.

Penny looked at her again.

'Maggie. How are *you*? Would you say you get overwhelmed a lot?' She paused, briefly, then continued. 'How are you sleeping? Do you have a support network you can call on?'

Flashbacks from when Elliot was born and the post-natal depression questionnaire crashed into Maggie's mind. She had known what the answers needed to be in order to 'pass' and she hadn't wanted to admit to her failings. To admit them to others would be to admit them to herself. Believing in the professional experience of the health visitor to know of maternal subterfuge, Maggie had answered 'correctly'.

'Okay, Mummy, then that's great! I can officially discharge you!' the health visitor had said and ticked the box.

Maggie hadn't known whether to feel relieved or crushed. She had mostly just felt broken.

This time, beyond fearful of what consequence a 'wrong' answer might result in, Maggie took a deep breath and smiled straight at Penny. 'I'm sleeping okay, as much as you can with two such young ones. I have my sister, as you can see, and my husband is on his way here now. He won't be long,' she said, editing out the lack of practical or emotional support she had from him. 'It had been a long day and the children wanted to be near me while I prepared dinner. It was an accident.'

Penny met her gaze, trying to work out whether this was a one-off, an accident pure and simple, or the result of failings elsewhere.

'Maggie, I know it's hard work being a mother.' She looked down to check her notes once again. 'I see that they're two and one years old. Close together. That must be nice for them, if hard on you. Look, I know that the days are long...' Penny said, not completing the cliché she fell back on. 'Parenting brings plenty of challenges, as I'm sure you know. So how can we make sure this situation doesn't get repeated?'

Maggie couldn't look Penny in the face. She dug her nails into her hand to stop her from losing her tenuous grip on her composure. Sullenly, quietly, Maggie replied. 'I will make sure from now on that they are not in the kitchen when I drain hot water.'

Maggie then sat in silence. What could she say? Penny was right. It had been her fault.

'Okay,' Penny said suddenly, closing her notebook and tucking it under her arm as she rose. 'I'll chat things through with the team. We will follow up with you in a few days, make sure everything is well.'

She held her hand out to shake Maggie's, which she reciprocated in shock. 'Nice to meet you, Maggie. You too, Rose.' And with that, she turned and left.

Rose got up off the bed and came over to Maggie. Maggie felt like a piece of laundry, wrung out and draped on the line.

'See?' Rose said, quietly and reassuringly. 'It was an accident.'

Maggie let Rose hold her up whilst she felt she was splintering apart. What was she supposed to do now? Mothers are supposed to *know* but she never did. She'd read all the books she was supposed to, and yet this instinct that she was supposed to have just wasn't there. In her life before, as a costume designer, she would look at material, at buttons, zips, fastenings, and just *know* what needed to go where and how it would look when it was done. What sort of person can create a dress but have no idea about another human? Maggie had never stopped to consider that her design instinct was moulded by years of training and experience that as a mother, she just didn't have yet. She only saw the flaws – as though she were a dress with poorly stitched seams and uneven hems, waiting to come apart with a single pull on a loose thread.

'Maggie!'

She snapped round at the voice to see Stephen, pink in the cheeks and slightly out of breath.

'There… were no cabs, so I… ran. I knew it'd be faster. How – how are they?' he breathed, as a sheen of sweat formed on his face. It was cold outside, but overly warm on the ward and he looked almost soggy as he stood there in his work suit and wool coat. Literally suited for somewhere else.

'God, Stephen,' Rose admonished, 'you and your bloody running!'

Rose stepped forward to explain the latest, it being clear that Maggie was in no fit state. The two of them walked together to the children, who were excited at their father's arrival.

Maggie was pale, trembling and mute. Now Stephen had arrived, she could switch off, shut down. The children were no longer her sole responsibility. Looking at the tableaux before her – two children, Stephen and Rose – moved Maggie into action. Slowly, without wanting to bring attention to herself, she picked up her bag and walked out of the door. She did not look back. She could not look back. The door closed behind her, with barely a sound.

2

Maggie wandered, directionless, down residential streets darkened by the late November sky. Winter was starting to take hold, before the defensive festive lights pushed back the encroaching darkness. Several houses had curtains open, the lives being lived within them shown off like shadow puppet theatres. Family dinners being eaten, school children finishing homework, happy couples enjoying time together. Each one a slap in the face. She didn't deserve a family. Her family didn't deserve her. She stumbled onwards, not looking where she was going. She could barely see straight. Her mind was running through all the reasons that she *had* to keep walking, keep going, keep putting distance between her and her children. She had to keep them safe.

Even before the horror of the dropped pasta, the hospital, and the safeguarding lecture, she could list error after error. She had not remained calm, she had shouted, she had made them cry with harsh words. Maggie felt ashamed. Day after day, she was coming up short and letting them down. They were saddled with a tired, sad, impatient mother who failed to sit and enjoy them without half an eye on something else.

'Enjoy every moment,' she was so often told, usually just at a moment that even a saint would struggle to enjoy. 'It goes so fast,' was another regular comment. This made her panic. That in the day-to-day stumbling through motherhood, desperately trying to get it right – she was missing it. Missing the joy, the love, the wonder, that the same people told her she must be experiencing. Was she? Maggie asked herself. Maggie thought of all the times she had yearned for her life before. Had she ever really felt the same love for her new life that she clearly felt for her old? The question hit Maggie in the guts. She felt guilty for even asking it but guiltier still when she couldn't bring herself to answer. Certainly, she wasn't happy with her life right at that moment, but was she *unhappy*? Everything had happened so quickly, marriage then Emily, then Elliot, all within two years, that she hadn't had time to think about anything, she had just been reacting to circumstance.

Maggie felt a wave of despair wash over her, cold and cruel. *What the hell was she playing at? What the hell did she think she was doing?* Her injured children were still in hospital, Stephen and Rose would be worried at her disappearance, and here she was, wandering the streets. She should go back. Back to her family. Except family to Maggie was where she felt like she was failing, every single day.

Tears welled in her eyes at the thought of the mess she had created. She loved her children with every shred of her soul, but she also knew that she was a terrible mother. She couldn't even get the basics right. Neither of them slept well, they were often tired. Neither was a great eater. Emily was at the stage where every single thing became a battle. She might have blinded Emily, might have disfigured them both for life. She was a worthless mother. Defective. Her own mother obviously wondered why Maggie was finding it so hard when she had managed perfectly well in her day. Little comments lanced at her: 'Well, you know what I'd say, but...' And then a long pause, followed by a defeatist sigh. 'But you have your own ways and apparently that works for you.'

Maggie remembered when she had been floored by a sickness bug. Stephen was away and she had begged Rose to help her as Maggie could barely leave the bathroom. Rose had taken both children out for a while so that Maggie could rest.

'You should have seen us, Maggie. The kids were perfectly behaved for me and everyone we met commented on what a perfect family we were,' Rose had said when they got back. Maggie recalled feeling both proud of her sister, relieved that it had gone well but also annoyed at her for rubbing in how easy it was. Rose often had limited patience with people in general and yet she seemed to have endless patience and understanding for terrible-two behaviour and could stay calm while the children raged.

Hot tears cascaded down Maggie's face as she realised that her sister, a difficult person to handle, an easy person to love, would be a better mother for her children. Rose was the one with them now, after all, whereas she was a tear-stained mess, stumbling through throngs of people on the street.

'I'm a disaster,' she whispered to herself. 'I should just do everyone a favour and disappear.'

She wiped her face on the sleeve of her jumper and desperately tried to think clearly.

Disappear.

If she were to go, then Rose would *have* to step in to look after Emily and Elliot. They were the only people Maggie had never seen Rose be selfish with. For the children, she was always her best self, maybe because they were what she wanted. She'd always wanted a family.

Stephen... well, he'd cope. Maggie wasn't sure that he cared any more anyway, not since the birth of Elliot. He always had his mind on his job, the idea of being the breadwinner so important to him.

'We could send Emily and Elliot to a nursery, just a few hours a week. I could do a little freelance work, bring some money in. It'd take the pressure off. Off us both. Or a nanny, they could stay home with a nanny,' she had begged.

'No. It's okay. I am fine. We're fine. They're still little, they need their mother, they don't need a stranger. It'd confuse them. They need not to feel abandoned.'

He hadn't seen her desperation, desperation for some space to breathe. He hadn't seen her drowning. He loved the children fiercely. They were what mattered to him. He'd be fine.

Her babies. Her dear babies. She wanted the best for them and she knew now that the best wasn't her. It would be horrible, hard, of course it would, but they *would* be safe.

She could do this. She *had* to do this. She *had* to keep them safe. Penny had said it. It was the single most important thing she could do for them.

But how many nights would they cry for her? How many days would they go to the door expecting it to be her and be disappointed?

Maggie stopped suddenly, nearly causing the man behind to crash into her. He muttered at her as he swerved past. 'Idiot!' She tried to calm her breathing, trying to calm her mind.

She hadn't said goodbye. She couldn't not say goodbye.

She hadn't prepared herself for this. This wasn't right – just leaving them at the hospital.

But.

It was *her* fault they were there in the first place, wasn't it? Maybe they hated her, maybe they would even be *scared* of her. Maybe they would cling to Stephen, to Rose. The ones they knew loved them but had never hurt them. She felt sick. The idea that her children no longer trusted her to keep them safe. She no longer trusted herself. She had to go.

Images of Emily and Elliot, all smiles and giggles, came to her. The thought of never seeing them again made her stomach contract and bile rise up in her throat. Could she walk away from them, from their faces nuzzled against hers, breathing in their sweet breath as they fell into sleep, their limp trusting bodies relaxing against her as they drifted off? Could she walk away and pray against all hope that one day they would understand that she did this for them? Would they ever forgive her?

She loved them so much, but she was failing them. She couldn't love them *really*, because she was drowning just trying to care for them. They deserved better than she could give them. Maybe she was justifying it to herself, maybe it was the truth.

For the first time in what felt like years, Maggie had a plan and she could see it clearly in her mind's eye. She *would* disappear.

Suddenly, as if the universe had been bringing her to this understanding, she turned the corner to find that she had walked to the coach station. Its noise and lights were a shock to her, and she recoiled. She needed calm, quiet, dark. Nothing.

It was late now, Stephen and Rose would be worried and the children would be needing to go to sleep. Were they home? Or in hospital still? Maggie hoped that Rose would remember how to get them to sleep wherever they were. She hoped that Emily's hair would be stroked as she snuggled down in bed. That someone would have brought Elliot his favourite blanket to hold. That Rose would mother them. Maggie couldn't any more. She had done them so much harm. She had to cut them from her mind, if such a thing was even possible. She knew that she couldn't think clearly here, so close to home. She needed their apron strings to stretch so far that they had to break. Only then could she decide how to end things, how not to get it wrong again.

No. No! This is wrong! I have to go back to them. They need me. They need their mother.

Maggie shook her shoulders to try to shake off some of the heaviness that she felt and put her hand into her pocket to get her phone to check tickets and timetables, her mind working hard to focus on the necessary logistics, shutting everything else out. Her fingers closed around space. Her phone. At first, she panicked but then recalled dropping it and walking away. A feeling of weightlessness briefly washed over her. She was disconnected. This was the right thing to do.

Maggie made her way to the information kiosk, hoping that it was still even possible to buy a ticket in person.

'How can I help?' the lady asked, still chirpy at what looked like the end of a long day if the number of empty mugs littered around her was any indicator. They reminded Maggie of the half-drunk cups of tea, cooling, as she desperately tried to get Elliot to feed properly, or to calm Emily as another tiredness tantrum tore through her. 'Yes, love, can I help you?' the lady asked again, gesturing at a queue forming behind Maggie as she stood, mute and motionless.

'Oh, sorry. I'd like a ticket to... to, um, to Glasgow, I guess. Please,' Maggie found herself saying, shocked at the words coming out of her mouth. She opened her purse and found that she had money.

'Cambridge to Glasgow – you'll need to change at Birmingham.'

She paid the lady, took her ticket, and walked to her stop.

Standing by the coach, a visceral wave of pain shot through her, squeezing at her chest as if a band had tightened around it. Maggie struggled to stay upright. She swallowed it down and forced her resisting legs to take the three small steps up into the coach. The door shut behind her, the driver wanting to keep the warm air inside, stale though it was, rather than let in the evening chill. Maggie sat down and pressed her nails into the back of her hand in order to stop herself from getting off. She needed to cancel out her brain until it was done. It wasn't working. She could feel herself wanting to tear her body off the seat – warm and overly patterned, so as not to show how grubby it was – and run back home to her children.

But something was holding her firm, refusing to let her get up. This was *for* them, they would be better, more rested, happier. Safe. Better with a different mother. Happier with someone else. She was bad for them, she was bad for their development, for their happiness. *She* was bad. Maggie pushed harder into her hand, the pain stopping the tears coming as her blood started to leak out of the tiny cuts she was making in her skin. She held her breath, her body shaking as the doors opened and shut one more time and the driver started the engine. The coach moved back and out of the depot, and she was away. She was gone.

3

Rose stepped through the door into the darkened house, followed by Stephen, carrying both children, half-asleep, over his shoulder. It was late and the house was silent and cold.

'She's not here,' Rose said, looking worriedly at her brother-in-law. He shook his head, his expression a mixture of concern and annoyance, and something else Rose couldn't put her finger on.

'I'll take these two up to bed and then we can sort things out,' he replied, as he gingerly headed to the stairs, trying not to jolt Emily and Elliot, who clung to him. Rose stepped forward and kissed them on the top of their heads, breathing in the scent of childhood – warm, and scented like crayons and soap, with an additional unwelcome medicinal tang.

'Night-night, my darlings.'

Rose watched as the three of them disappeared into the upstairs darkness, their outlines silhouetted from light that streamed in from the street through the landing window. It should have been a sweet scene; two sleepy kids being tucked into bed by their loving father. Rose swallowed hard. The children were going to be okay; the hospital had assured them that Maggie had done all the right things, the burns would most likely heal without scarring and the local nurse would check up with them to arrange changing dressings and to see that all was healing well.

'Paracetamol,' Rose said out loud to the empty hallway, reminding herself that the nurse had suggested they have some ready for when the hospital painkillers wore off in the night. She walked into the kitchen to where the medicines were kept in a high-up cupboard and turned on the light.

'Jesus...'

The scene in front of her caused Rose to take a sharp intake of breath. It was carnage. There was a burnt smell which Rose managed to track down to the pan of what might once have been pasta sauce but was now charred and stuck fast to the bottom of the pan. The floor was covered with sticky pasta water and cooked pasta, apart from two distinct areas where there was none, and the starchy residue had been wiped at. Rose felt sick. It was like looking at those chalk outlines of a body, only the marks were where her niece and nephew had been, the boiling water sticking to their delicate skin rather than to the floor.

'No, Daddy, it hurts! Don't go, no!'

Rose turned back to look at the hallway, hearing the cries of Emily and Elliot.

'Okay, it's okay.'

'Daddyyyy,' Emily wept from upstairs.

Should she go up? Did Stephen need help? Where on *earth* was Maggie? Unsure of what best to do, Rose started picking up the mess around her. The chaos wasn't just from the accident either, there was laundry in piles everywhere, some dirty, some clean. The washing up was half done, there were toys all over the place. If tidy house, tidy mind was a thing, Maggie was clearly in a bad place.

She'll be home soon. She can't have gone far, Rose thought as she picked up the pasta, wiped down the surfaces and tried to clean away any trace of the awful scene that the room held within it. The children didn't need to see this, neither did Stephen. They had enough to deal with. Rose felt a sense of satisfaction as she brought the room back into order.

She looked up at the clock above the kitchen door. It had been a housewarming gift from Stephen's father, Edward, and Rose recalled the moment Maggie had unwrapped it, the memory sharp in her mind.

Stephen's father had laughed when Maggie pulled back the stiff, smart wrapping paper and beautiful ribbons. 'Now you have no excuse for being late all the time!' He had looked around the room, expecting humorous agreement with him on this perceived flaw of his daughter-in-law's. Maggie had tried hard to smile politely. Rose had winced. Stephen's father never seemed to have a kind word for her sister. Nothing she did was ever good enough, and that was before she'd had the children.

She was late now, though, Rose thought. She should have called back; she should have come back to the hospital. She should be here.

'Where *are* you?' Rose said out loud.

Had something happened to her? Or was she roaming the darkened streets in distress? Rose shivered and wrapped her arms around herself.

Rose had known for a while that all was not well with her sister's marriage. But today it had been loud and clear for anyone who knew them. Thinking back, at the hospital, did they even speak to each other? Both she and Stephen had been so focused on the children that neither saw Maggie leave.

Not sure what to do with herself, but not feeling that she could sit down either, Rose wandered from room to room. She'd been here a million times, but had she ever really *looked*? What had she missed all those other times? What signs had she been oblivious to? She stopped by a photo on the living room mantlepiece, all of them sat together on the floor of the photographer's studio. A family, a group, a unit. Looking more closely, Rose saw a tautness to Stephen's jaw and a redness to Maggie's eyes. Not all happy families then on this day either, it seemed. Elliot looked like Maggie but Emily was the spitting image of her Aunt Rose with the same green eyes and blonde wavy hair she'd had as a child. Rose picked the picture up, wiped a thin layer of dust from the glass and gazed longingly at it as she wondered if her own children would look the same. She wanted *this*. She wanted a family of her own. She was the adored baby of the family and she was used to getting her own way. Charming, even as a child, she had a way of knowing how best to present a question so as to get the answer she wanted. She understood what made people tick and how that was useful to her. She expected everything and she usually got it – in all things but this.

It hadn't passed Rose as unironic that her sister, without effort, had ended up with a husband and two children. A family that she knew that Maggie was never 100 per cent sure that she had wanted. Whereas she absolutely did want a family but was single and had not met anyone lately that suggested this would be changing anytime soon. Rose wouldn't admit it, to herself or anyone else, but she was envious of her sister. The children were beautiful and funny and obviously adored their mother. Maggie had everything and Rose felt that she had nothing. Nothing that mattered. She could see how it would suit her so much better than Maggie. Sometimes life just wasn't fair.

'Rose?'

Stephen's voice, tight with stress, called from upstairs, breaking Rose's train of thought.

'Yes?'

'Can you come up here? I need you.'

Rose ran upstairs to the children's bedroom with a hint of pleasure at being needed. The door was open, throwing light into the dimly lit room where Stephen was struggling to get pyjamas onto the children. Drawers were left opened and messy, where he had rifled through them to find what he was looking for. He looked up at her, ruffled and exhausted. Something inside her jolted but she pushed it away.

'Not enough hands. I can't get them over their heads gently enough and hold it away from the sore patches.' He looked pained, desperate.

Elliot sniffled. 'Ow!'

'I know, lovely,' Rose said, nodding sympathetically. 'What we need here is a team effort!' she said, taking things under her control. Her bright smile spread to the others in the room and there was a shift in the atmosphere. Rose was here, so everything would be okay.

'Arms up, lovely,' Rose said gently as she and Stephen eased first Emily, then Elliot into their PJs. *This would have been easier with Maggie here, someone who knows what they're doing*, Rose thought, silently admonishing her sister for wandering off. Rose tried not to nudge the sore skin on Emily's face. It had been so close to being so much worse, the burn right next to her eye. Rose shivered as she thought of the 'what ifs...' and knew Maggie must be feeling the same.

Rose checked her watch again. What was keeping Maggie? She'd been gone for hours now. It was cold and dark out there. A tingle of misgiving ran down her spine.

'Into bed now,' Stephen said, giving Rose a grateful look.

'Where's Mama?' asked Emily. 'Mama does stories, Mama puts me to bed. I want Mama!'

Stephen looked panicked. He said nothing. He clearly didn't know what to say.

'It's a Daddy story time tonight. It's special. Mama is out at the moment. She'll be back as soon as she can,' Rose said, knowing this to be vague enough to be true and reassuring. She dipped down to kiss them both on their heads. 'You two snuggle down now and get comfy.'

'Ow! Ow!' Emily yelled as she snuggled into her usual sleeping position. She leapt up again.

'Ow,' Elliot echoed.

'Oh, darlings, I know... The paracetamol. I left it downstairs. Back in two ticks.'

Where have you got to? Rose thought as she went downstairs. She took her phone from her pocket. Dialling Maggie's number, Rose leant wearily on the doorframe. The phone rang and rang and rang... then went to voicemail.

'Hi, it's Maggie, leave a message and I'll get back to you!' her sister's voice rang out.

'Mags, it's me. Where are you? You can't just walk out of a hospital and leave your kids, for God's sake! What are you playing at? Call me back, or better still, come home!' Rose snapped as she hung up. She immediately felt bad. She called again but it went to voicemail once more. This was not a normal day and Maggie was not in a normal place. She didn't need to be yelled at.

Rose took deep breaths as she walked back upstairs with the medicine. Stephen was struggling to get them to settle. Elliot had turned into a limpet and would not let go. It was impossible to do anything but hold him. Emily was also very clingy and was tired and teary.

'Where's Mama? I want Mama. Mama!'

Rose sat on the floor between the two beds and stroked her niece's head.

'She'll be back, poppet, she'll be back.'

The reassurance was both for Emily and for herself. Rose gave both children some painkillers to help them to sleep.

'Let's all hop into bed and we can snuggle down and read a story while we wait for her, shall we?' she whispered into the darkened room. She laid Emily into her bed and arranged Elliot next to her, careful not to nudge any of the dressings. The siblings wriggled close to each other, comforted by the other's presence and the familiarity of their room.

Stephen stepped back, clearly happy to have someone else in charge here. He may have been wonderful at his job, but he was clearly clueless when it came to the kids. This was not his domain. Here, Rose happily commanded the room and he backed away, leaving her to it.

She picked a book that she knew they both loved and started to read. Mid-way through the story, Rose paused as she noticed a change in the children's breathing. Both had fallen asleep. A peace washed over the room like a switch had been turned off. Rose understood why exhausted parents lived for this moment. You could pause, you could take a breath. Sleeping children were as close to angels as anything in this world could get.

As Rose started to get up, Emily grabbed at her. 'Mama... Mama,' she murmured through her sleep. 'Yes, darling, Mama's here,' Rose said, not wanting to deny the comfort that the word offered, liking how it sounded when said to her. A few moments later, Rose slid off the bed, hoping the closeness of their sibling would mimic the presence of their missing mother.

Tiptoeing out the door, Rose rubbed at her temples as she stood in the hallway. She needed a big glass of wine. She hoped that despite the chaos in the kitchen there might be a bottle in the fridge. She walked downstairs, trying to ignore the heavy feeling in her chest, when she heard a clink of glass in the kitchen.

'Maggie?'

Rose rushed down the rest of the steps and rounded into the kitchen.

'Where the hell have you been?' Rose yelled to confront her missing sister, only to find a shocked-looking Stephen standing by the counter, pouring two glasses of wine.

'Oh,' Rose said, embarrassed at yelling. Or at least yelling at the wrong person. 'I thought you were Maggie, sorry,' she said, not looking him in the eye. Without the children, it felt weird to be on her own with him. They had been so just a small handful of times. He was clearly uncomfortable too and the atmosphere was unsettling.

'No, just me,' Stephen muttered. He took his phone out of his pocket and checked it. 'Nothing. Yours?'

Rose shook her head and glanced above Stephen's to the clock. 'She's been gone hours now. I thought she might have taken a walk to get some air.'

She felt a burning at the back of her nose as her eyes started to fill with tears. She blinked them away. 'Something's not right, is it? No one in their right mind leaves their injured children at the hospital and just walks away, do they?'

Stephen looked at her, nonplussed.

'She obviously wasn't okay,' Rose continued, 'but I presumed that was the shock. She didn't say she was going. I'm worried. Aren't you worried?'

Stephen clearly wasn't listening.

'Um, hello?' Rose snapped, irritated both by Stephen's apparent lack of concern but also, his lack of attention to her. 'She's been gone hours! Something must have happened to her.'

'I know! I know... sorry. Do you think she's okay?' he asked as though just by being her sister, somehow Rose would know.

Rose shook her head. The possibilities of what might have happened to Maggie had been going through her mind once she admitted to herself that her sister had been gone too long. Her instincts were rarely off, and they were screaming at her that something was wrong.

'No, no, I don't think she's okay,' Rose snapped. *For a clever man, he could be bloody stupid sometimes.* His wife had walked out of A&E hours and hours ago. His wife had not come back. His wife was missing.

'I'll, umm... I'll...' he stalled, clearly not knowing what he should do. 'I'll think who might know where she could be.' He got his phone out of his pocket again and started scrolling through the contacts.

'I called her phone, but it rang out twice. I *told* her to call me!' Rose fumed. *When Maggie got home, she would have words with her. This was not funny.* She took a sip of wine and it burned in her throat as she swallowed it.

Stephen, with his glass of wine in one hand, his phone in the other, looked for all the world as though he were simply ordering pizza. He was focused on the screen, frustration clearly building.

'I don't know!' he finally said, throwing the phone down onto the counter with a clatter, clearly angry with someone, whether Maggie or himself. 'I don't know who to call. Your mother? Laura? Maggie never mentioned anyone in particular. I don't know who she sees while I am at work. She never says.'

'You don't ask?' Rose replied dryly.

'This is not my fault!' Stephen shouted.

'What isn't?' Rose retorted. 'We don't know what we're dealing with here, so how do you know it's got nothing to do with you? And keep your voice down. The kids are exhausted. They don't need you waking them up with your yelling. This isn't about you anyway.'

Rose felt sick. She tried to remind herself of her overly dramatic nature, always presuming the worst, and yet she couldn't shake the feeling that this time... this time she was right to be worried. Surely Maggie knew that the children would be distressed and that she and Stephen would be concerned? She wouldn't just walk away. Something must have happened to her. Even a minor incident, she would have called, would have found a way to let them know that she was all right. Suddenly exhausted, Rose walked into the living room and sat down. Stephen followed. They were silent, staring ahead at the fireplace, trying to work out what to do, what to say. Rose was the first to speak.

'Where is she? Did something happen between you two? Why didn't you come to the hospital straight away? Your family needed you,' Rose said, refusing to look at him.

Stephen whipped his head round to his sister-in-law, his face twisted in anger. 'What do you mean? I was at *work*, but I got there as soon as I could. The trains, I couldn't have got there any faster. I literally *ran* from the station!'

'Work!' Rose scoffed. 'You're part of this family but frankly it doesn't sound as though you've been pitching in. No wonder she looks broken! And you could have just got a cab *from* the office, straight there!' she spat at him.

'Maggie is the one at home. It's her job to look after the house and the children while I bring in the money for the family. Surely, if she had needed help, she would ask, wouldn't she?' Stephen said, initially confident in this explanation, but clearly losing the certainty the longer he spoke.

Rose read the doubt creeping into Stephen's mind as the expression on his face darkened and small frown lines that sort of suited his face, always slightly too serious, started to appear on his forehead.

She looked at him properly, in a way that she hadn't really done since her sister had brought him home to meet the family. He had the almost permanent look of an overgrown sixth-form head-boy, meaning that he looked both younger than his years and somehow always middle-aged. She had always been nervous around him, unsure as to why, as she was confident with everyone, especially men, who usually fell at her feet in compliant heaps. But Stephen had seemed oblivious to her and Rose hadn't been sure how she felt about it.

Doubt, then fear slowly crept across Stephen's face and Rose took the opportunity to ask the question that neither had wanted to ask.

'She *is* okay, isn't she? This is just some misunderstanding? She's got held up or something?'

Stephen turned, pale-faced, to Rose and said, ever so quietly, 'I don't know. What do we do? Should we call the police?'

The potential seriousness of the situation had clearly sunk in for them both. Rose looked at her feet, which she had not been aware were tapping the floor.

'Okay,' Rose said, taking control of the situation as she stood up. 'I think it's a little early for the police just yet. She can't have gone far. I'll call her friends. You call the hospital just to check that there's not been an accident. While we do that, she'll most likely waltz in the door, with some explanation as to where she has been, and everything will be fine.'

She picked up her phone and then put it down again, looking down at Stephen who had yet to move. 'Um. Who are her friends now?' She chewed a little on her lip, trying to think, the realisation that she knew as little as Stephen did about Maggie's new life beginning to dawn. 'Should I call her old friends? Like you said, there was Laura, from uni. They used to hang out all the time before the kids.'

'Can't hurt. She did mention her from time to time. I just don't remember how recently. Things at work have been really busy and...' Stephen stopped as Rose looked at him, one eyebrow raised in a *don't make excuses* expression. 'I'll call the hospital...' he said. 'Shall I call the safeguarding team?'

'No. No, just A&E. I don't want the safeguarding team sending someone here before we know what we're dealing with,' Rose said firmly. 'The children *are* safeguarded, they're with us. Just call A&E. We can update anyone else when they come to see the children.'

Rose nodded to indicate he should get on with it and he walked through into the hallway, as though it were a confidential business call. Rose could hear the muffled sounds of the one-sided conversation. His long explanation, the pause, the 'I see,' and the 'You're sure?' and the 'Well, thank you anyway,' before Stephen ended the call. He didn't come back.

Rose tentatively moved to the doorway and peeked around. Stephen was sitting, slumped on the stairs, the phone abandoned beside him, his head held in his hands as he rested his elbows on his lap. The sorry sight of him made Rose start to panic.

'So...' Rose asked, almost not wanting to know. Stephen looked up at her and slowly shook his head.

'Nothing. They can't share details, but the receptionist would say that they had received no new admissions of anyone matching Maggie's description. I didn't mention the visit this afternoon. It seemed... unwise... to connect the two. Is that wrong? Should I have said?'

Rose screwed up her face and nodded. 'No. I think that's best. I don't think it would help things. She's not there. That's good, isn't it?'

'Well, yes. But it doesn't tell us where she is, though, does it?'

Suddenly Stephen leapt to his feet. Decisively he walked to the kitchen and returned holding his keys. 'I'm going to find her. She can't be far. This is ridiculous,' he said, switching back into work mode.

He was focused, professional, as though this was a black and white situation that a bit of no-nonsense common sense would fix. He stepped out before returning almost immediately.

'You'll stay here with the children, yes?' he asked.

He was obviously used to picking up his things and leaving the house with no concept of how easy that was in comparison to Maggie's experience. Rose watched him leave and her stomach sank. Just here and there, she was catching glimpses that she hadn't noticed before, tiny suggestions that perhaps her sister had decided enough was enough.

Rose tried to keep herself busy. She called Laura. She was nervous and a little relieved when it went through to voicemail. She left a brief, vague message. Rose had no idea what they could have talked about and the more she spoke of the situation out loud, the more real it was becoming. She wandered the house, hoping that the children wouldn't wake soon and ask again after their mother. She knew from Maggie that they often woke several times, so that she was never really able to switch off, always alert for the call of 'Mama?' from upstairs. Their burns were no doubt sore and Rose was nervous that the night would be a continuous stream of tears, reassurances that Mama would be home soon, medication and cuddles. She would stay. Stephen would never be able to cope by himself. Rose made a cup of tea, but it felt wrong to sit on the sofa and scroll through her phone, or switch on the TV while Maggie was missing. Missing. The word alone made Rose feel sick. She wanted to call their mother and tell her, but on reflection, decided to wait until the morning when there might be further news. No sense making her feel as awful as she and Stephen already did. She pottered about, trying to tidy but mostly just picking things up and putting them down again.

She tried to keep the noise down, but Emily woke and appeared at the top of the stairs, crying out, 'Mama?' in her small, sleepy voice.

Rose went to her.

'No Mama yet, lovely,' she said gently, as she tucked her tearful niece back into bed, 'but your Auntie Rose is here, and I will keep you safe until she gets back. Promise, promise.' She kissed her on the top of her head and stroked her hair until her breathing slowed and she slipped back into sleep, cuddling her bear. 'I'll keep you safe, my lovely,' she whispered again before creeping quietly back downstairs.

Rose returned to the kitchen and started to sort out the laundry that had been washed and dried. She sighed and thought how in any other circumstances this would have been wonderful. Two beautiful children sleeping upstairs, a lovely house and a husband soon to return. *If Maggie has chosen to walk away from this, then she's a fool*, Rose thought disloyally, as she folded the last of the tiny socks away.

4

She could hear them laughing. A cackling sound that came again and again from the trees on the shoreline. Perched on the top branches, swaying in the breeze that was whipping across the sea – the magpies were laughing at her. One mean-eyed little bird swooped past, dancing in the wind about her. It glared, then flew further towards the horizon. It was returned to the shore by the air stream that buffeted its black, white and green wings, fanning her face as it passed her.

One for sorrow, two for joy. How many for failure? Maggie thought, before pushing the question away. It wouldn't matter soon anyway. The water was ice cold around her. It had been painful at first, but then the beautiful numbness, a nothingness had crept in, shutting out the pain. She had waited long enough but the time was now.

Standing waist deep in the water, she was shivering violently as her body tried to fight against the enveloping cold. If anyone had glanced across the water, they could have misconstrued her as a piece of driftwood, stuck in the sand at the bottom of the waves, looking out as the sea headed towards the western horizon.

Maggie took another glance back towards the shore. She had thought that Ailsa would be here. That Maggie would not be alone here as she had been back home. Ailsa had said that she was at this beach at the same time every day and yet – not today. Another miscalculation. Another mistake. No more, Maggie couldn't take any more. She took a step further into the waves.

A loud 'bark' rang out against the rocks of the shoreline as a chocolate-brown dog bounded its way across the sand, followed by a lone woman, wrapped up against the chill. As she neared, she stopped and looked out towards Maggie.

'Hey!' she shouted.

Maggie didn't react. She heard her voice, one she thought she recognised, but the words, the details, were swirled away from her. The world was going fuzzy at its edges as her brain started to give in to the cold that the North Atlantic current had brought to this Scottish shore. 'Hey!' the lady called again as she got closer. She dipped down to her dog.

'Stay.'

She took off her shoes and jacket and waded in towards Maggie. Maggie turned to look briefly, then turned away and started to walk further into the sea. There was nowhere to go but under. The woman stopped and called to her again.

'Maggie? Maggie, is that you? What are you doing? Stop, please stop. Let me help you. Please, come back, we can get you warmed up...'

Maggie stopped. Now was the time to choose, to decide before the choice was made for her. She knew how unforgiving the sea could be, how the waves would come and take you before you'd even had time to see them coming. That was how she had planned it. She would offer herself to the waves and they would take her, dragging her down to oblivion. Her breathing was slow and shallow. All she wanted was to go to sleep and not have to do this any more.

Emboldened by her pause, Ailsa called again to her.

'Please. Maggie, please. Just don't go any further.'

She edged closer, reaching her hands out towards Maggie, beckoning her back towards her, the shore and safety.

'Please...' she repeated, her teeth chattering with cold. 'There is another way, this doesn't have to be how it ends,' she pleaded.

Finally, Maggie turned around to look at her, seeing the concern etched on her face now that she was close enough to see in the half-light.

'Don't you see? It's already over.'

5

Rose opened her eyes and blinked repeatedly to push sleep from them. Daylight was peeking through unfamiliar curtains, and she took a moment to work out where she was. The light in the room suggested that it was still early morning; cold but bright. The house was quiet. Rose pulled herself up and sat in bed. She was at Maggie's, the clutter of the spare room glaringly different to her own bedroom, which was minimalist and serene. Rose's bedroom was a sanctuary of calm. This room was not that.

As Rose moved, her head felt heavy after a night of interrupted sleep, waking several times to comfort the children. She and Stephen had both tried their best but all they really wanted was their mother.

How does she do this, night after night? Rose thought, registering how atrocious she felt after just one. She'd barely finished her glass of wine last night before Stephen returned from his search with nothing, and yet she felt hungover.

It had been a night of high emotion. Elliot in particular, too young to understand why his mother wasn't there, had cried until he had been sick, succumbed to exhaustion, and then whimpered still in his sleep. Emily had eventually refused to sleep unless someone was with her. 'Stay, Daddy!' she'd cried and so Stephen had, his warmth and heartbeat reassuring his daughter that someone was still there. Rose's heart had broken a hundred times overnight. It had been upsetting not to be able to tell them it was all okay and really know it. No one knew what the morning would bring, if Maggie would suddenly reappear, full of apologies for worrying everyone or if the police would call with news that would destroy them all.

Suddenly, a picture of her sister, remorseful and embarrassed, appeared in Rose's mind. Maybe she had already come home, as though just back from a long overdue night out, and had quietly crept into bed? Rose got up, grabbed the blanket from the foot of the bed, wrapped it around her and went to check. Nervous adrenaline overriding drowsiness, she quietly poked her head around the door leading to Stephen and Maggie's bedroom. It was dark, but light enough to see an empty bed with a tangle of sheets at the bottom.

Next Rose checked the children's room, as she knew that Maggie often slept on the floor, or in their beds, on nights when they hadn't settled. A desperate attempt for some rest, any rest, regardless of how poor quality. Stephen was slumped in the middle of a crumpled heap of pillows and duvets on one of the beds with both children draped across him. But Maggie was not there.

She had not come back.

It had now been too long. It was painfully clear to Rose that something very wrong had happened and that today was not going to be a happy one. She crept downstairs and put the kettle on. If the day was going to be hard, it might as well start with a good cup of coffee.

As she heaped grounds into the cafetière, the bitter aroma waking her up already, Rose heard Stephen upstairs, so she took a second cup out of the cupboard. The absence of a cup for Maggie made Rose falter and she had to try very hard not to lose her composure. *Tears before breakfast help nobody*, she reprimanded herself.

Above the wail of the kettle, she heard Stephen move from room to room upstairs and Rose felt its echo of her morning. The same burst of optimism followed by the same loss of hope. Emily and Elliot slept on, no doubt exhausted by broken sleep and worn out from all the crying. They had gone through so much in the past few hours, Rose hoped that they slept a while longer, to recover as much as they could before today. They would undoubtedly ask for Maggie as soon as they woke.

As the kettle boiled and bubbled on the counter in front of her, Rose realised that for the first time in her life, she had absolutely no idea what to do. Maggie – a mother, a wife, a sister – was missing. How do you even start to find someone? Someone who has been taken? Someone who doesn't want to be found?

A ragged-looking Stephen walked into the kitchen. His hair messy, his skin grey, tinted by the shadow of his morning beard, which Rose realised she had never seen before. The times they had woken in the same house, he had emerged downstairs fully dressed and groomed for the day and Rose remembered being struck by how someone could look so handsome so early in the day. She needed time to wake properly and get ready before she felt able to face the world, something she could do living alone. Here she felt exposed, wearing yesterday's crumpled clothes. This sudden and unexpected intimacy gave Rose a curious thrill as she handed him his cup.

'You look like shit,' she said, laughing, trying to lighten the atmosphere.

He smiled back, lifting his eyebrows as he registered the affectionate insult.

'Thanks. Yes. Well,' he stammered before regaining his composure. 'We can't all look as glamorous as you always do.'

Rose noticed just the hint of a blush rise on his cheeks before he looked at the contents of his cup. She enjoyed it.

'You're using *her* mug, by the way,' he said, gesturing to the bright yellow handmade mug in her hands. 'She always used that first thing in the morning. She liked to put her thumb in the indent at the top of the handle, fitting into where the potter's thumb had once been. She was...' he stopped.

He looked at Rose's face, which had dropped in horror.

Liked. Was.

Past tense.

Tears sprang to his eyes as he saw in her expression what she was thinking.

'Where the hell is she, Rose? What am I going to tell the children? What am I meant to say to them when they ask for their mummy?'

He looked at his feet, tucked into what Rose called grandad slippers, shuffling about the tiled kitchen floor, not sure in which direction they should go.

Rose thought about comforting him, putting her arm around his shoulders or hugging him. He looked so sad, so lost, stood there in his dressing gown, tightly holding a cup of coffee that he was not drinking. Something stopped her. That awful Christmas morning. She had pushed the memory of it to the back of her mind but now it came to the fore and she shuddered. That one time.

'I don't know. I guess, the truth, Stephen? But also, as little as possible until we know more.'

She stepped back from him, getting breakfast things out of the cupboard, keeping herself busy to stop her from going to him. She had to keep boundaries. Instead, Rose stood in her missing sister's kitchen and acknowledged how wobbly she was feeling. Maggie, as well as being mother and wife, had always been there for her too. She was her big sister, her protector. With her gone, Rose felt unstable. So much of her own identity was in relation to Maggie – the younger one, the glamourous one, dare she say it, the more attractive one. She felt like a vase of flowers, wobbling on the table after the tablecloth had been ripped away. Beautiful, but swaying in such a way that it was impossible to guess if it would fall.

'We have to call your parents, don't we?' Stephen asked, more downcast somehow, as though he would be calling to say he'd lost their daughter, as though he were her keeper and Maggie a naughty puppy.

'We need to call the *police*, Stephen. She walked out of the hospital. She barely had anything with her. It was cold overnight and she's been gone hours now. Something is *wrong*,' Rose said pointedly. 'I will fix myself up and wait for the children to wake. You – get yourself presentable and call them. Once you've done that, I will call Mum.'

'Mama?' a voice called faintly from upstairs.

Rose and Stephen looked at each other, then to the door. Neither moved at first. Then Rose walked towards the stairs, seeing that Stephen was more exhausted than she was.

Stephen stayed where he was, drained by his poor sleep and looking grateful to have Rose there to take up the reins. He was still in the kitchen, motionless as a shop mannequin when Rose came back downstairs with the children. Their little faces were puffy and their eyes rimmed red.

Emily reached out to Stephen, who then held her as she buried her face sideways into his neck. All you could see was the tangle of her hair and the dressing over her burn. 'I want Mama,' was all she would say.

Rose held onto Elliot, who was doleful, sucking his thumb and staring at the floor. He was usually such a cheerful little soul that

Rose's heart broke a million times over as she tried her best to hold him in a way that didn't aggravate his sore back.

Rose motioned towards Stephen. 'I've said that Mama has gone away for a bit and has asked me to look after you all until she's home. She sends all her love and kisses.' Rose gestured to Stephen with her head to back her up.

She was thankful when, after a pause, he worked out her meaning, and added, 'Yes, Mama is away for a bit. We'll be okay, us four.'

Rose felt the warmth of being included. She smiled at him, and he returned it.

Then, like a dad in an advert, he picked up the cheer in his voice and said, 'Who wants pancakes?' He was smiling a little too widely.

This was not the daddy they were used to, and it showed on their little faces. They looked confused, unsure how to be. Seeing the bewilderment in the room, Stephen looked at them all in turn.

'I'm doing a "Yes Day". Mummy used to... does them. Days when you say "yes" and do all sorts of fun things. I thought we could do with one this morning... No? Is that wrong?' He looked concerned, his previous certainty falling away.

'No. Yes. Pancakes are great. Why not?' Rose joined in cheerfully. They needed a distraction of some sort for the little ones, and this seemed as good a way as any, even if it did feel like Stephen was delaying facing the situation.

'I need to call work, let them know I won't be there today,' Stephen said solemnly. He stepped out into the hallway where Rose heard the brisk one-sided conversation, before he came back into the kitchen, said nothing and then set about getting things ready. He opened one cupboard, then another and a third, before finding what he was looking for. Rose looked on, less than impressed. Clearly, cooking was another thing her sister had done alone.

Stephen kissed both children on their heads.

'Daddy time,' he said, cracking eggs into a bowl.

'Who wants to add the flour?' Rose chipped in, standing on her tiptoes to get it from the cupboard. She wasn't quite tall enough and without asking, she and Stephen danced around each other, her taking the bowl, him reaching for the flour. In different circumstances, it would have been a wonderful morning, a family together, enjoying each other's company.

Sitting around the table, the four of them tried to eat a normal breakfast. But it was not normal, and they all felt it. Emily took the opportunity to add far more syrup to the pancakes than Maggie would ever have allowed. Elliot mostly tried to paint with it. Stephen ate in silence, a furrowed expression on his face. Rose was having difficulty eating at all. Pancakes made by someone unused to cooking and served with a two-year old's enthusiastic addition of topping meant that they were thick, stodgy, and unbearably sweet. The nervous energy coursing through her body was making Rose feel nauseous and she was finding it hard to swallow anything.

In the near silence of the room, the doorbell rang out loudly, making Rose jump. Stephen whipped his head to her, embarrassed, and gestured to his pyjamas and generally messy appearance. Rose, not having brought any nightclothes with her, was already dressed. She was clearly best placed to answer the door. Thankful for a reason to stop moving the pancakes around her plate, Rose pushed it away, stood and walked to the door as Stephen disappeared upstairs to get dressed.

When he returned, transformed from his scruffy earlier self, he stiffened when he saw who the caller was. Rose stood next to another woman, who was clearly as uncomfortable as Stephen was for her to be there.

She was taller than Rose, with cropped black hair and bright red lipstick. She was dressed in black skinny jeans, a slouchy grey t-shirt and a leather jacket with a huge yellow scarf wrapped around her neck, barely leaving enough room for her face to peek over the top of it. She looked utterly out of place in this domestic setting. She smiled kindly at the children, who were fascinated by her.

'Laura,' Stephen finally said, breaking the stifling silence. 'It's been a while.'

There was a terseness to his tone that Rose couldn't quite place. She knew a few of Maggie's close friends from before had disapproved of her keeping the baby that turned out to be Emily, and of her marrying Stephen, and she recalled a huge row one night that ended in Maggie crying her eyes out on her, scared that she had lost her friends by choosing a family. Rose couldn't remember exactly who Maggie had argued with but now she realised it must have been Laura. She had never paid much attention to Maggie's fashion industry friends. She thought them flaky and too pleased with themselves. Rose didn't like people like that. Perhaps she recognised that a hive only needs one queen bee, and she knew who that ought to be.

Emily was spellbound by Laura. She shoved her plate towards her.

'Am saving for Mama,' she said, displaying a plate of leftovers carefully set aside. Emily looked proudly at them, then took just one more bite before leaving the rest.

'That's kind, Emily. She will be pleased with you,' Laura smiled.

Rose placed her arm around her niece territorially. Stephen moved to place his hands on Elliot's shoulders. A family unit closing against what felt like a potential aggressor.

Laura turned to Rose.

'So, nothing, I presume? After I got your message last night, I called a few people, but no one has...'

Rose coughed dramatically, making Laura realise that she was talking in front of the children who were both still staring at her as if she was an exciting new exhibit at the zoo.

Rose smiled at Laura, the smile not quite reaching her eyes. If anyone had looked more closely, they would have seen her clench her teeth together and her jawline tighten. Laura had once referred to Maggie as her 'sister' and Rose had never quite forgiven her for treading on her toes.

'Well. Laura. I haven't seen you since, well, when was it now? Was it before Emily was born? You certainly haven't met our lovely Elliot yet,' she said, picking him up from his highchair and giving him a gentle cuddle. 'I remember Maggie being quite hurt by that,' Rose said accusingly, yet light in tone.

She handed Elliot to Stephen, then picked up Emily and set her down from the table. She ushered the three of them out of the kitchen.

'Time to brush your teeth, you two. Stephen, they need more medicine now they've eaten,' she instructed.

Once they were all out of earshot, Rose returned to face Laura.

'So now you care?' she spat at her as she recalled the upset that Laura had caused Maggie. 'You abandoned Maggie when she had Emily and didn't even bother to visit once she had Elliot too. That devastated her. She cried. I held her while she cried.' Rose stood, arms crossed, waiting for Laura to try to defend her past actions.

'*You* called me!' she started to argue but then stopped. 'I know. I'm sorry. I didn't know what to do or say. She was so wrapped up in her new world...' Laura trailed off. 'We argued. I wasn't sure how to...'

Laura looked down at the floor.

'Yes, well, so you know how it feels to be the one left out of things. She came back to *me* when you dropped her. I told her then that you weren't to be trusted.'

Rose huffed her breath out and shifted her feet, trying to find a way to move things forward. This was not the time for petty arguments. Maggie was in trouble somewhere.

She was ready to move on but then Laura spoke again.

'There's no need to get on your high horse, though, Rose. I remember perfectly well, the times that I did visit after Emily, Maggie being upset with you. You always focusing on the baby and never on her, making snide comments about how she'd ruined her figure, so she'd have to stick with Stephen whether she wanted to or not. Maggie said she couldn't work out if you were being deliberately cruel or thoughtlessly selfish. Either way, you can't be "Saint Rose" now. It may have been more than a year since I last saw you, but you haven't changed. You do nothing if there is no benefit to you.'

Rose stood open-mouthed in shock. She was poised to strike when the sound of the children now playing in the front room reminded her that this was not about her.

Rose knew that this was about Maggie, the children and Stephen. They needed her now. The coming hours, days or weeks were likely to hold news that they might not want to hear, and it benefitted no one for Rose and Laura to be bickering like this. Rose uncrossed her arms and took a deep breath. She could be the bigger person here.

'Maybe you're right. If we both mistreated Maggie in the past, then we both need to step up now, don't we? We have to work together, for *her* sake. For her children's sake. So, shall we call bygones and move on?' Rose smiled. The smile that always, *always* worked. Laura paused, perhaps aware of being worked on. She, too, took a deep breath and let it out.

'Fine,' Laura said. 'You're right. This is not about us. So, what do we do now? For Maggie?'

'We call the police,' Rose said. 'It's time.'

6

Stephen closed the door behind the departing police officers and leant against it. Laura had taken the children upstairs, so the adults could talk openly with the police. It was just the two of them now. He looked broken

'What next?'

'We have to call my parents now. They need to know that she hasn't come home. I've missed three calls from Mum already asking after us all...' Rose faltered. 'If she has gone, if she has *chosen* to leave or to... or worse...'

Stephen's head snapped up.

'This is not my fault!' he barked.

Rose continued, looking directly at him, unmoved by his temper.

'... if, well, they may have some idea where she has gone.'

It needed saying. Maggie *could* have left. She could have had enough.

'We have to consider that possibility, the police just said so. It's more common than you think and far more common than abduction. Some people just want to disappear.'

Stephen walked away, unwilling to listen. Rose watched him go, wondering if he was always so averse to discussing things that he found uncomfortable. How had Maggie dealt with that? Or had she?

Rose thought back to the last time she and Maggie had an in-depth, real conversation. The sort of chat that dismisses the surface bullshit, one that ignores the 'I'm fine' and 'We're okay' to get to the real point. Rose felt sick when she realised that she couldn't recall it. All her memories of such times were from before the children were born. Once her niece and nephew had arrived, she could only recall lightweight chit-chat, jokes about sleep deprivation and baby brain. She was beginning to understand that it was entirely possible that her beloved sister might have been having a very difficult time, could have been desperately unhappy and she would not have known. What kind of a sister did that make Rose? How had she stepped out of her sister's life to such an extent?

Rose was astute enough to acknowledge how jealous she had been of it all. Maggie had what Rose herself wanted so badly. She had made jokes at the wedding about shotguns and how big the wedding dress had to be to fit in the baby bump, but that had been her trying to lighten the situation. Wasn't it? She hadn't come to the hospital as soon as Emily was born, but that was her trying to give Maggie and Stephen space to be a new family together. Wasn't that what you were supposed to do?

With all that space she had given her, Rose realised that she had effectively replaced Maggie within her own social circle. All the things she had once done with her sister – dinner and drinks, weekends away, theatre trips – she'd moved on to doing with other people, leaving Maggie to flounder in the chaos of early parenthood without her. Rose recalled being annoyed at Maggie for not being there for her, but now she considered just how the opposite might have been true.

'Did you not want to invite Maggie?' Rose's friend, Pete, had asked, when she'd offered him tickets to her latest event.

'No, she'll be busy with the baby. She'll need to be in bed by nine!' Rose had laughed.

'Couldn't she bring her with her? Everyone likes babies.'

Rose had shuddered.

'No. No, I think it's best to keep things professional, don't you? Now, do you want these tickets or not?' Rose had snapped. She hadn't wanted to ask, in case Maggie had turned her down, choosing the baby over her. So Rose had made that choice for her, whether Maggie liked it or not.

Rose sat down, suddenly light-headed and dizzy. In thinking she was being a good sister and giving Maggie space for her new life, by throwing herself into her work and spending time with her friends instead, had she actually abandoned her sister at the most difficult time of her life?

It had hurt Rose to watch Maggie live a life that she wanted for herself. Seeing Maggie struggle with it would be a further slap in the face. Rose wasn't oblivious to her flaws, she knew that she could be self-centred and that she wasn't always the greatest friend, particularly to women, who seemed to find her a threat. But it wasn't like that with Maggie. They had each other's backs, didn't they? A cold feeling swept over her. Everything was suddenly taking on a new hue as she looked back with fresh eyes. She felt a little sick.

She could hear Stephen on the phone in the other room. From the tone of his voice, she knew that he was talking to her parents. Probably her mother. He was trying to get sentences out and the person on the other end of the conversation kept interrupting. It was clearly a difficult call to make, and her heart went out to him.

At some point, they would have to tell the children. But tell the children what? They were too young to understand the complexity of it all. All they would know was that they wanted their mummy and she would not be there. And only Mummy would do. Rose had seen the pressure of being a mum first-hand, a few weeks after Emily had been born.

Maggie and Rose had met for lunch in a café near Rose's work. 'What are you working on now?' Maggie had asked, trying to juggle a wriggling baby, a cup of coffee and have a conversation. Doing all three was impossible, so Maggie put the coffee down.

'It's a really exciting project!' Rose said, sipping at her coffee. 'I'm running an interactive event at an art gallery. It's going to be so amazing.'

'That's brilliant. Well done!' Maggie said.

'Thanks! It's everything I love about my job in one project. There's always something different. My boss isn't great – he likes to micro-manage – but we get along well enough.' Rose tucked a loose tendril of her hair back into her smart up-do. She dressed the part. Professional creative. She was the one who made sure that an event ran smoothly but also that it was interesting and unusual. She made both sides work, and everyone had a good time.

Maggie didn't say anything.

'Maggie? You still there?' Rose asked teasingly.

'Hmm? Sorry. Bad night,' Maggie replied, looking longingly at her cup, just out of her reach.

'Shall I hold her?' Rose gestured towards Emily.

Maggie almost flung Emily at Rose, apparently relieved to have empty arms and free hands.

'And how is my beautiful little niece? How are you? Are you clever yet? I'll bet you are. All of us Richardsons are!' Rose laughed, staring adoringly at Emily. 'Though I suppose you're a Fairfax, but we won't hold that against you!' Rose knew she looked utterly out of place, her high fashion outfit perilously close to a drooling baby, and yet, totally right. Babies suited Rose.

Maggie smiled as she quickly drank her coffee. But after a while, Emily started to fidget and wriggle, no longer happy to be in her aunt's arms and soon after, she started to cry. The crying intensified until Rose was embarrassed to be holding her, making such a fuss in public. She tried all that she had seen Maggie do, from ssshing to bottom patting, singing to swaying from side to side but nothing worked. Rose admitted defeat and handed her back.

'It's okay, little one, Mama is here,' Maggie whispered to the top of Emily's head, nuzzling her downy baby hair as she did so. It took a short while for Emily's breath to settle back down again but her distress was over. Maggie was there. That was all Emily had needed, had wanted. Her mother.

Looking back, Rose felt awful because she had been annoyed at her niece for rejecting her and irritated at her sister for being able to do so quickly what Rose herself had failed to do. At the time, Rose had felt pushed out and hurt. Looking back, she hadn't seen the flip side of that bond. As much as it was wonderful to be the only person in the world who could calm Emily, the only person in the world that Emily wanted, it was also an impediment. A tie that meant you couldn't do what you wanted or go where you needed because it also wasn't about you. Nothing was about you any more. It was about the baby. And if it wasn't about you any more, would it ever be? Was that what Maggie had been feeling?

The words of the police rang clear in Rose's ears.

'With a lack of evidence to suggest foul play, we have to look closer to home. Some people don't want to be found.'

If nothing indicated that something untoward had happened to Maggie, then she must have *left*, mustn't she? Why? She must have known that the children would be distraught without her. She must have weighed that up in her mind and yet still decided to go. None of it made sense. Did someone *want* it to look like a choice?

Rose sighed. It was all too real now. This morning, it had

almost felt exciting. Like she was living in a film, and it was thrilling. Now, having met with the police and her parents on the way over, it was sickening. What were they going to *do*? How should they behave? The situation in which they found themselves was so far from normal. Usually Rose worked out what she wanted and then worked backwards in order to achieve it. That was her *modus operandi*, but here, that didn't work. What she wanted was for none of this to be happening. And she couldn't have that.

Rose walked upstairs and into the master bedroom. She sat down on Maggie and Stephen's bed. It felt wrong to be in such a personal space without either of them. She had been in the room before, helping Maggie decide what to wear or holding a baby whilst Maggie sorted laundry. Today it felt like trespassing. She was an intruder. But she needed information. The police had said so. So, she sat, and she properly looked, took everything in.

Rose was talented at working out what made people tick, and she was good at getting them to do what she wanted, especially if she knew that they loved her. Maggie was a terror for letting her baby sister get her own way most of the time, though she could also put her foot down and refuse to budge. That was when they butted heads like only family can do. Their fights were as legendary as their closeness.

Now, sitting in her sister's empty room, Rose wondered for the first time if this wasn't how things should have been. She'd always assumed that her big sister was happy for Rose to be happy. *Maybe* her big sister was just used to being passed over in favour of her. She would have said something, surely? Maggie was no pushover. She must have been okay with it all?

Doubt nagged at her insides. Rose loved Maggie more than she loved anyone, and the idea that she had taken her sister for granted their whole lives made her feel sick to the stomach. Was she a horrific sister? No. No, Rose had always been there to defend

Maggie if she needed it, ready to stand up for her if someone was treating her badly. Rose always shared the perks of her job with Maggie – free tickets, VIP passes, all that fell at her feet. She had always offered them to Maggie. Well, almost always, before Emily. She loved treating her. It hadn't all been one-sided. Yet Rose had a heavy feeling knotting in her core. She couldn't wholly work out why, but it was there, and it was unmistakable. Guilt.

Attempting to shake the feeling, Rose got up from the bed, straightened the covers where she had wrinkled them by sitting and opened the wardrobe doors. She stood looking at the clothes, hanging like flattened versions of Maggie. What was she looking for? Would she even recognise if anything was missing? It didn't look as though anything had been taken. There were no empty hangers. Nothing seemed obviously absent. Maggie's luggage was still there at the top of the wardrobe. If she had packed anything, it wasn't apparent.

Standing on her tiptoes and reaching behind all the shoe boxes, Rose grabbed the old-style hat box where she knew Maggie kept all her documents. Rose noted that the shoe boxes were dusty and untouched. A sign that the document box hadn't been moved lately, but also that Maggie hadn't worn her beloved high heels recently either. Beautiful shoes brought Maggie joy. She kept them in their original boxes. A curated collection of happiness. Happiness that had been left to gather dust.

The dark blue hat box weighed barely anything, and Rose felt a rush of blood to her head as she considered what might be missing. Travel documents, money? But as she opened the top, she could clearly see the passports were still there and, on sifting through, so were the birth certificates of the children, Maggie and Stephen, and their marriage certificate. People's lives documented by flimsy pieces of paper. It felt so insubstantial.

Where are you? What's happened? Are you safe?

Rose couldn't find anything missing but as she searched through the intimate space, there *were* things that shocked her. Maggie had always been sceptical of self-help books but there was a pile of them, admittedly immaculate and unread, by her side of the bed. *How to Be a Good Enough Mother, Find Your Family's Way, Finding Your New Self*. Then there was a crumpled pile of discarded clothes by the window. Maggie felt about clothes the way she did about shoes. They were part of her, her personality, and yet here were some things Rose remembered her wearing. They were broken, discarded, awaiting repair. This wasn't the Maggie that Rose knew.

She sat back down on the bed and tried to work out what, if anything, this told her. On one hand, surely unworn high heels and unfinished mending wasn't unusual. Plenty of people, parents to young children, would be the same. But it niggled at Rose. Absentmindedly she opened the bedside table drawer.

'What the hell…?' Rose gasped.

Inside were packets and packets of pills. Caffeine ones that she remembered from all-nighters at university. Sleeping tablets. A prescription packet, which on closer inspection and in Rose's limited understanding was an antidepressant. Whatever combination Maggie might have been taking these in, it was not an indication that all was well with her. *Maggie wouldn't have done anything stupid would she? How many of these pills did she have? Were they all still here? Were any missing? Had she been taking them at all?* She clearly needed to talk with Stephen. What on earth had they missed? She gathered the pills in her shaking hands and took them downstairs.

Stephen was hanging up the phone as Rose walked into the living room holding the stash of medications. He turned to her, looked down at the hands that she was holding out towards him and then back up to her face, his expression one of confusion.

'What are those?' he asked, looking perplexed. 'Do you have a headache? I know I do,' he half-laughed before realising that nothing in the scenario was funny. No one knew how to act any more, as though Maggie had taken all the social tent poles with her when she walked out the door and nobody else knew how to hold everything up.

'I did what the police said we should. I've gone through her things,' Rose started, and she lifted one hand to stop Stephen as he began some sort of protest. 'I know, you should do it too, but I'm her sister, we might spot different things,' she continued. 'I can't see anything obvious missing, but these... please tell me you know all about them and it's absolutely fine for Maggie to have what looks like the contents of a whole damn pharmacy and God knows what else, all mixed up together in her nightstand drawer?'

Stephen took the bottles and packets from Rose, turning them over to read what they contained. At first his expression was blank, but it turned to a look of horror as he realised just how out of step Maggie must have been. 'These... these are all hers?' he asked, looking up at Rose. He had clearly had no idea. 'I mean, I know she's tired. We both are. I know it's not a competition, but I work long hours, work is really stressful, and I get woken too when she gets up to the children and...' He stopped when he saw Rose's expression. It was not one of sympathy and it was turning more hostile with each word uttered.

'We are not talking about you,' Rose said, her voice like stone, before gesturing for him to continue.

'I didn't know. I'd suggested sleeping tables once as she struggled to get to sleep. She used to toss and turn, and it was really frustrating, so I said maybe she needed a little help. She was exhausted. She didn't want to. In case she didn't hear the kids.'

Rose looked at him, her face not even trying to conceal her distaste at his lack of empathy.

'But these,' he continued, oblivious that his pill-by-pill excuse for his behaviour was not gaining any sympathy. 'These, what are they?' He looked again before the penny dropped. 'Antidepressants?' He looked up.

'What has she got to be depressed about?' His face scrunched up like paper as his temper built. 'We have a good life. I work hard for it. She has no money worries, our own house, she doesn't want for anything! All she has to do is look after the kids and the house! I work *all* hours. The department is restructuring, and I am trying to hold on to my bloody job!'

This stopped Rose in her tracks. She had never seen Stephen like this before. He was always so placid, so calm, dull, if she was brutally honest. She had been able to see what Maggie saw in Stephen physically. Physically he was just her type, but personality wise, she had always been stumped. Maggie was fun, spontaneous, silly. Stephen was... not, and though this rant was not exactly attractive, Rose felt that she was seeing a hint of a passion that might have been what Maggie had seen when no one else was looking.

Still. He was being completely unreasonable.

'You know it doesn't work like that, Stephen. You're not an idiot!' She shook her head at him. 'You do know that pregnancy can mess with your hormones. You do know it's *hard* looking after small children, don't you? Monotonous. Repetitive. Lonely. Even I know that, and I will admit, I haven't been here as much as I should have been, but it seems you have been here even less.' She laughed at him.

'Who do you think you are? Get out of my house, Rose. Get *out*!' Stephen shouted.

Rose was saved by the doorbell ringing, quickly followed by a knock on the door.

'I hate it when people do that,' Rose said, breaking the tension with a laugh. 'Do they think we can travel to the door at warp speed?' She smiled at Stephen, who, rage spent, looked at her and smiled back.

'I'm sorry,' he said sheepishly, 'this is a lot to deal with. It's like, I just... I feel like I don't know my wife any more and I don't know whether to be angry with her, angry with myself, angry at someone else. I don't know whether to be worried *for* her or furious *with* her or both. All the while trying to work out what the bloody hell I can tell our children!'

Rose stepped towards him and instinctively wrapped her arms around him. She held him in silence for a few seconds until his tension at the sudden closeness relaxed. Rose held him until he surrendered to it.

'I'm here, Stephen,' she said, 'and we can work this out together. For the kids. For her. For us.' He broke away from Rose but held her at her shoulders and smiled.

'Thanks. That means a lot,' he said, before looking at the door as the bell rang again. 'That'll be your parents. We should probably let them in.'

'If we must!' Rose laughed, and together they walked to the door.

Rose opened the door and her parents bustled in. Her mother, Elizabeth, was jittery. She walked around in little circles, trying to take her coat off. Her father, Bill, was silent and stony faced. Rose's stomach swirled with nerves. Her family had never been great at conflict. They were a 'least said, soonest mended' sort of family. She and Maggie had developed different methods from this standpoint. Maggie was a people-pleaser, avoiding conflict arising in the first place. Rose was a charmer, turning any conflict round to her advantage and usually winning over her adversary in the process.

'Darling,' Elizabeth leant to kiss Rose. 'Any news?' she added anxiously. Concern was etched on her face, nervous energy clearly keeping her going. 'Where are the little ones? How are their burns? Are they all right?' she asked, wringing her hands. She looked around as though expecting them to run to the door to greet their granny.

'They're okay. Laura came over this morning and is helping to keep them occupied. You remember Laura? Maggie's friend?' Rose said, noticing but choosing to ignore the look of disapproval that flickered across her mother's face. Not directed at Laura as such, more that perhaps she and her husband had not been the first ones to know about the situation in which they found themselves.

'They don't know anything yet,' Stephen chipped in. 'We haven't worked out exactly what to say,' he said, gesturing his in-laws into the living room. Unusually, they seemed happy to act as guests, whereas Elizabeth was more often found pottering about as though it were her home too. Tidying, plumping cushions and checking on the state of things.

Sitting down on the sofa, Bill finally spoke. He looked the same as usual, sensibly dressed in his grey trousers and navy-blue jumper over a collared shirt. His hair, once brown, was now a variety of greys that gave him a distinguished look. He had a kind face, but one that clearly didn't take any nonsense. A look that had come in useful during his years of teaching.

'So, what did the police say?' he asked, and Rose knew immediately that he was going to be the practical to her mother's emotional in their response to the situation. 'We should have been there for that,' he complained.

'Bill...' Elizabeth reproached. 'We agreed we wouldn't...'

'She's our daughter! And she's missing. God knows what could have happened to her, she could be...' His voice wavered.

'Don't, Bill. We can't think like that. I'll go mad if I do,' Elizabeth said, her voice shaking. 'We have to keep positive.'

Rose stood by the window, keeping to the edges of the scene

unfolding in the room. She knew that her father adored Maggie, his eldest child. She was most like him in personality, keeping all emotions bottled up inside where they did less harm. Or at least less harm to others. Rose felt sorry for him. It couldn't be easy keeping your thoughts inside you all of the time. You can't swallow it all up forever, it has to come out. Perhaps that was what happened with Maggie. Had her unhappiness finally spilled out of her?

'They mostly listened to what we could tell them and asked lots of questions. When we last saw Maggie, what happened with the children. Her state of mind. Our home circumstances. If she'd taken anything from home or if it looked as though she had been back here before us. They were obviously trying to work out whether she left by choice or by... or by force.' Stephen choked the last words out.

'And which is it? What are they doing?' Elizabeth demanded.

'Mum,' Rose said calmingly, 'they're just trying to work the situation out. They only know what we do. That the scalding incident was an accident – the safeguarding team are happy that it was, even with Maggie now missing. That we think she left the hospital by choice and hasn't come back here since. We told them what she was wearing and how upset she was. No one knows any more.' Rose sat by her mother and took her hand in hers. Elizabeth squeezed it affectionately.

'So what is the plan?' Bill said.

'They asked colleagues to run a check for any incidents or accidents involving anyone matching her description. Nothing as yet. They took a look around for any leads, things that look out of place, maybe things that might have been removed. They spent a long time questioning me, I'm definitely on their radar for something, though I have nothing to hide,' Stephen said, crumpling his hand into a fist that he kept clenched at his side.

'They said that they've found no indication of any foul play as yet. There's very little CCTV footage of her at the hospital, and what they do have shows no evidence of any struggle, nor are there any witnesses to any argument or disagreement. They said that, that...' Stephen choked a little and took a moment to regain his speech, '... that no remains have been found.'

There was a small, horrified gasp from Elizabeth, and she dabbed at her eyes with the tissue she was grasping onto so tightly her hands had gone white.

'They have nothing, basically,' Rose finished, seeing that Stephen needed to take a pause.

Rose realised that her parents hadn't really had time to process what they might be looking at. There was a chance that Maggie wasn't here because Maggie was dead. Whether dead by her own hand or by someone else's, no one knew, but her sudden disappearance and abandonment of the children had to at least suggest that possibility.

Bill put his hand on Elizabeth's and gave it a small squeeze. Elizabeth visibly calmed. Rose's parents had the type of relationship that she wanted so desperately for herself. They balanced each other out. Even in a horrific situation such as this, Bill knew what Elizabeth was feeling and knew how to help. They were a partnership, a team. Rose wanted a team of her own.

Stephen continued, 'We've given them all the information that we have, though I need to update them on a few things.'

He glanced at Rose, who met his eye and nodded discreetly to agree that this would be a good idea. 'We've found a selection of, um, medications that she may have been taking, that she may still need to take. The police are going to talk with the safeguarding team at the hospital to gauge how high-risk a case they consider her, if they feel she may be at risk of, um, of self-harm.'

Elizabeth's hand tightened on her husband's. She was clearly trying very hard not to cry.

'They are going to check CCTV at various transport hubs and get back to us if they find anything. They've got a description and a recent photograph.' Stephen's face looked strained and pale as he tried to remember all the information from the meeting with the police.

Trying to bolster everyone with the positives that the police had left them with, Rose interjected. 'The good thing is that they said in most cases people turn up again fairly quickly. That most need some space and come home once they're ready. As Maggie is an adult with no significant mitigating circumstances, it is most likely that she has decided not to return just yet and we have to wait for her to choose to come back. She will come back.'

Stephen did not look so sure, and on seeing the fear and doubt on his face, Rose felt her conviction waver.

Bill and Elizabeth sat still and silent and looked up at their son-in-law. Elizabeth's face pinched as she started to sniff, trying not to cry. Bill nodded slightly to indicate that he understood what he was being told.

'So. We wait,' he said. 'We wait and see if she comes back. No news and all that.' He nodded again, more emphatically this time, as though he was agreeing with himself.

No news, no drama, all would be well, Rose knew he was thinking. She looked at her mother, to see what she was making of all this. Elizabeth's face was starting to colour, a blush tone that started at her chest and was rising slowly up her neck as her hackles rose.

'We do nothing? We just sit and wait and hope that she comes back? Surely there is something we can do, ought to do! What if she's in danger? Or hurt? Or upset? Or worse? My baby is out there, and I don't know where, and I'm supposed to sit and drink tea?

That's ridiculous! We have to *find* her. The children need us to find her!'

Rose said nothing. She looked from Stephen, stoic but clearly very rattled, to her father, calm and ready to be patient, to her mother, furious and desperately worried. These were Maggie's life-lines and all of them were like Hansel and Gretel, with only scattered breadcrumbs to follow in a desperate attempt to find their way out of the forest they found themselves in.

'I think we should put up posters,' Laura said quietly from the hallway. Everyone whipped round to look, wondering how long she had been there. 'Getting Maggie's face out there can only be a good thing.'

She paused, then glanced upstairs.

'They're sleeping, must be exhausted.' Laura paused, bit her lip and then continued, 'That friend, the one who runs the print shop I mentioned earlier? I hope you don't mind but I asked them about it. They've just messaged and said they'll run up some posters if we send over a photo and text. We could use the same one as you gave the police. They've said we could go and get them now if I emailed them an image. They'll print them while we're on our way. What do you think?'

The atmosphere in the room was strained and Rose was glaring straight at her.

'I suppose...' Rose said, through gritted teeth, 'though we really ought to let ourselves be guided by the police, don't you think?' She glanced around the room, expecting her family to agree with her.

'I think anything we can find out can only be helpful. I think it's a good idea,' Bill said, nodding at Laura awkwardly.

Rose was affronted by being contradicted by her father. She wanted him to be on her side. 'Okay. Let's go. Let's do it now,' Rose said, immediately standing up, trying to take back control. The atmosphere in the house was oppressive and she needed some air anyway. She had forgotten how Maggie made social situations with her parents and Stephen flow, and now she was not there, it was borderline painful. If she took Laura and left, then her parents could look after the children, Stephen could search the house and she could step away for a moment.

Laura looked surprised at Rose's sudden change of heart but stepped back into the hallway to gather her things, stopping to get the photo and details from Stephen before leaving. Rose followed her. Outside on the doorstep, the chilled air seeped its way into Rose, making her wake up with a speed that she had failed to achieve all day. She was tired and drained, but the coolness on her face was refreshing. Soon enough, she would be yearning for the warmth of indoors, but right at this moment, it was perfect.

'Do you want me to collect the posters and meet you afterwards?' Laura asked, clearly not wanting to spend time with Rose.

Rose nodded, feeling the same.

'See you in a while then. I'll call you?' Laura said, turning to walk away.

'I'll head towards the hospital then, see if there are any shops or businesses who might have seen her.' Rose said, not wanting to be seen to be doing nothing while Laura was on the case.

Rose felt her shoulders lift as she walked away from the house and from Laura. Despite feeling that it was all on her to make things okay, it was exhausting having to have all the answers when she felt as clueless as the rest of them.

She walked haphazardly towards the hospital, its tall towers beacons on the skyline. It felt surreal to be showing strangers a photo of her sister, uttering the word 'Missing' again and again. Each time she looked into Maggie's eyes, she felt accused. She should never have let her walk out of the hospital. Stephen had been there for the children, why hadn't she been there for Maggie?

It had been nearly two days. Where could she be by now? Had

something happened to her? After a handful of enquiries, she found that she couldn't look at Maggie's picture any more. It was all too much. Rose texted her mum to say she was heading back to her flat to sort out a few things.

She got home, closed the door behind her, curled up on the sofa and wept.

7

Maggie's hands shook as she clasped them tightly around a steaming cup of tea. She tucked herself further into the garden chair and closed her eyes, lifting her face to the bright, late winter sun that washed over her, bathing her in its warmth. Despite it being two weeks now since she had been coaxed out of the freezing sea, Maggie still felt cold. She had slept for days but the core of her was still ice, and she didn't want it to thaw. She needed to be numb.

'You know, hen, you need to drink it, to get the benefit of it,' Ailsa said, smiling encouragingly.

'Thank you,' Maggie whispered. She tried her best to return the smile. The result was well-intentioned but hollow. Maggie turned away, retreating back into her thoughts.

Ailsa had talked her out of the sea, taken her home and called the local doctor. He had checked Maggie over, declared her physically unharmed but admitted that local mental health services were struggling, and he was not aware of a place that could take her.

'If she were to... *try* again, well, then I could find her a bed, I suspect,' he had said, hands aloft in a *I wish it wasn't so* sort of way.

'I'll keep her here with me a while,' Ailsa had replied. 'I have the space and the company would be nice. I've lived alone so long. It'd be nice having someone around and besides, it looks as though she needs some proper looking after, don't you think?'

'Is that wise? You don't know her from Adam, after all. Who is she? A woman you met *online*, on some chat group, and who turned up practically on your doorstep, unannounced?' he said with concern and distrust in his voice.

Ailsa paused while she considered a reply.

'That may be true, yes. But sometimes, Doctor, the universe delivers people to each other just at the right time. She needed help. She knew I would help her.'

Ailsa had settled Maggie into her spare room and set about trying to help her deal with what was troubling her.

Ailsa knew how Maggie had been struggling through the conversations they had had first online, and then at times by phone. They had met on a parenting forum, one Maggie had joined, desperately trying to reach out to someone who understood her conflicted feelings and who wouldn't make how *she* was feeling somehow about them, like Stephen had done. Ailsa had been like a fairy godmother, someone who had been there before, understood and just *listened* while Maggie talked. Though, in the days since she had been pulled from the sea, Maggie had barely said a word. The pair sat in silence in the garden. Ailsa sipped at her own tea, blowing gently on its surface to cool it before drinking. Her wisps of breath played with the steam rising from the cup, which swirled upwards and melted into the cooler air.

'You know, hen,' Ailsa started, 'I think you've done the right thing. Sometimes when something is troubling you, stepping away for a bit, getting a break, can help you see more clearly. Talking it through with someone who understands helps too.'

Silence.

'What I mean to say is, I'm here to listen. Whatever it is, it can't be so bad that it can't be put right, can it?'

Maggie mumbled, not wanting to speak.

'I won't force it, love. I won't make you share anything you don't want to. Life has very clearly ground you down and you need time to build yourself back up. You can do that here. I can help you if you let me. I meant it when I said it in our chats, and I mean it now. No one should have to cope alone, and you are not alone. I'm here.'

Maggie looked at Ailsa, at the care and the eagerness to help on her face, and she felt cold. She did not deserve this. Not after what she had done. Nothing could fix that. She did owe her, though. Ailsa had brought her back from her darkest moment. She had brought her into her home and she had asked nothing of her.

Maggie breathed deeply and then replied quietly, as though, if she did not speak up, then it might not be true.

'I have done something terrible that cannot be undone. I cannot be forgiven. I will not ask to be.'

Ailsa took the hint. She stood up, her joints creaking from sitting in the cool air.

'I understand. Like I said, I won't pry. Tell me when you're ready, if you're ready.' She paused, then continued. 'You have found your way to somewhere you can rest, somewhere you can rebuild yourself, come back stronger. There is always another chance to start over.'

Maggie scoffed. She knew there was no way back.

'Until you find it, please stay. Rest. I'll be here.'

There was something about Ailsa's refusal to push, about the space she was willingly giving to Maggie, that made something inside her give a little. A tiny flicker of a light that she thought had gone out.

Maggie looked as Ailsa turned to busy herself, tidying things away as the daylight faded. So far north, the winter crept in faster and was slower to leave than other places. Ailsa had told her that those who lived here knew to put themselves in daylight's grasp whenever they could.

'It's... it's the children...' Maggie whispered.

Ailsa put the tray she was holding back down, pulled her chair closer to Maggie's and sat.

Maggie paused.

'What happened?' Ailsa prodded gently.

Maggie's voice cracked as she thought of them. Of the chaos, the ball and those screams as the scalding water tore into her babies' skin. Maggie could barely get the words out as she recounted that evening, every inch of her shaking, like a delayed shock. 'And I just, I knew. When Stephen finally arrived, when Rose was there. I knew.'

'Knew what?'

Maggie stopped. She bit her lip so hard she tasted blood. Good. She deserved that pain.

'That it was my payback.'

'Payback? For what?'

'For...' Maggie shuddered. She was petrified that Ailsa would no longer be understanding once she knew the whole truth. After all, Ailsa had never disfigured anyone the way Maggie had. Her kindness would be replaced with revulsion, anger, disgust. All things that Maggie knew she deserved and yet couldn't bear to face.

In the smallest voice possible, Maggie confessed.

'For not wanting them.'

Tears welled in her eyes. Slow tears filled with regret.

'Emily was a mistake. Unplanned. I – I had an abortion booked. I wasn't ready. But when I got to the clinic, I couldn't do it. I went home again. Time somehow split itself into fragments, coping moment to moment. The hormones, the tiredness, the nausea. I wasn't myself. Then suddenly I was married, and she was here. I was a wife and a mother without really being sure that I wanted to be either. I was… gone.'

Ailsa moved her chair closer in order to reach out to Maggie. She said nothing, but reached across and squeezed Maggie's shoulder. Maggie glanced up at her, fearful of the hate she would find looking at her, and was relieved to find nothing but empathy staring back.

'Then, before I had a moment to catch my breath, Elliot was on his way. The only time between the two that Stephen and I… I was trying to work out how to be a good wife. And then. God. I remember when I did the test. I was violently sick. I absolutely didn't want another baby. Not then. But then I felt so guilty, like I was wishing Emily away. I did love her. I *do* love her. I just wasn't ready to give myself up like that. I had already turned into someone I didn't recognise. I made another appointment. I didn't tell Stephen. But who could I leave Emily with? I couldn't exactly take her with me, could I? So I didn't go,' Maggie half-laughed.

'Such a mess. Somehow, in two years, I'd gone from being me to being a shadow of a mum; a bad and empty wife. I spent my days wishing for sleep, wishing I could turn back the clock and do it differently. Which was to wish away the kids, which I didn't want to, but I also did. I love them. But did I want my life the way it was with them? No. No,' she whispered. 'Even with the joy they brought, the light they have. I wasn't happy. Which makes me selfish, rotten, wrong. And what happened to them was my payback. It was my fault.'

Ailsa sighed, took Maggie's hands in hers.

'No one is perfect. It was an accident. You didn't do it on purpose.'

'Maybe not. But maybe my mind wasn't on the job in hand.' Maggie's anger at herself rose. 'Maybe I was miles away, wishing I was back at work, or out with my friends. Not making dinner that two over-tired children wouldn't eat, before putting them to bed where no one would get enough sleep. Only to wake up and do it all over again. Maybe if I'd been more engaged. Maybe if I'd appreciated them more.' Maggie shook her hands and wrung them over and over and over.

'We can't live on maybe. Nobody knows how differently things could have turned out. Everyone is just trying their best, after all.'

'I could have disfigured them for life. Their screams, Ailsa. I can't unhear them. But what have I done? I hurt them and then I left? I walked away. It's been two weeks. After I... after the beach, I don't know. I couldn't think, I couldn't function. Everything was numb. But now it's been two weeks. How do I reach out? How do I... They must all be out of their minds with worry. Emily and Elliot won't understand. Stephen will be furious with me. Rose, too. I keep thinking about calling but then I can't. What would I *say*? What can I say?'

Ailsa nodded, taking it all in, considering her response.

'Two weeks is long, but also it's no time at all. You needed to rest. You *need* to rest. You've been through the wringer with it all. The children are with their father and their aunt, they'll be all right. It's not as though you've left them in a box in a doorway somewhere, is it?' Ailsa smiled, trying to bring some levity.

'I should call them though, tell them I'm okay. They'll want to know when I'm coming home...'

'Do you feel ready to go back yet, hen?' Ailsa asked, looking unsure. 'You're only just starting to deal with everything. Sometimes space is what everyone needs.'

'I shouldn't have just walked away, though. I should get in touch to let them know I'm alive at least.'

'Could you write? You could take your time, put it all down, make sure you get your thoughts across clearly. If you called, wouldn't the children get upset that you were there but not?'

Maggie paused, considering. She wanted to hear their voices but knew that Ailsa was probably right. She'd upset them enough as it was.

'I guess so. I could explain everything in a letter.'

Aisla nodded and stood up.

'Come inside, let's get some paper and you can get something down.'

Maggie picked up her things and followed. She sat down at the old wooden kitchen table that wobbled a little on the uneven stone surface of the floor. Her heart was racing, and she tried smoothing her fingers over the whorls of the wood to calm herself down. Ailsa came back in with a notepad and a pen and placed them in front of her, touched her lightly on the shoulder and then busied herself in the room.

Maggie picked up the pen in her shaking hands and turned to a fresh page of paper. She paused, the tip of the pen poised above the blank sheet, and then she opened her soul onto the page. Her love for the children, her sorrow for what had happened and her promise, her absolute promise that she would come home as soon as she could, a healed, happier person. A better mother.

She turned and looked up at Ailsa, moving the letter so that she could read what Maggie had written.

'What do you think? I don't know what else to say right now.'

'I think it's fine. You're letting them know you're safe, you're going to take some time and that you'll be back. They'll understand, I'm sure. They love you after all, don't they? They want you to be well too?'

Maggie nodded, though she wasn't so sure about Stephen. She knew he'd be furious with her for walking out.

'Stephen, he... I guess he might come and insist I come home?'

Ailsa pursed her lips.

'That had occurred to me, sweetheart. He didn't seem the most supportive of husbands from what you said. But you needn't put an address on it. I, well, I could post it for you when I go into the city? So the postmark isn't from here? You know yourself how easy it is to track someone down without an address around here!' She laughed kindly.

Maggie looked abashed.

'Yes, I'm sorry, I just didn't know where else to go. You'd told me so much about this place and how peaceful it is and how you walked your dog on the beach every day...'

'Ack, no, I wasnae complaining but explaining why it might be worth being cautious. You will go back home when you're ready. You can keep in touch, and you can work on you for a while. Get you better. After all, your children need their mother healthy, don't they?'

Maggie nodded. She felt herself relax in a way that she could barely remember. It was all going to be okay. She could get herself better and then go home to be a better mother for Emily and Elliot. They were fine with Stephen and Rose for now.

It was all going to work out.

8

Rose stood on the doorstop, ringing the bell and knocking. The house was silent inside, no movement, no voices. She sighed impatiently. *Stephen would have called if he had a different plan for today, surely?*

The past few weeks had seen them settle into a routine. The children's burns had healed well and they were nearly back to their normal selves. Rose had taken on the main parenting of the children. Though it had meant quitting her job when her manager had not succumbed to Rose's way of thinking when she'd asked for extended leave. Rose had lost her cool and shouted, 'If you have so little empathy then maybe I should just quit!'

She had been appalled. She and her boss had never really seen eye to eye but she was shocked at how little he seemed to care that her family had been torn apart.

'Look, I appreciate it's a difficult situation. But it's not like they're *your* kids, is it? Why can't the grandparents step in or something?'

'They're my *family*!' Rose had snapped, her face crinkling in disgust at his dismissal of how important she was in their lives. He obviously didn't get it. He had kids himself, not that you'd ever know it from his manner. At work, they simply did not exist for him, and Rose did not think it made him any more professional. It made him seem cold, and in a regrettable moment of angry honesty, Rose told him so. He had not taken this well and had simply shown her the door. She had been late enough and absent enough lately that he could terminate her contract without a moment's pause.

Rose called Stephen in tears.

'What am I going to do? I mean, I know I can always get another job when it comes to it, offers always pop up now and again but right now, my flat, my bills...'

'I see,' Stephen said calmly. 'This is partially my fault. You've been away from work to help us out. And we appreciate it, we really do. You're so good with them.' He sighed, sounding concerned. 'Look, let me worry about the finances. I'll take care of it, okay?' Stephen assured her.

Rose stopped crying, sniffing as her tears dried up. 'Are you sure?'

'Yes. I'm sure. Work is... well, it'll be better if I can actually *be* there, if I can focus when I *am* there. My boss is understanding but, still, he pays me to get stuff done and I haven't been doing. In this climate, that's... not good. You looking after the kids helps me to keep my job. Consider it payment for childcare?' Stephen suggested.

Rose thought it rather chivalrous of him. She had rescued him by taking care of the children, he was going to rescue her by taking care of her. He was a good man, really. Rose briefly found herself wondering what it would be like to be his mistress before reminding herself how utterly inappropriate that was, particularly in the current circumstances.

Rose felt that she was doing something significant by handing in her notice to help her family. With a glimmer of self-awareness, she noted how much she enjoyed being the centre of the drama and there had been enough drama to experience in the days following Maggie's disappearance. The police had opened a missing persons case and all available evidence had been reviewed thoroughly. Maggie's phone had been located, abandoned by the side of the road, with no other DNA or fingerprints found on it other than hers. There was some blurry CCTV footage of Maggie by the local shop, and again at the coach station where she could clearly be seen buying a ticket. The staff there, when interviewed, recalled Maggie being confused and distracted when buying a ticket to Glasgow, but nothing significant. The police had spoken with other forces across the country, but the trail had gone cold. There was not enough information to trace where she might have gone from there, if she made it there at all, only enough to deduce that the journey had most likely been taken voluntarily, unless she was being coerced by a third party who had left absolutely no trace whatsoever, which was unlikely. They couldn't guarantee that she was safe and well, but they had no evidence to the contrary either.

'Some people don't want to be found,' the pragmatic constable had said. He was trying to be reassuring, to suggest that nothing untoward had happened to Maggie, but Stephen was furious when he closed the door behind him.

'It isn't good enough!' Stephen raged. 'She could be hurt or in trouble! She clearly wasn't in her right mind. She wouldn't have just walked away. That's not *her*. Why have they stopped looking?'

'Stephen, there's nowhere else they can look,' Rose said gently. 'If the police are right in their understanding that Maggie has chosen to step away for a while, then we owe it to her to keep things as normal as possible here.'

'There has to be something else we can do! I can't just sit about waiting, presuming it will all be fine. The kids are a mess. I can't pretend it's all normal. I've called everyone I can think of and anyone *they* suggested as well. No one has heard or seen anything. It's like she's disappeared off the face of the earth!'

'The police don't have the resources to trawl CCTV footage all over the country. You have to understand. They know that she bought a ticket for Glasgow, but she could have got off the coach before then. Or doubled back on herself or gone somewhere else entirely.' Rose went to stand next to him, putting her hand gently, reassuringly on his arm. 'They don't have any evidence that anything bad has happened. We need to hold on to that and believe she will come home. Maybe, maybe we have to let her go for now... give her time to come home.'

'I know,' Stephen said resignedly. 'I need to do something, though. I just don't know what!' The strain on his face was clear to see.

Rose knocked on the door again, with more force this time. Surely someone would hear her? Why wasn't Stephen answering? She tried to look in through the window but all she could see was the front room as she had left it the night before. What was going on?

Rose walked the perimeter of the house with rising concern. The car was still there, she didn't think they'd have gone for a walk, not on a weekday, nor without letting her know. Stephen struggled with the night parenting. He wasn't used to being tired. It had been Maggie who had gone to each night-time call, soothing bad dreams, providing comfort and settling the children back to sleep. Stephen wasn't coping with being back at work, trying to put in the hours and stay focused when he was so exhausted. His manager had begrudgingly offered unpaid leave but that felt financially unwise, especially now he was also supporting Rose. Christmas was just around the corner and he'd never had to do any work to make that happen before. The pressure was clearly getting to him.

He wouldn't have done something stupid, would he? Rose tried to shake the thought away. But then again, she wouldn't have imagined in a million years that Maggie would walk out on them all.

Rose tried the back door. It opened. Stephen must have forgotten to lock it the night before. She was breathing hard as she stepped into the kitchen. The atmosphere was calm. She didn't sense anything untoward as she moved through the silent house. She came to the foot of the stairs and stood for a moment, listening. Nothing. Apprehensively, Rose started up the stairs.

She reached the children's room first. It was dark inside and as she pushed the door open to see more clearly, she swallowed hard in nervous anticipation. She exhaled with relief when she found the room empty. The beds had clearly been slept in but there was no sign of anyone. The bathroom was empty too, the bath containing only a collection of brightly coloured toys.

I'm being silly, Rose told herself as she stood and took a moment, leaning against the bathroom door. She held her hand to her chest as she tried to control her breathing, to stop herself feeling light-headed. There was still no movement from anyone, from anywhere in the house.

'Hello?' Rose called out, hoping for a reply. None came. Her stomach was doing somersaults. The atmosphere was wrong somehow but she couldn't put her finger on why. There was only Stephen and Maggie's room left. Rose steeled herself and then pushed the door open, straining to see in the half-light creeping in around still closed curtains. On the bed she could see an outline of a pile of bodies, all twisted around each other and the bedclothes in a tumbled pile. There didn't seem to be any movement and millisecond by millisecond, terror rose in Rose's heart. She turned on the light to see the details of what her mind had already written.

'What have you done?' she whispered, as the light flashed on.

'Hm, ug, what?' Stephen mumbled, as the light burned into his eyes and he sat, bolt upright, confused and tangled in his children, who were slowly coming to, abruptly woken by their father sitting up so unexpectedly.

'Oh,' Rose breathed out as she leant against the wall and slid down to sit on the floor in a crumpled pile, sobbing and laughing, relieved, shocked and angry. Unable to get words out, coughing, crying and smiling.

'You have *got* to give me a key!' she finally said, once she had regained her composure. 'And get a better alarm clock!' She pointed at the clock, knocked to the floor. 'You scared the living daylights out of me. I thought...' She faltered.

'You thought what?' Stephen asked, embarrassed to be seen by Rose in such a state. 'We've had a bad night. They wouldn't settle without me. So, we all piled in here and read stories...' He pulled a bent storybook from the tangle of covers on the bed.

'I thought you'd... to yourself, to... never mind,' Rose faltered, not wanting to say it in front of the now wide-awake children. 'You're going to be late for work,' she changed the subject. She looked at the three exhausted people on the bed. She was tired herself from leaving Maggie's house late and coming back so early each day.

'This isn't working, is it?' Rose looked at Stephen.

He shook his head gently in agreement with her.

'You have a spare room. Why don't I stay a few nights a week to help? We can share the childcare and you can get more rest.'

Stephen ran his hand through his rumpled hair.

'I mean, that would be great. I... I was thinking of maybe getting a night nanny but... if you could then...'

Rose turned and smiled at the children. 'Who wants Auntie Rose to come and stay for some sleepovers?' she beamed.

'Me!' Emily bounced over for a cuddle and Elliot gurgled a

smile. Rose's heart leapt. Mere moments before, she had feared the worst but here they all were, safe, warm and with her. She closed her eyes as she hugged Emily, grateful for the family she had with her and trying to ignore the building fury she felt towards her sister for leaving such beautiful children, whatever her reason.

'Right. Let's get everyone ready for the day, shall we?' Rose said brightly, her composure recovered. She scooped the children up in her arms and took them downstairs for breakfast. By the time Stephen came downstairs, showered and dressed immaculately for work, Rose had cleared the kitchen and sat feeding Elliot his breakfast whilst Emily ate hers. 'There's coffee...' she said to Stephen. He looked gratefully at the scene in front of him and poured himself a cup before joining them at the table.

'I was supposed to be at work today.'

'I know.'

'I've just called in. There was an important meeting, I missed it. They've said to take the day off,' Stephen said morosely.

'That's good, surely?' Rose asked him, looking at his worried face. 'Your bosses have been really supportive.'

'I'm not sure it was a "take a day", it felt more like "don't bother".'

'This is not a normal situation. Your wife is...' She stopped, not wanting to shatter the currently peaceful breakfast time. She spooned another mouthful of porridge into Elliot's waiting mouth and reached out to stroke Emily's head.

'Look,' she continued. 'It hasn't been working. You've been doing too much. But I'm here now and I'll stay. I will support you all until we know where we are with things. However long that takes, okay?' she smiled at him. Her stomach flipped and she tried to ignore it. Now was not the time.

For all his faults, Stephen is a good man, she thought. He genuinely cares for the children and he is committed to his job. I've been hard on him. He's just trying to work it all out. Rose looked at him as he sipped his coffee. She thought she could see the tension in his shoulders loosen a little the longer he sat at the table with her. They were a team now and they would survive this together.

'As you're not going to work today, stay here with the children and I'll go back to my flat and get a few things. I can set myself up in the spare room. You'll need to move a few things, though. I can't live in a box room.' She smiled and Stephen smiled back. He took her hand for a moment, a gesture of appreciation. Rose felt a warmth wash over her.

'Okay,' he replied.

Back at her own apartment, Rose opened the door to silence. But this time the silence wasn't concerning or peaceful, it was oppressive. Rose loved her flat. It was in the centre of town; everything was close by, and her friends could come round whenever. She had filled it with beautiful things, everything she could possibly want. Apart from other people. The flat felt lonely. Rose had not really considered it this way before, but since spending so much time at Maggie's house, she realised that her flat reflected that no one here cared if she was there or not. Even her house plants had been chosen for their ability to withstand neglect.

Rose had always considered her freedom to pack up and head off wherever and whenever to be a bonus. She had no ties. Now, standing by herself in her empty flat, one that she hadn't even bothered to decorate for Christmas, she considered the flip side. No one missed her when she was gone. Her friends might miss her coming out for drinks or to unpick another bad date with, but there were other friends for that. She was no one's number one. She missed the chaos back with Stephen. It was awful, it was upsetting, and everyone was worried about Maggie, but they were worried together.

Rose whipped through her things, packing up what she

thought she might need for the next few days. It was difficult to pick clothes, as her wardrobe tended strongly to the glamorous and that didn't really suit crawling around the floor with Emily and Elliot. She rejected a few dry-clean only things and focused on practical clothing. Sure, the things she picked still showed off her figure to its best advantage, but she could be practical and look good. Once the essentials were packed and she realised how little she actually cared about the *stuff* in the apartment, Rose closed her suitcase and headed out the door.

With the large suitcase at her feet and a handful of other bags from her flat, Rose stood on the doorstep of Maggie and Stephen's house, not quite sure what to do. Stephen had given her a key that morning, but she wasn't sure whether to ring the doorbell first or not? Was she a guest still or did she live there now? She shook her head at herself. This wasn't like her – all this second guessing and trying to work out what to do. Rose had always followed her instinct and her instinct told her that she was always welcome. She turned the key in the lock and let herself in.

'Hello! I'm back,' she called.

There was a sound of tiny feet rushing to the top of the stairs.

'Mama!' Emily cried as she started down them, only to stop, crushed at the sight of not her mother, but her aunt. It had not occurred to Rose that she and Maggie sounded so alike and that by letting herself in and calling, she had briefly given false hope, a cold and cruel thing, to her beloved niece. Emily stood, statue still, as tears filled her eyes and toppled down her cheeks. She was shaking with the effort of not crying, of not showing her sadness, of being a 'good girl'. Rose's heart broke for her, she was barely out of babyhood and here she was trying so hard to understand such grown-up things. She looked up at Rose, eyes cloudy behind her tears. She opened her mouth to whisper, 'Where's my mama?

Where my mama gone?' She trembled, her lower lip shaking as she tipped over into crying.

Rose dropped the bags she was carrying and went to her niece. She wrapped her arms around her, as if by holding her tightly she could somehow make it all better, she could make her feel safe again. She held her while Emily's little body racked itself with tears, her breath ragged and uneven as she shook out all of her confusion and fright at where her mother had gone. They had been so intent on keeping things as normal as possible for them that Rose realised they hadn't given the children permission to grieve, to be sad, to let it all out. Rose kissed the top of her head and stroked her hair over and over as Emily howled.

'I don't know where Mama is,' she told her truthfully. 'I don't know. But wherever she is, I know that she loves you. We all do. I love you. *I'm* here, Emmy, I'll look after you until Mama comes back, okay? I won't leave, I promise. I *promise*.' She rocked her back and forth as they sat in a heap halfway up the stairs.

Rose became aware of someone watching and she looked up to see Stephen, his face in pain as he watched them. He put his hands to his head to indicate that Elliot was sleeping. They were both grateful for that. In sleep, Elliot was missing this, missing this grief, grief that he did not understand. Rose turned back to Emily and wrapped her up again, holding her close, keeping her own breathing calm in order to calm Emily, who was now slowing down her sobs, all cried out.

Gently, slowly, Emily rose her head to look at her aunt.

'You my mama for now?' she asked, desperate for something to be sure, to be solid and unchanging.

'Mama for now,' Rose whispered, her heart soaring, as she held Emily close to her, willing for her to know just how much she was loved, even in the absence of her mother. Rose knew right then that she would do anything for these children, she would never let them down and she would do absolutely everything in her power to make it all right again. Whatever it took.

The rest of the day was sombre. The children were low in energy and enthusiasm, and it felt false for either Stephen or Rose to try to create a fake happy when they themselves didn't feel it. Maggie was gone, she was either safe or not, she was either coming back or not and there was absolutely nothing any of them could do about it. They had to cope with those facts as best as they could whilst also not denying them. Rose had always treated Emily and Elliot as capable of much more than some might think and she felt no reason to change this now. She would do all she could to make things easy for them, knowing that this would not actually *be* easy. But she would be there for them – strong and reliable. She would be there. She would tell them that and show them that, over and over, until they believed her.

Usually, a quiet, calm bedtime was a thing to be celebrated but that evening it was disconcerting. Neither Emily nor her brother complained about dinner. They just ate. Neither splashed about in the bath. There was no joyful playing. They allowed themselves to be bathed and got out without protest. It was not a happy thing to witness.

Rose glanced at Stephen, concerned, and met his eyes, the same expression of worry on his face. She hoped he could read her thoughts and that he shared them. *Were the children too sad to be happy, grumpy, or frustrated? Were they trying their hardest to be 'good', not to push or to need anything, in case Stephen or Rose left too? Did they think their mother's return would be their reward for good behaviour? Did they think her leaving was their fault for being 'bad'?*

Rose wished beyond anything that she could read what was going on in their minds so that she could reassure them, to squash any blame that they might be feeling. She knew that she felt blame, at least in part, for Maggie's departure. With so little information from the police, they were all left in limbo, scrabbling around for anything that explained it, any shred of information that would give them an idea of whether this was it, or if Maggie might come back and, if so, when. It was hard to know what to feel in their situation. Anger was easy, but it was dismissive of Maggie's obvious pain. Sorrow came too but it was diminished by the fury that Rose felt on behalf of those left behind. Without knowing *why*, it was impossible to know what to feel and, by extension, what to do.

Dried and dressed in their matching pyjamas, Emily and Elliot went to bed without protest. They were too worn out. They both fell asleep quickly after Rose had told them that she would be there all night and there in the morning and if they needed anything, they just had to call out for her, and she would come. Rose knew that this was what Maggie had done. The children often woke in the night, and rarely at the same time, so Maggie's rest was taken in snatches where and when she could. No wonder she had broken. Rose knew she would have to be careful not to break too, despite not starting from the same post-pregnancy state of exhaustion that Maggie had. She would see if they could add another bed into the children's room so she had somewhere to sleep nearby if needed and insist that she had rest at the weekends. Perhaps Stephen could do one night a week. Something to make sure history did not repeat itself.

Rose sat in the darkened room, listening to the sounds of the children's breathing, heavier and drowsier than before, and tried to empathise with her sister. At what point had the overwhelm come? Had she planned to run away? Had it been a spur of the moment thing? Rose looked at the children's calm faces and her heart melted. Sleeping children were a gift. Being able to be here now for them felt like a gift to Rose. *How exhausted do you have to be, how completely spent, to look at such peace and see only something to escape from? What had they missed? Was Maggie running to something, or someone, rather than running away?* Rose sighed. There were so many unanswered questions, and it was exhausting to have them on repeat in her brain.

As quietly as she could, Rose crept from the children's bedroom and slowly walked downstairs and into the living room. It had been tidied, as had the kitchen, and Stephen was sitting on the sofa, staring at the walls. He was miles away and, as she looked at him in the moment, before he registered her presence, Rose wondered what he was thinking about. *Was there something that he knew, did he feel the same guilt as she did?*

Stephen jumped as he caught sight of Rose in his peripheral vision. Rose was grateful that she didn't look like Maggie, despite apparently sounding like her. She was painfully aware that her presence was a reminder of what was missing. She sat down in the chair opposite him and waited for him to speak. She used the moment of silence to look about the room. The pale grey walls and neutral tones of the upholstery were so Maggie. Rose's own apartment was saturated with colour. Colour everywhere and as bright as possible. Maggie liked monochrome. She said it made the contrasts greater. Maggie was also a fan of kitsch and, despite Stephen's hatred of it, had added small touches. There was a peace lily planted in a gold-coloured frog-shaped pot, nestled into the fireplace The tastefulness of the room, the tiled and cast-iron fireplace and the lush green of the plant all clashing with the deliberate ugliness of the frog. Rose smiled. Maggie always surprised people. They thought she was one thing and then would discover she was something else. Rose winced at the thought. She had thought Maggie a happy and devoted mother. Rose had clearly been wrong.

Stephen broke the silence.

'Ugly, isn't it? I hate that frog thing. It isn't plastic but it looks it. God knows where she got it from,' he laughed. 'Maggie loved it.' He caught himself. 'Loves it. Maybe I should get rid of it, if only to summon her home to yell at me for it.'

He smiled at Rose, who was grateful for this attempt at conversation. The atmosphere was strained. One-on-one was still not something they were accustomed to. There was a tension that Rose couldn't quite place. It felt wrong. Mind you, everything felt wrong.

Stephen was quiet again, lost in his thoughts. Rose looked at him, trying to get an insight into his mind. As if he had heard her, he said, 'I think this is my fault.'

She looked at him, her face expressionless to try to encourage him to open up.

'Why do you think that?' she asked.

'Well, you know how she was when we met. At university. She was always making things, creating outfits, sewing. It was the only preparation for the babies that she seemed to find any joy in, making things for them. The rest, well, it seemed to scare her. But when they were here, she stopped. There wasn't time. But that was such a big part of who she was. Should I have encouraged her to keep at it? She talked about getting a part-time job, but I wouldn't hear of it. It was my job to bring home the bacon, after all, and I do that well. But... it wasn't just about money, was it? I didn't see that. Or didn't want to. I felt she needed to be at home with the children. We're so different, she and I. I was so scared that she'd see that and change her mind about our family so, well I, I let her sort of... fade. Does that make a terrible husband?'

Rose widened her eyes at him. Stephen had always been confident. He had graduated top of his year at university and gone straight into a good job with a high-profile firm. His upbringing had installed the belief that success was to be expected. He had gone along with things, presuming all was fine, as it should be, never stopping to check if that was true. He had curated a vision of himself as a strong father, reliable, supportive husband and a decent family man, providing for them all while they grew under the nurturing eye of Maggie. Each role clearly defined and happily undertaken. It was clear now, in the way he looked at Rose questioningly, like a child wanting reassurance of their goodness, that this vision of himself was crumbling under the scrutiny that Maggie's disappearance had put it under.

'Truthfully?' she asked him, raising her eyebrows in a way that she hoped was sympathetic. He nodded, mutely, preparing himself for an onslaught from a defensive, angry sister.

'No,' she said. 'But I don't think you were a *great* husband either.' Rose checked her manicure and chewed on her lip whilst she formed her next sentence in her mind. She looked back at Stephen. He looked exhausted. Perhaps this wasn't the time to clarify her point. But when would it ever be?

'You know I couldn't ever really see you two together, don't you?' Rose said bluntly. She was too tired for niceties.

Stephen nodded, and his lips curved upwards at the corner, the smallest of smiles, but one that did not meet his eyes. More of a wince.

'She is social, and poised and fun, and you... well, you're sensible and... so very *English*. I couldn't ever work out where you met in the middle. I had hoped that you might bring out the good things in each other, but now? Now, I think, perhaps you crushed her.'

Stephen twisted in his chair, a pained expression on his face.

'Not necessarily intentionally,' she said, 'but... you're right. The person she was with you and the children was not who she wanted to be. She never talked about the family thing. She raved about designing, about costumes and the productions she wanted to work on. Then – bam – the kids were here and that all stopped. Maggie became Mum. But... if she felt she wasn't herself any more then, well, who was she? Who was left?'

Rose stopped. She was going too far. She didn't want to revel in her ability to make him squirm. That benefitted no one. So, she stopped, got up from her seat and sat down next to Stephen on the sofa.

'I'm sorry,' she said, looking directly at him. 'I'm grasping at straws. I don't know what went on in her mind any more than you do. I just... I can't compute what I know of my sister, of what she was like... is like,' she corrected herself '... of what I thought she was like, with this. With her leaving. And I wonder if any of us knew her at all? Or if we did, at what point did we fail to see what was happening?'

Stephen shifted a little away from Rose, distracted by her proximity.

'I can't think that she would hurt herself, but the police said we have to consider every possibility, and that includes considering that she may well have, she may be...' Rose faltered. She didn't want to say it out loud. She swallowed and continued. It had to be said. 'That she might be... be dead.' Rose exhaled, letting the words hang in the air.

'Don't say that. Don't!' Stephen pleaded. 'The children, she wouldn't... I know. It's all so confused. All questions and no answers. Still – I have to believe she is still alive. I can't look the children in the face if I believe she's gone. For them, I have to believe that she will be back. And soon.' He paused and then said, 'Tea?'

'You're so bloody English!' Rose laughed as she nodded at him.

He walked into the kitchen and busied himself with the kettle. Rose looked at him as he distracted himself from the situation with the everyday task. He had no clue just how much of a mess they were all in.

9

Stephen stood in the hallway, smartly dressed, as Rose handed him his newly polished shoes. He took them from her and tipped his head quizzically.

'They needed polishing, so I polished them while you were getting ready,' Rose said. 'I hope that's okay. Seems like work needs a little reminder about who they are lucky enough to employ. Suited, booted and ready for success.'

'Thanks.'

Rose saw something like pride flicker across his face and she tipped her head in a 'no problem' sort of gesture. She called the children to her and the three of them said goodbye as Stephen put on his coat and headed for the train. Rose felt that Stephen needed reminding of all he *did* have. Three weeks into this new arrangement and Rose already had things running like clockwork. New year, a new regime. Just, this time, it wasn't a new exercise regime, it was a whole new life.

Back in the living room, Rose got out a selection of toys for the children, which Emily immediately tipped all over the floor, splashing colourful plastic over the pale carpet like a dropped can of paint. *Embrace the chaos*, Rose reminded herself as she settled onto the sofa to watch them play for a bit and to decide what they would do with the day. She had barely sat down when the doorbell rang. The children stopped and looked up at Rose, their faces betraying their hope that it was their mother. Rose smarted. It hurt every time they hurt, a daily occurrence.

'It's okay, kids, I'll see who it is,' she said as their eyes followed her to the front door. Rose took a look through the view finder. She didn't want to be caught off-guard. 'It's Laura. Again,' she called back at them, before swinging the door open with her best smile on her face.

'Laura!' she cried. 'Come in! You've literally just missed Stephen,' and she put out her arm to take her coat from her.

Laura smiled, unsure of how to take such a welcome. 'Did I? I didn't see him...' She handed her coat to Rose and allowed herself to be ushered into the living room.

'Can I get you a drink? Something to eat?' Rose asked, a little too brightly.

'Bisskit, Mama?' Emily said hopefully.

Laura looked shocked but said nothing.

'Yes, all right, darling. One biscuit. No more, though. Okay?' Rose smiled at Emily, who followed them to the kitchen for it and then went back to playing quietly in the front room.

'Um, so, how is everyone?' Laura asked, as Rose bustled about putting the kettle on. Rose stopped. She turned and rested her back on the kitchen counter. What was Laura *really* asking? Rose decided to go for a breezy answer. She'd noted Laura's reaction to 'Mama'.

'It's a mix. Stephen seems to be doing fine, though mostly via denial. He thinks she'll be back any minute, unharmed and things will go back to normal.'

Laura nodded knowingly.

'That sounds like him. Everything always went his way. He doesn't know how to cope with anything else. And the children?' Laura questioned further.

Rose could feel the chat turning into an interrogation. Laura had turned detective, coming round every week without fail with updates of her so far fruitless search for Maggie, asking for more information that might help. Now it felt like she was focusing her investigative skills closer to home.

'As can be expected. The children don't really understand. They're either fine or they're distraught. I spend most of my time saying over and over that she's gone away for a while and reassuring them that I will be here until she's home. Every little glimmer of hope they have that gets dashed is brutal to watch. I can barely stand it. I don't know what to say. What can I say? Emily calls me her "Mama for now", which seems to be helping,' Rose said, watching for Laura's reaction.

Laura nodded mutely.

'It's a lot for all of us to take. The children desperately need someone to take care of them and for some reason, that person isn't Stephen. They need a mother. These past few weeks, the night-time terrors and the tears have been horrific. Christmas was the worst. But they're starting to accept that when they call in the night, it is me who comes to them.'

'That's good, I guess,' Laura replied. 'And you? How are you doing?'

Rose glanced downwards. She didn't want Laura to see her face. It would betray her true feelings. The children relentlessly asked for Maggie and still knew that 'Mama' was gone but occasionally both Emily and Elliot would slip and call Rose 'Mama'. She didn't correct them, but she was conflicted when this happened. Her heart leapt – she loved being their number one. She loved them. But her stomach sank, too. How was this going to work?

Everyone had lost someone important to them. Stephen, his wife – the children, their mother. Rose had lost her only sibling. Laura had lost a friend too, but Rose wanted Laura to understand just how hard this was for her. She had admiration from Stephen, love from the children, but Rose wanted some sympathy too. She needed a friend and she wanted Laura to perhaps be that person. Or if not a friend, then at least not an enemy.

Rose looked up at Laura, painting all her sadness and worry onto her face and she let a tear fall. She had not cried since that time back at her flat and it felt good to let it out.

'I...' Rose croaked out as she stood there, letting her tears fall, letting Laura feel her pain. Surely Laura would be moved by such a display? Rose couldn't imagine who wouldn't. It would cement Laura as being on Rose's side. On Rose's team – right where Rose thought Laura ought to be.

Laura stood, her arms locked to her side as she worked out what to do and eventually, she did what Maggie would have done. She stepped forward and held Rose while she cried and looked about the kitchen for tissues.

'God. Sorry. I am *such* an ugly crier!' Rose laughed, relieved that Laura had reacted how Rose had wanted her to.

'It's okay...' Laura said, stepping back, clearly a little uncomfortable. 'I was wondering if you might not be all right. You've been so... well, so *fine* that I almost wondered if you were happy about all this,' Laura laughed.

Rose's tear-stained face shot up, rage glowering from every pore. *How dare she?*

'You... I beg your pardon?'

'No. No, no, no, I didn't mean it like that!' Laura backtracked. 'I'm sorry. It was a joke. It was poor taste. I'm sorry. Of course you're scared for her. We all are. Of course you're not fine. You just do a better job of not showing it, that's all I meant. This all, well, this all seems to come naturally to you.' Laura ran her hand through her hair, strands falling over her face as she did.

'Okay. Fine. Sorry.' Rose sniffed as she reached for a tissue to dab her face, removing any smudged make-up.

Still embarrassed, Laura said, 'And the police?'

Rose shook her head and looked at Laura, her composure fully regained.

'Nothing. They have no new leads, no new suggestions. They interviewed anyone that we could think of, anyone who might have seen her or know anything. They clearly think she left by choice, and they don't have the resources to be chasing down anyone who just needed a change of scenery,' Rose scoffed.

Laura wrinkled her brow at Rose, which Rose took as disapproval. That wasn't fair. Maggie was in a bad place, yes, but she had also dropped everyone in it. Rose was beginning to see that she ought not be too open with Laura. Rose wasn't wholly sure of what she wanted, of how she wanted things to play out now Maggie was gone. She was confused. She needed to keep Laura in her pocket in case she needed her, even if right now, Rose didn't know for what.

'There is nothing we can do now but wait. She isn't deemed at risk. Despite the A&E visit the night she left, there is nothing in her records to suggest that she wasn't coping. You know that the police put us in touch with a missing persons charity, but the advice is the same – keep channels of communication open and wait.'

'That's... disappointing,' Laura said tersely.

'It's frustrating,' Rose retorted, 'but I can't see what else we can do. We've put out an appeal on social media. It's been shared all over the world and still, nothing. Well, nothing concrete. It's like she's stepped off the face of the earth.'

Laura nodded and then started blinking strangely.

'Are you okay?' Rose asked.

'Yeah, sorry. My contact lens has moved. Um, could I use a mirror to check it?' Laura asked.

'Of course. Use the bathroom, the light is better in there. Do you know where it is?' Rose asked. Laura's diminishing visits once the children had been born was a sore point and she could have sworn she saw Laura flinch at the question.

'It's just at the top of the stairs, you can't miss it,' Rose said as Laura walked towards the hall.

Rose went to the children while Laura was gone. 'Isn't it nice that Laura has come to visit?' she asked with a bright voice, hoping Laura might hear her but not clearly enough to register how forced it was.

Laura returned, looking sheepish.

'Um... Rose?' Laura said, clearly trying to work out how best to ask something, irritating Rose. She hated when she could see someone making an effort to be polite. It usually meant they were about to be insulting, regardless of their intention. Rose raised her eyebrows in a way that answered and her lips hardened into a firm line. She was not about to be criticised.

'It's just that...' Laura continued. 'Well, I couldn't help but notice that your things are in the bathroom. Or at least, I presume that they're yours. And, well, I looked in on the spare room on the way past. I wasn't snooping, just the pile of your clothes caught my eye. Did you move in?'

Rose looked up at Laura and tried not to feel guilty, which should have been easy as she had nothing to feel guilty about.

'Yes,' Rose said firmly. 'I've been here every single day since Maggie left and everyone was exhausted with all the coming and going. It was too much, especially over Christmas. We all needed some stability. The children are much more settled with me here and it helps Stephen too. He and I decided I should move in full-time for a bit. Until Maggie's back. And in the spare room, obviously.' It was nothing like that, there *was* nothing like that, he was her sister's husband, wasn't he? But the second Rose said it, she wished she hadn't. Rose blushed and Laura noticed. Rose knew it by the way she was looking at her now. Just the tiniest inkling of suspicion.

'I'm sorry, Rose, I didn't mean to suggest anything,' Laura muttered, unconvinced.

Rose replied only with a disapproving expression, all thoughts of hospitality long forgotten, the tea cooling rapidly in the mugs on the kitchen table.

'I know you've given up a lot to step in and help. I know whatever Maggie's reason for leaving, or staying away, or whatever has happened to her, I know she would be happy to know you're taking care of her family. Until she gets back,' Laura said conciliatorily. She looked flustered but Rose's expression gave her nothing to go on.

Elliot toddled over to Rose and she picked him up. He snuggled into her shoulder, shyly peeking back at Laura, this lady who had caused an atmosphere that he was too young to understand but astute enough to pick up on. He was calmed by Rose rocking from side to side and stroking his back. She looked a natural, as though Elliot was hers, despite their different colouring.

Laura caught Rose's eye and smiled. 'It can't be easy to reassure them over and over. It must be emotionally draining, especially when you're so worried too. You really are holding everyone together. I'm so sorry. I didn't mean to suggest... I...'

Rose held up a hand to stop her.

'It's okay,' she said. 'I was going to take the kids to the park. Give them some fresh air. They've been cooped up too long. They need airing. They're like puppies!' Rose tried to smile. She found Laura and this forced deference grating and was finding it hard to hide it.

'Do you want to come? I need another pair of hands for the swings. We can talk more there,' Rose suggested.

'Oh. Um, yes, okay,' Laura said, looking surprised at the invitation.

Rose bundled the children into their coats with some resistance and the four of them walked around the corner to the little play-ground. This place had been a lifeline for Rose. The park was easy. 'Swings!' Emily yelled and bounded towards them. Elliot made it clear that he agreed. Rose lifted each in and then stepped back to allow Laura to push one.

'We'll be here for most of the morning now,' Rose said. 'This is their favourite and it's not easy pushing two at once, so get pushing!'

The two women stood in silence for a while, pushing the swings back and forth, back and forth. It was almost hypnotic. A literal breath of fresh air, though the chill would spread into their fingers and toes soon enough and long before the little ones would be ready to go home.

After a while, Rose turned to Laura, picking up the thread of their earlier conversation.

'The police have stopped looking. There's nothing else they can do or are willing to do. We have to accept this and just wait. The police said that she bought a ticket to Glasgow and that's all we know.'

'Glasgow. So...' Laura stopped. She looked thoughtful.

It was exhausting having Laura visit all the time, asking after any new information. There was none. There never was. All her visits did was stir things up, things that were beginning to settle. In an ideal world, Laura would just leave them be to work things out on their own.

'I get why the police have stopped looking,' Laura said, 'but that doesn't mean *we* have to stop looking, do we? There are leads that we might have that they wouldn't follow up. I mean, if she's in Scotland...'

Rose looked surprised.

'Are there? What? And we don't *know* she's in Scotland, there's been no sighting of her there. That's just where the bus she got on was going.'

'Well, it's just there's...'

Rose cut in.

'Stop! What if this is what Maggie *needs*? This time, this space away from it all. What if she chose to go because she needs something that she can't get here? What if we chase her down and drag her back when she's not ready? How is that helping her?'

'No, I'm not saying we should *force* anything, just that if we knew she was okay, we could...'

'If we *love* her, like we all say we do,' Rose tried not to be too pointed but she needed Laura to feel that she was the one being selfish here, 'then perhaps we need to be patient and wait for her to do things on her terms?'

Rose was conflicted. Her new situation was exhausting but it was also the most fulfilling thing she'd ever done. She didn't need to worry about work, or money, or deadlines or anything. She had her own little world, her own kingdom, and it ran as she wanted. She'd never had this before and Laura turning up with more 'leads' or 'suggestions' just threw a spanner in the works.

Rose stopped pushing the swing, looked at the ground and sighed deeply. She closed her eyes. Laura stood looking at her, confused.

'Rose, are you okay?' she asked.

'I'm fine,' Rose said, still facing down, her eyes still shut. Her lack of sleep was making it so hard to stay patient. Chasing after Maggie wasn't doing anyone any good.

'Push me, push me!' Emily cried.

Rose took up pushing the swing again.

'I'm just tired. I'm tired from lack of sleep, waking for the children and reassuring them that I'm here, even if Maggie is not. From trying to decide if we *should* be looking for her and we're just sat waiting. I'm tired of trying to work out whether to be angry with her. I'm tired of being scared that she's dead. I'm tired of trying to work out how we are going to fix this, *if* we can fix it at all. I'm tired of worrying that I won't be enough, and that these beautiful children are going to be broken by this.'

She looked straight at Laura.

'I think we let her down. I will *not* let her children down too. But I am so *angry* at her for leaving them!' Rose dropped her voice, angry as she was, she didn't want the children to hear. The forced hard whisper felt more aggressive than shouting. Enough. This was not the time nor the place.

'Time for something else, kids! My arms are sore,' Rose said as she helped the children out of the swings. They toddled off towards the mini trampolines and Rose followed, jumping gently with them, holding hands in a circle.

'Now your turn, you two. I need a rest.' Rose sat Elliot down, with Emily bouncing him gently and stepped off, standing back with Laura.

'I'm impressed,' Laura said, nodding towards them. 'You've more patience than I would have for this. I'm... I'm surprised, to be honest. I always thought you'd be more hands-off,' she said kindly, no malice in her voice. 'I remember when you came to stay with Maggie, the two of you would be planning your world domination. All the places you would go to, the things you'd do. You barely mentioned a family. I know Maggie didn't.'

'Well. It's not like you and I bared our souls to each other now, did we? Maybe I just didn't tell you,' Rose said pointedly. 'I still want to do all those things. Just this, now, is more important,' she said, shutting the conversation down.

They spent the rest of the afternoon focusing on the children, Rose waiting for Laura to excuse herself and leave, which she didn't do. Rose felt wrung out by the time Stephen arrived home. He breezed in the door with a smile on his face and a large bunch of flowers in his hand.

'Daddy!' Emily said and bounced over to him. He put his arm around her.

'Oh,' he said, shocked at finding Laura in his home. Rose hoped that he wouldn't be angry with her for allowing Laura to stay. Memories of Maggie and Stephen's wedding day came to her mind, of when Laura had practically begged Maggie not to go through with it, telling her that she was making a big mistake. Stephen was, understandably, not a fan of hers.

Rose looked from Laura to Stephen, who had frozen on the spot like a deer in the headlights. Rose let him hang for a moment, before breaking the silence that was beginning to swallow them all.

'Laura came for another update,' Rose explained. She looked at the flowers. They were pink lilies. They were not her favourite flower; the strong scent always gave her a bit of a headache. She, of course, favoured roses. Lilies were Maggie's favourite, though not in pink. Just one more subtle way that Stephen was missing the mark.

Stephen nodded and cleared his throat. He handed the flowers to Rose, almost sheepishly, not looking at her, as though he was a shy schoolboy handing flowers to his teacher.

'These are for you,' he said, unnecessarily. Then he added, 'For all you're doing for the children. I, um... I realise that perhaps Maggie didn't or doesn't know how much I appreciated all she did for our family. I know that, um... maybe that may have made her feel, um, unsupported or, um, alone...'

Stephen fell over his words. The speech was a struggle for him, but it was obviously something that he felt he needed to say. Laura was looking at him, her expression both shocked and surprised. This was not Stephen being *Stephen*. This was new. This was not the silent, unemotional man both women knew.

He stopped talking and looked up at his audience. 'I don't want to be flippant. I am still very much aware that my wife is missing.' He slipped back into the stiff upper lip of his upbringing. 'I just don't want anyone else to think that I don't care.'

He blushed and looked at his feet. Rose was surprised. She'd never seen this from him before, an actual expression of his feelings. He'd always been so closed, so uptight. Did he have hidden depths after all?

'Emily, darling?' he said to his daughter, who looked up at him with adoring green eyes. 'Can you put this in Daddy's office for me?' he asked, handing her the evening newspaper he had tucked under his arm. She did as she was asked, beaming from being given such an important task.

Elliot, too young to understand, was sitting in his highchair, enjoying making a terrible mess with some crayons. He was blissfully oblivious to the grown-ups' conversation. With Emily's listening ears out of earshot, Stephen continued.

'I am not demonstrative. It's not in my nature. But I have to say this.' He looked out of the window, aware of all eyes on him, voices silent, waiting to hear what he had to say. 'It pains me beyond words that Maggie may have walked out on us all, have left of her own free will. Though it is better, only just, than the thought that someone may have done something to her. I should have been a better husband, a better father. I was trying to sleep last night, after you had resettled them, Rose, and I couldn't. I couldn't get all of the "what ifs" out of my head and it just hit me.'

He stopped, the weight of his thoughts etched on his face.

'This is what it was like for *her* when they were born, and I left her to it. I left her to do all of that by herself. I thought we were okay. I thought she was happy.' He stopped. He looked broken at the worry grinding him down.

Laura shifted her eyes away from him, clearly uncomfortable at seeing Stephen exposed like this. Quietly, she said, 'So maybe she wasn't happy and needed to get away for a bit. I could try and find her? We know she probably went to Glasgow. I could see what else I can find out?'

'Yes. Glasgow.' He shook his head. 'Means nothing to me. We have no connections there, nobody I can think of. Why would she go there? I...' Stephen said, 'It does feel wrong, doing nothing, but I just can't be in so many places. Work, the children...'

Rose jumped in. 'You're doing all you can, no one can do everything.' She glared at Laura.

Sensing that toes were being trodden on, Laura added, 'You two need to stay with the children, I get that. But I'm self-employed, I can work anywhere. I could head up and just ask some questions, see what I can find. It can't do any harm, can it?' She looked from Rose to Stephen and back again, like she was trying to work something out.

Rose nodded, without saying anything. A twinge of sibling animosity told her that she didn't want to go gallivanting all over the highlands to drag Maggie back, when she had dropped them all in it when she left. Rose swallowed. That wasn't fair, but it was hard not to be angry with her sister.

'What would we do if we found her and she doesn't want to come back? Do we force her to come back, so all can go back to *normal*? How does that fix anything? Surely, if she needs time, we should give it to her?' Rose crossed her arms, as awkward silence met her statement.

'I hear you, Rose, but I can't do nothing,' Laura argued.

'Right. We each play our part then. Stephen, you keep going to work and keep that normal. I will stay here with the children and look after them. Laura, you go and see what you can find. But please do bear in mind that the police said she may not *want* to be found. We have to tread carefully.' Rose was done with this discussion.

'You *do* want to find her, don't you?' Laura said, offended by Rose's apparent disinterest in locating her sister.

'Of *course* I do! Don't be ridiculous, Laura. God, you always were so dramatic! I am just saying what the police said and if she is okay, and she's somewhere taking time, getting ready to come home, we don't want to undo that, we don't want to scare her into doing something rash. That's all I mean. Go, look. But please be careful.'

Considering the subject closed, Rose picked up the flowers that Stephen had left on the kitchen counter.

'Thank you. The flowers are lovely. Maggie's favourite too. A reminder that she is still with us, even though she is not here.' She threw a pointed glance at Laura. 'But Stephen, for what it is worth, I am right here with you. You are not alone. I am not alone. We will learn from Maggie and make sure that the family stays together.'

Rose glanced back towards Laura, who could not hide her unease.

'I have to go,' Laura said suddenly and she turned to pick her bag.

Emily wandered back into the room. Laura patted her hair affectionately and blew a kiss to Elliot, who gurgled chirpily back at her. Then she left the room and let herself out of the front door, closing it firmly behind her.

Rose and Stephen barely noticed she had gone.

10

'It's my birthday!' Emily sang out, dressed in a sparkly party dress and bouncing around the room, playing with the balloons that Rose had filled the space with. Colours floated around the room like a rainbow. Emily started singing 'Happy birthday to me' to anyone who might be listening as she walked through the preparations that were going on around her.

There was a birthday banner draped across the window. Cards covered every surface. Everyone was making a huge effort in an attempt to mitigate the elephant in the room. Maggie was not there. Laura's searching had turned up nothing so far. Months ago, the police had said that often people who chose to leave are pulled by significant events. Would Maggie be drawn back by Emily's birthday?

If Emily had been missing Maggie particularly on this day, she hadn't shown it. She was giddy as only a three-year-old can be on the approach of a day that means presents and unlimited treats. She was now old enough to understand why the day was special and, importantly, that it was all about her.

Rose sat on the carpet, immaculately dressed in a pale grey

dress that somehow made her green eyes stand out even more. She was sorting items into brightly coloured party bags for the guests who would be arriving later that day. She was nervous. She wanted Emily to have the perfect day. It had been so hard to see her struggle initially with the absence of her mother. Rose had seen the pain, the confusion and the grief. Rose had hugged out the sadness and she had tried her best to comfort Emily and make her feel safe and secure again, as Maggie had once done. It was working too. Rose was good at being mum and the children were returning to the happy souls they always had been. Too young to really know what was going on, they lived day to day.

The social workers who had visited to check on the children were concerned that Maggie had gone missing but there was no question hanging over the safety of the children. Their visit was just one of many official visits in the week that Maggie had left, and it blurred into insignificance against the many calls from the police. From initial reassurances that Maggie would return, Rose had slipped into not mentioning her at all. The children seemed happier with this as their memories faded. Stephen, if he disagreed, said nothing.

The birthday party had been a welcome distraction for everyone. Rose was always the perfect hostess, and this party would be no different. Every guest had been individually accounted for, every party bag with a different gift chosen for each child attending. There would be party games with beautifully wrapped prizes, food prepared with all tastes in mind. Rose had spent several days making and decorating the birthday cake of Emily's dreams. A fairy doll with a cake dress, beautiful piped icing and decorated with all the sweet jewels that it could possibly need. Emily had been excited to watch Rose make each stage.

'What should it taste like?'

'Chocolate!'

'What colour should it be?'

'Blue!'

She had been so happy to see the final result that she could barely go to sleep the night before for all the excited anticipation coursing around her body. Rose had managed to stay patient. It was wonderful to see joy rather than sorrow keeping her niece from sleep now.

'All done,' Rose said, handing the bags to Stephen to keep out of sight until the end of the party. Emily bounced off the sofa she had been clambering over.

'Party!' she shouted as she rushed into the kitchen, where her dad was now looking confused at all the paraphernalia that Rose had acquired. Rose came into the kitchen and smiled amusedly at Stephen who was holding a packet of small glittery 'Happy Birthdays'.

'It's table confetti,' she said, motioning with her head to his hands.

He looked up, 'Oh, okay. I don't know what that is!' and Rose laughed again, kindly, taking it from him and collecting up all the things before taking them to the kitchen table.

Emily ran around the kitchen, followed by Elliot, who was as excited as his big sister, even if he didn't really know why. The pair of them looked so happy that Rose's heart ached. They were more resilient than everyone had feared, yet Rose was aware in each and every moment of that morning that someone was absent. And that that someone could just show up as unannounced as she had left. Rose wanted so much to be Mother on this day, for Emily, but she was nervous and she had imposter syndrome running through every fibre of her being.

It didn't help that Rose barely knew the guests, all newly acquired friends. Maggie didn't appear to have known many people, not people with young children like her. Rose had been shocked. No wonder Maggie had felt isolated. It seemed that she hadn't made an effort to meet people at all. Rose had barely had to reach out and already she had a small gang of fellow mothers to spend time with. They all knew Rose as the children's 'Mama', and it was easiest not to correct them.

Rose was still worried that people might not come and that Emily would be disappointed. That made her feel sick to the core. Her niece had experienced so much sadness in just three short years and the thought that her first big birthday party would be a disappointment was too much.

The doorbell rang and Rose jumped. Emily whooped and shouted all the way to the door, to find her granny and grandpa standing there with the most enormous present she had ever seen.

'It's my *birthday*!' she shouted at them, as if this was news to them.

'I know, my darling Emmy! How big are you now?' Elizabeth said, as she stepped into the hallway, handing her coat to Rose.

'I'm *threeeeee*!' Emily yelled and dragged her granny into the living room.

Bill, smiled tightly and nodded at her.

'How is, um, how are things?'

Rose smiled back. He never knew what to say, even at the best of times. Rose had never known him to say anything that didn't need saying. She took the huge box from him while he took off his coat. She put it down and hugged him. He held her tightly, as though his hug could stop her from leaving too.

One by one, the guests arrived, allaying Rose's fears, and the party got underway without issue, Rose running party game after party game with boundless energy. Her parents stood back, watching, supporting and being as enthusiastic as only grandparents can be.

Stephen hovered, trying to be useful but not really knowing

how. He did a lot of tidying up and following instructions from Rose. They worked well as a team. The games were done, and it was time for the party tea. The children all gathered round the table and devoured their meal. The parents stood politely, sipping tea and coffee, and nibbling on the biscuits and cakes that Rose had Stephen offer around.

The lady who lived a few doors down approached and held Rose gently by the elbow as she said, 'You're doing such a wonderful job, you know? You'd hardly know her mother wasn't here.'

Rose strained a smile across her face.

'Oh, I'm sorry. That was the wrong thing to say,' she continued. 'It's just, well, if I didn't know that Maggie was gone, I would have thought *you* were Emily's mother. You're so good with her. It must be hard,' she said, releasing Rose, unsure if she had upset her or not.

'It is hard, yes. But days like today make it easier.' Rose smiled welcomingly. 'Thank you so much for coming, it's made Emily's day that your daughter is here.'

In the absence of any idea how to respond, Rose fell back on a role she knew well – perfect hostess, kind, polite, enthusiastic and welcoming. Always make your guest feel comfortable. Rose offered her another drink just as the telephone rang.

'Excuse me. I must get that,' she said, grateful for a reason to move away from the conversation.

Out in the hallway, it was calm and quiet. Despite the insistent ringing of the phone, Rose took a second to stand still and close her eyes, then picked up the receiver.

'Hello?'

There was a slight crackle on the line, a connection to somewhere, but no voice. No one spoke.

'Hello?' Rose said again, a little impatient. It was nearly time for the cake and Rose had somewhere else to be. Still nothing.

'It's a bad line. I can't hear you. Can you hear me?' Rose asked into the void. No reply... Rose closed her eyes and strained to listen. Was it, was there breathing on the line? Was that a whimper? Was it...?

'Maggie?' Rose said softly. 'Maggie, is that you? Did you call to speak to Emily? To wish her happy birthday?'

There was an intake of breath. Rose's stomach fluttered. She ached for her intuition to tell her if it was Maggie or just some cold call with a flaky connection. If it was Maggie, then she was alive! She was alive and well and able to call. Rose looked back at the party, they would be wondering where she had got to, but she didn't want to rush things. This could be pivotal in getting her sister home.

Home.

Rose stopped.

If Maggie came back now, it *would* be wonderful, wouldn't it? She could go back to her own life, her own flat, a job. She had walked away from these things without much thought, her typical 'act now, think later' behaviour. Did she miss them? Things would be as they were before. The children would have their mother back, Stephen, his wife. That was what everyone wanted, wasn't it? *Wasn't it?*

Rose waited, then continued.

'It's Emily's birthday party today. She's got friends here. Mum and Dad are here and there's a big pile of presents. Stephen is making tea and coffee for our guests. I've made Emily the most sparkly birthday cake you've ever seen – one of those ones with a doll in the middle and the dress is the cake. It's covered in sprinkles. She's so excited. She's having a lovely day. Elliot is wandering all over the place now, can't keep my eyes off him for a minute. He's started talking lots more too.'

Was the breathing still there?

'Maggie? Say something! Is that you? Do you want to know how we are?' She was angry now. If this *was* Maggie, then why didn't she speak?

Suddenly, something in Rose snapped. If Maggie didn't want her family, then fine, but Rose did. Rose *really* wanted them. What could she say?

'We're all fine here. It's all under control. You gave me the children to look after and I'm doing that. They're fine.' Rose found her voice sounding harder than she had anticipated. 'You are clearly not – making silent phone calls! You've seen what happens to the children when you're not in a good place.' She winced as she said it, even though it was true. 'You're obviously not well, you need to get better. Take this time, we can handle things here. I've told the children you've asked me to look after them. I'll take care of it all.'

She took a deep breath.

'I have to go. It's time for the cake. We're fine. We're all fine. You don't need to call again.'

Rose hung up. Immediately she regretted it. She snatched up the receiver in case she hadn't disconnected the call. The dial tone rang out in a monotonous peel. Whoever had called was gone.

She hung up again to reset and then dialled the last caller number. It did not connect. Caller unknown. Whoever it was, if it was Maggie or not, was either calling from abroad or did not want to be traced. They wanted their anonymity.

She stood there, torn. Worried that she might have driven Maggie away, yet almost hoping that she had. Whatever Rose had done, it was too late now.

She smoothed down her dress, regrouped and walked back to

the party. 'It's time for cake!' she announced as she walked through the door.

'Who was that on the phone?' Elizabeth asked, noticing that her youngest daughter was rattled.

'No one,' Rose said, looking away. 'I think someone called by mistake.'

Rose signalled to Stephen to turn off the lights and as he did so, she started singing, 'Happy birthday to you, happy birthday to you...' as she walked to the table holding the cake, the candles burning brightly as she placed it in front of Emily. She kissed her on her head, finished the song and stepped back to allow her to blow out the candles.

'Wow, Mama. Wow!' Emily said, as she looked at her cake and then back to Rose, her face absolutely beaming with happiness. Rose's stomach shifted as she was aware of eyes on her from around the room, waiting for her response. She could feel the heat of them on her. She couldn't ruin this moment of joy for Emily. She didn't want to. For Emily, but also for herself. Rose kissed Emily again and said, 'Happy birthday, my darling girl.'

Once the children had eaten their cake, Rose took the rest away to slice it up and put it into the party bags. Her mother followed her to help. At first, they stood in companionable silence as Rose cut the doll dress into pieces and Elizabeth wrapped them into napkins and placed them into the waiting party bags. There were no questions. Rose closed her eyes briefly, tired from the effort of keeping the party going. When she opened them again, her mother was looking at her. Her face gentle, open. Whatever Elizabeth was about to say, she was not angry about it. She was Rose's mother and she loved her. However, Rose also knew that expression. She was about to be parented. To be honest, Rose felt so lost that she welcomed it. To be guided in untangling the mess. She was trying hard not to cry.

Elizabeth's face held a mixture of emotions. She paused visibly and then said, 'You know that I'm proud of you, don't you? How you've stepped in here to help, how you have loved Emily and Elliot when that's exactly what they needed in this awful mess. You've helped them be as all right as you can be when... when your mother di.... disappears.' Her voice cracked.

She was trying to be a mother to Rose but also being a mother to Maggie was making this terribly hard.

'None of us know what has happened to Maggie and we need to keep faith that she is alive and well and will return to us, that she will come back to her family. *Her* family.' A look of pity crossed her face.

Pity. Anger started to rise in Rose. She had done so much and had given so much, and she was getting pity?

Her mother wasn't done, and as she placed her hand on Rose's shoulder, Rose flinched as she continued. 'The children love you. They adore you, that's clear. But this is not *your* family. I know, my lovely daughter, that you want your *own* husband, your *own* children and I know that when you get them, you will be brilliant at it. You are born to be a mother. But not now, not here. Here, you are an auntie. And you must wait for Maggie to come home. I know my child, mothers just do. She will come home.'

Fury fluttered in Rose's stomach. This *was* her family. She wouldn't hear any different. Not from her own mother, not from anyone.

Elizabeth squeezed Rose's shoulder again and turned back to the party bags. She had said her piece. Rose understood what had been said and what that had implied. As the younger sister, Rose had spent a childhood wanting what her older sister had. Toys, then clothes, then boyfriends. And the love that Maggie had for Rose meant that Maggie usually stepped aside for her. There had been quarrels, of course. They were sisters and they fought like cats and dogs, but Maggie adored Rose and would do anything for her. But Rose doubted even Maggie would step aside and give Rose her family.

If their mother was right and Maggie did eventually come back, then she would be the centre of attention, with all efforts on making sure she was okay. Despite having done all the work in keeping things going here, Rose would be pushed to the side. Just like that horrendous Christmas when Maggie was pregnant. Rose had never admitted she'd made a drunken pass at Stephen that one time. He'd rejected her then.

Would he choose differently now?

A smile flickered across her face. The situation had brought them closer together and Rose could see how much better she suited this life than Maggie had done. She made a better wife for Stephen. She was far more his type. Was he hers? She didn't exactly know, it was too difficult to separate out what she felt for him from what it was that he offered. The life that he offered. She knew she wanted that. Wanted this. Stephen was the key.

The increasing noise from the living room, as the excited children tipped from happy into over-tired, brought Rose fully back to the present and she looked at her mother filling the party bags. Elizabeth had clearly heard what Emily had called her and wasn't happy.

Rose found that she was furious. Maggie was the one who *left*! She had chosen to go, possibly forever. The part of her that loved her sister knew that she had been in a bad place, distraught and not in the right frame of mind. But the part of her that had been left to deal with the mess that Maggie had left was angry. Maggie had abandoned her children, her husband, her life. She had left Rose to pick it all up and now their mother was reprimanding her for handling it too well? She bit back her response and smiled, determined not to make a scene, and squeezed her mother's shoulder in supposed agreement. Rose knew in a way that Elizabeth was right, but she also knew that this meant nothing. Things would be how things would be. She would *not* walk away from everything she wanted when Maggie clearly no longer wanted it herself. Whatever the consequences.

11

The doorbell rang and Maggie went to answer it. Today was tough. She had been away for four months, it was Emily's birthday and it hurt to think she was missing it. She comforted herself with the knowledge that she'd sent her something special, that Emily would know she was thinking of her. She was getting better. Before she knew it, she'd be able to go home.

The light from the window above the door streamed in, bringing early morning sunshine into the dark corridor of Ailsa's cosy cottage. Maggie opened the door and on the step was a woman, a similar age to herself, with a young girl, almost three years old, who was trying not to fidget.

'Maggie. Sorry we're a bit late,' the lady apologised.

'No, it's okay. Come in, come in,' Maggie smiled, though she looked nervous. This was still new to her and being face to face with a girl who was roughly the same age as Emily shook her more than she'd expected.

They walked through into the front room where Maggie had set up her things. The makings of a dress were draped carefully over the back of a tall-backed chair. The lady put her bag down and Maggie took their coats.

'Heather? Is that you?' Ailsa called from the other room. 'Tea?'

'Yes, and yes, please!' Heather called back, tilting her head towards the doorway that Ailsa's voice had drifted through.

'So, hello, Katy, I'm Maggie,' Maggie said, crouching down on her haunches to make eye contact with the child. 'This will be your special dress. For being a bridesmaid?'

The little girl nodded, shy, still holding her mother's hand. She was clearly excited but being in a new place with someone she barely knew was making her cautious.

'It's okay. What I'll do is show you what I've done. It's roughly stitched together but I need you to try it on so that I can make it perfect just for you!' Maggie smiled at her. She was still guarded, but the girl loosened her grip on her mother. 'Is it your favourite colour? Yellow?'

'Yes! That and pink, but everyone likes pink, so my fave-rit is yellow!'

'What a good idea. My favourite colour is yellow too. Just like the sun. And lemons.'

'And bananas!'

'And bananas. You're right!' Maggie encouraged.

'You're so good with her,' Heather said, 'do you have any of your own?'

Maggie flinched. It was the question she dreaded. Questions like this were why it had taken her some time to agree to Ailsa's suggestion that she take on seamstress work.

'It'll do you good to make something again. To use your hands, remind you what you're good at, what you love. Remind yourself who you are,' Ailsa had said.

'No. I don't have any children,' Maggie replied, it was easier that way, but the sadness that she couldn't keep from her voice prompted Heather to say, 'Ack, there's time still, pet. You're still young. You'll be brilliant at it. I can see that.'

She meant it kindly, but Maggie couldn't reply. Heather took the hint and changed the subject.

The waiting lists for counselling were long and she had no funds for any private support, so Maggie was doing all she could to get strong again by herself. She had taken on some work, aware that she was wholly dependent on Ailsa otherwise. She was writing to the children regularly, telling them all her news and asking about them even though there was no way to receive a reply. It was hard, she just wanted to hear from them. But she knew they would be okay with Stephen and with Rose. Maggie knew that right now she had nowhere else to go and there really was nothing else that she could do. She was a designer, that was who she had been. That was who she could be again. Maybe then she could also be a mother, maybe it would finally fit.

And so here she was, designing dresses for the bridesmaids of a local wedding party, who had been let down by their other dressmaker. Maggie had stepped in at the last minute. The adults were mostly done but they'd saved Katy until last due to children's habit of outgrowing anything made too far in advance. 'They grow like weeds, don't they?' Ailsa had said and Maggie found herself wondering what Emily and Elliot looked like now. Every month makes such a difference when they're so young. She locked the thought away, refused to let it sit with her.

Maggie talked them both through the fitting, explaining all the time to Katy what she was doing and why. She thought back to when her mother had reprimanded her for talking at the babies all the time.

'It's not like they can talk back!' she'd laughed.

Maggie had been affronted. They could listen and surely that's how they'd learn and learn to trust her. But their trust had been misplaced, she hadn't kept them safe like she'd promised she would.

Maggie felt happy doing what she was good at: taking the spark of an idea and seeing it develop into a real thing. She loved this. She was herself. Just after Elliot was born, she had felt so strongly that she would never do this again, that this part of her life was over. The idea had physically hurt her. She knew sacrifices had to be made and that the children needed her more. Yet it had felt like too much to give. She wondered now whether she could do this at home, for Emily and Elliot, but Ailsa had urged caution.

'At home, you'll get dragged back into the chaos of before. A little time yet, hen, stay here, get your old self back, let Stephen take on the lion's share for a change. It will reset the boundaries for when you *do* go back.'

Maggie was working through this logic in her head, trying to make it sit as well as Ailsa clearly thought it should do, when she became aware that Heather was still talking to her.

'She is desperate to wear it, aren't you, poppet?' Heather said as they were putting their coats back on, getting ready to leave. 'It's her birthday next week and I can't convince her for love nor money that she won't be wearing it then. It's for...?' She turned to her daughter.

'The wed-dink,' Katy sighed.

'The wedding,' Heather replied smiling. 'Thanks so much. Will you let us know when it's done?'

'Can I come and play again? I like it here!' Katy asked, looking hopefully at Maggie.

Katy's open expression and innocent enthusiasm cut Maggie to the core. It was like looking at Emily. Maggie had to force a smile onto her face, she didn't want to let this little girl down like she had let down her own.

'Of course,' Maggie said, her voice starting to shake. She

needed them to leave. She was barely holding it together. 'Next week sometime? Okay, lovely to see you again, bye!' she said, too brightly, as she ushered them out and closed the door behind them.

Maggie staggered to the stairs, her legs giving way beneath her, folding to the floor like a house of cards knocked over. Specks of dust floated in the air as her tears came thick and fast.

'Och, hen, what's wrong? Didnae she like the dress?' Ailsa said, coming at the sound of Maggie's tears.

'No,' Maggie said between gasps of air, trying to catch her breath. 'No, it's not that. It's...'

Ailsa sat next to her and put her arm around her. Maggie knew she wouldn't push. In the past few months, she had shown Ailsa just how stubborn she could be.

'Birthday... today is... today is Emily's birthday. She'll be three. And I'm missing it. I – I should be there. I promised I'd make her cake. She wanted one of those ones where the cake is the dress of a doll. What – what if she hasn't got one like that? What if...?'

'Oh, love...'

The two of them sat, side by side in the quiet hallway. Alan, Ailsa's dog, came and found them. He looked confused as to why the humans were so sad and sat down on the cold stone floor beside them.

Maggie was first to speak.

'Maybe – maybe I could call her?' she said softly. She didn't want to offend Ailsa by suggesting she didn't want to be here. She was beyond grateful but today, today she wanted to be somewhere else. She wanted to be with them.

Ailsa looked sceptical.

'I understand, I really do. But is that a good idea? Today?' She looked to Maggie for some kind of rational thinking. 'It's been four months. Calling suddenly out of the blue, on her birthday...

wouldn't it just upset her? Unsettle her? Maybe even ruin her day?' She saw the hurt on Maggie's face. 'I don't mean she wouldn't want to hear from you, they all would, I know it. Just perhaps, not today? After all, today is Emily's special day, isn't it?'

'Maybe it would make her day?'

'I guess it might do...' Ailsa let the alternative idea hang in the air unsaid. She clearly thought it was not a good idea.

'What do I do, Ailsa? I thought I had it under control. Writing the letters helps, so I know that they know I haven't given up on them but am getting myself strong again *for* them, so I can be the mother they deserve but... I should *be* there!'

'Because you're their mother,' Ailsa said gently as she got up, 'you need to think what is best for them. Is your need to call today about them or about you? You're still very fragile, my love. You wouldn't want to frighten them, would you? Maybe wait and call when you're a bit stronger, a bit more yourself, eh?' Ailsa nodded kindly at her and went back into the kitchen, leaving Maggie to consider her words.

Maggie chewed her lip in contemplation. *What would Rose do?* She wondered. Rose was always impetuous, following her instinct. Maggie's instinct told her to call and so she stood up and with shaking hands, she took the phone off the cradle.

Maggie felt sick. She wanted to speak with Emily, with Elliot and them all, more than anything. Maybe she *could* do this. Maybe she could reach out. Maybe it would be okay. Maybe she had made a mistake in leaving and in staying away. A spark of happiness flared inside her. A teasing, tantalising suggestion that perhaps, just perhaps, a phone call could give her the answers she craved. Gingerly, she dialled her home number and held the phone to her ear. It rang several times.

'Hello?'

Maggie immediately recognised Rose's voice and the shock of it took her own away.

'Hello?' Rose said again, with a hint of annoyance in her voice. Maggie recognised that tone. This was a mistake. Clearly, Rose was angry.

'It's a bad line. I can't hear you. Can you hear me?' Rose asked.

A whimper escaped Maggie's lips.

Then, softly, 'Maggie? Maggie, is that you? Did you call to speak to Emily? To wish her happy birthday?'

Maggie took a breath. She held it. She wanted so much to say how she missed them and how sorry she was and just how much she loved them all. There were so many words to say and yet Maggie could not utter a single one of them. It was as though her mind had tied her tongue into so many knots that to speak was an impossibility.

'It's Emily's birthday party today. She's got friends here. Mum and Dad are here and there's a big pile of presents. Stephen is making tea and coffee for our guests. I've made Emily the most sparkly birthday cake you've ever seen – one of those ones with a doll in the middle and the dress is the cake. It's covered in sprinkles.'

So, Emily *did* have the cake she wanted. Maggie smiled with relief. She ought to have known that Emily would have asked and that Rose would have stepped up. That's why she had left, because she had known that Rose would be there. What could Maggie say? 'Thank you' felt trite, even though it was what she wanted to say. She missed her sister so much she ached, and on top of the pain she felt at missing her babies, it was too much. She felt sick.

'She's so excited,' Rose continued, telling Maggie all about the day and how they were, that they were all okay. She was her sister; she was her support.

Maggie opened her mouth to speak but a 'tsk' of irritation came down the line from Rose and she clammed up again. Rose's temper was rising. Maggie could feel it. When they were growing up, Maggie could always spot when Rose was losing her cool, long before anyone else noticed. It was like her voice was coated in ice – sharp and cold. Maggie was barely still listening. This was a mistake. She shouldn't have called. Images of Emily assaulted Maggie's mind. Her daughter blowing out her birthday candles, her face puckered and scarred from her burns, one eye not as it should be. Rose hadn't mentioned anything about the burns. Maybe she was leaving out anything that might upset her? Maggie nearly let the phone slip from her hands. She was sweaty and shaking. She had to hold on tight to keep it in her grasp.

'Maggie? Say something! Is that you? Don't you want to know how we are?'

Rose paused, her impatience growing in the silence. She snapped at Maggie, though Maggie barely heard her. 'You're obviously not well, you need to get better. Take this time, we can handle things here.'

Maggie was close to tears. Rose was right, she wasn't well. She did need more time.

'I have to go. It's time for the cake. We're fine. We're all fine. You don't need to call again.'

The line went dead. Maggie dropped the phone and Ailsa came running at the noise. Seeing the phone on the floor, Ailsa's face dropped.

'Oh, you didn't...'

'You were right. I should never have called. It was a mistake. They're fine, Rose has it all under control, but me? Look at me, I'm a mess!'

She held out her hands to show Ailsa. They were white and shaking.

'I'm not ready. I shouldn't have called. I need more time.'

Ailsa nodded in agreement. 'I think you're right, pet. If a phone call is too much, how would you cope if you went back now?'

'I... I wouldn't?' Maggie asked, unsure of herself. She had wanted so badly to talk with them, to hear Emily enjoying her special day, to let them all know how much she loved them. And yet one small conversation with Rose had brought back all the overwhelm, the fear, the panic. The terror that she would get it wrong again, that she'd do something stupid.

No, Rose had it under control, like she said. She was looking after them all like Maggie had hoped she would. It was okay to take his time. Maggie needed it.

'Love?' Ailsa asked, concern on her face.

'I didn't get to ask if Emily liked my birthday card,' Maggie said, bursting into sobs. 'What sort of a mother am I that I forgot?'

'One that needs time, lovely, one that still needs rest.' Ailsa put her arms around Maggie's shoulder. 'Everything at home is fine, you said so yourself. So you're free to take the time you need. For you, for everyone.' She stood up. 'I'll go and make us a cuppa,' she said, nodding, letting Maggie know this was the best solution all round.

Maggie remained standing, motionless, the cold seeping up from the stone flags keeping her alert. She clearly wasn't well. How she would get better she didn't know. There was a niggle at the back of her mind that all was not right, but she refused to let it in. It was just her anxiety gnawing at her. Rose was taking care of things back home. She could stay here, write often and rest. Recuperate. Find her old self and then go back. Yes. This was the best plan.

It is hard to know the difference between anxiety and fear and Maggie had long ago stopped being able to listen to her own instincts.

She should have tried harder.

12

In the days following the party, her mother's words echoed in Rose's mind every time there was a glimmer of feeling like she belonged. This wasn't hers, no matter how much it felt like it, no matter how much she wanted it to be. Every morning when she woke, with one or both of the children draped over her, her presence enough to lull them back into dreams, she felt grateful. This was how things were meant to be. Rose always went with her instincts, grabbing what she wanted with both hands, and really she was what was best for the children. She took the children to the park one morning, bundled up in their layers, and let them run themselves ragged, their little faces going pink in the still chilled spring morning air. She pushed them on the swings until her shoulders were sore, helped them onto the roundabout and spun it gently as they giggled. They were both so worn out by all this fun that they practically put themselves down for a nap after lunch. Rose had the house to herself. She sat on the sofa and sipped hot coffee. A feeling of a morning well done washed over her. She *was* where she was meant to be. Then again, her mother's words niggled at her.

She stood up and walked to the mantlepiece where the photograph from Maggie and Stephen's wedding had been pushed to the back. She picked it up and tried to read the expressions on both their faces. Two people who she now knew intimately. Rose looked at her sister, resplendent and glowing in the wedding dress that she had made for herself, draped to accommodate her growing bump. Rose smiled at the thought that the photograph included Emily. She looked at Maggie's expression with a focus that she had not done before. The anxiety behind the smile was clear to see for anyone who knew Maggie at all. She did not look happy. She did not look unhappy. She looked uncertain. As though her 'I do' needed a question mark alongside it.

Stephen was holding one of her hands with both of his, and what at first glance had looked like an affectionate clasping of hands by a newlywed, in retrospect looked more like a desperate gesture: 'Be mine. Stay.' Rose had always seen his smile as a happy one, but looking now, now that she knew him and his ways better, it seemed nervous. Like he wasn't sure that Maggie was actually going to do it, as though at that moment when the guests are asked if anyone has any reason why they shouldn't be married, he had fully expected someone to speak up. Maybe Maggie herself. Had he known that the moment was coming? Did *he* know where she had gone?

Rose had spent so much of the past months seeing things purely in the here and now and thinking of the children that there had never been enough space for her to really consider Stephen or rather Stephen before Maggie had left. The husband that Maggie had decided she didn't want any more. Wasn't he part of the family package Rose now enjoyed? Could you have one without the other?

Rose put the photo back in its place, wiped a little dust from the frame and turned away from it. She stood in the middle of the room and thought about her sister. She brushed her hand along the chair arm that she had sat on when Maggie told her, with a tremble in her voice, that she was pregnant again. She sat there again and remembered Maggie sitting opposite her. Rose tried to picture Maggie as she last saw her. Tear-stained and strained, exhausted and on edge. Unhappy and desperate. What had Maggie wanted when she got on that bus? Did she even know herself? Their mother was adamant that she would eventually come home but Rose was not so sure. Maggie had rejected this life, the one that Rose had so happily taken up. That phone call on Emily's birthday, what was it for? What had Maggie been calling to say? Had it even been her? Rose hadn't told anyone about it, hadn't talked it through. There was nothing to tell, after all, was there?

Rose sighed. It was impossible. She couldn't separate all the different things she was feeling into a single truth. It was too messy and too complicated. She loved her sister. She wanted her sister happy and safe. And yet Rose didn't want to leave. She loved the children as though they were her own. She *wanted* them to be hers. She wanted them to see her as their mother. She wanted a husband. Did she want *Stephen*? Maybe.

Rose wanted all these things but knew she could not have all these things together. She couldn't have her sister back and keep her sister's children. Could she? A cold feeling wrapped itself around her as she stood in Maggie's house with Maggie's beautiful children asleep upstairs and admitted to herself that she wanted all of this for herself. But this was not a new pair of shoes you borrowed. This was unforgiveable. And yet... was it worse than Maggie walking out? Was wanting it worse than not wanting it at all?

Rose sat back down, exhausted. It was all ludicrous. She got back up, walked to the kitchen, opened up the fridge door, covered with childish drawings and photos of them all, as curated as any art gallery. She took out a bottle of champagne. Despite her life being utterly altered, she had retained her habit of always having a bottle ready in case a celebration was in order. She unwrapped the foil, tearing it in a perfect spiral as she always did and slowly eased out the cork. It came out with a satisfying 'pop'. She took a gulp straight from the bottle and the bubbles fizzed in her nose. She raised the bottle to her missing sister and then drank again, longer this time but stopping before she went too far.

'Well done, Maggie,' she said to the ghost of her sister who was everywhere and nowhere. 'You've fucked us all.' She took a final delicate sip, a toast, before placing the champagne back in the fridge door. She laughed emptily as she turned and started to sort out the laundry.

Finally, evening came around. Exhausted from playing, reading, crafting, drawing, tidying and generally entertaining two little people, Rose took fish fingers and chips from the freezer and threw them into the oven. They were happy enough when their plates were placed in front of them and ate contentedly while Rose sat with them and drank a large glass of water. The pounding in her head from earlier was beginning to subside but she was bone tired. The cumulative effect of interrupted sleep night after night, the drinking and the stresses of parenting meant that all Rose wanted to do was curl up on the sofa and have a nap. Her train of thought was interrupted by Emily.

'Sorry, darling, what did you say?' Rose said, stroking Emily's hair.

Emily looked at her with a wrath so complete that it shocked Rose and there was barely a pause between registering her anger and Emily throwing her plate to the floor with such force that it shattered into pieces, mixing its broken fragments with her dinner, rendering it inedible.

'What did you do that for?' Rose shouted at her. 'Now it's

ruined, you silly girl!' She went to the floor to pick up the pieces before anyone got hurt by the sharp fragments. She cursed inwardly for refusing to use the brightly coloured plastic plates that she knew most other parents used. She was a prototype parent, learning moment by moment and she was playing major catch-up.

She was reminding herself that it was just a plate when she realised Emily was crying. All rage dissipated; this was different. She was quietly sobbing in a way that looked wrong on a pre-schooler. It was too restrained, as though she was trying not to cause any more trouble, like she knew bad things could happen if she cried more loudly. It made Rose catch her breath. She felt awful. She couldn't just lose her temper like that. These kids had gone through a major trauma. Their mother had abandoned them. She couldn't give them any inkling that there was even a possibility that she would do the same. She wouldn't ever do that. Rose dismissed the tidying immediately and went to Emily, scooping her up in a tight bundle.

'I'm sorry. I'm sorry, lovely, I'm so sorry,' she whispered into Emily's hair. She felt her tremble as the little girl tried to calm herself. She kissed her head and hugged her as tightly as she could.

'I shouldn't have shouted. It's just a plate. You shouldn't have thrown it, that wasn't kind. But it's okay. I'm here, I love you, it's okay.' She rocked her gently. The sobs subsided. Emily looked up at Rose with big pale eyes brimming with tears and her face red and blotchy.

'Sorry, Mama. I'm sorry,' she whispered. She held on tightly and Rose held her back, certain that she would not be the first one to let go. She had to make Emily know that she would not break away from her.

By the time Stephen arrived home that evening, Rose and Emily and Elliot were all asleep together on the king-sized bed in his room. Rose was half-dreaming when she was aware of movement close by. The room was dark, but she had not drawn the curtains fully, so the moon cast some light into the room.

'Stephen? Stephen, is that you?' she whispered.

'Yeah,' he replied, his voice not sounding like himself.

Rose wriggled her way out from the tangled pile of sleeping children and tried to get her brain to wake up and focus. She turned the bedside light on, just a touch, to help her see. Stephen was sprawled on the floor, tangled in his own clothing. Even in the half-light, Rose could see that he was drunk. She gently picked up the sleeping bodies of Elliot and then Emily and returned them to their own beds, their limp limbs draping against her as she carried them to the room next door. She tucked them under the covers, kissing them on the forehead and pulling the door to, leaving a small gap for the light from the hallway to flood into the room reassuringly. She paused momentarily, trying to shake sleep off her, to smooth down her hair before going in to deal with Stephen.

He was a mess. He was still fully dressed, coat and all. Rose turned the bedside table lamp up fully, casting light across the room. The atmosphere in the master bedroom, Maggie and Stephen's bedroom, her in her nightdress, with Stephen, had a strange energy about it that Rose couldn't place. Was it uncomfortable? Was it tension? She couldn't tell. She went to him and crouched down beside him. He was tear-stained with a tang of whisky on his breath. Rose looked at him and her heart jumped. He was lost. They both were.

Rose sat down next to him, put her head onto his shoulder and took his hand in hers. He didn't move or shift away. He didn't look at her either. He was in a different place.

'Where is she? What's happened to her? Why did she go? What did I do so horribly wrong that she would just walk away from us? I work hard, I work *so* hard for this family and she just walks out the door? I have walked the streets looking for clues of her, I have driven miles and miles in what feels like pointless circles. I have called and asked everyone and anyone I can think of. And nothing! Where is she?' he paused. 'Where *is* she?'

He turned to Rose and cried onto her. She took his frustration, as she took the children's sadness, and she held him as he cried. Rose looked at him and she hardened her heart against her sister.

Maggie had a family. She had people who loved her, who depended on her and she walked away. *You did this*, Rose thought angrily. *I know you were unhappy. I know you were struggling, but this? This is your solution, to tear your family apart?* Whatever Maggie had been feeling, she had clearly decided that it was more important than her two beautiful babies, who for weeks after her disappearance had bawled and screamed and struggled to comprehend where their mummy was. It had been Rose who had been the one to absorb that grief for them. It had been she who had dried eyes and been there for reassuring hug after hug, to kiss away nightmares and day terrors. It had been she who had made them feel safe again. Stephen had done his best, but it was not in his nature, he was not one to deal with emotion and it embarrassed him to talk about it. Rose had taken the pain suffered by Emily and Elliot and she had been drained by it, some nights collapsing into a bed that was not hers, in a house that was not her home and she had sobbed into a pillow with all the worry and the anger and the frustration. Maggie had abandoned her family and by doing so had broken it, and it was Rose who had the difficult job of trying to put it back together. What did she get in return?

Rose held Stephen close. She had expected this moment to come. No one could experience what he was going through and feel nothing. He was a kind man, not cold or unfeeling. He had just been trained not to show feelings. But there came a time, and there always would be, when he just couldn't do it any more and it all came pouring out like a river bursting its banks.

Rose looked at Stephen and saw her chance. She took Stephen's tear-stained face in her hands and gently kissed his tears. She peppered his face with little kisses that said, 'I'm here. I will heal you. You are not alone.' She kissed his closed eyes. She kissed his cheeks and she very gently kissed him on the lips. He looked at her and she swept the hair back from his face, wiping away a tear or two as she did so. He had absolutely beautiful eyes, Rose noted. Both the children had them, and she was used to staring into theirs. Now she was staring at where they had come from and she felt love wash through her. It did not feel like she was doing anything wrong.

Stephen shifted. She stopped. He was still for a moment. He closed his eyes. Perhaps his clouded brain was trying to think clearly, then he opened them again. He looked at Rose. And then he kissed her back. A kiss of friendship at first, a 'thank you for all you have done' kiss, in lieu of the words that Stephen found so difficult to find. But then, again, not gently, not gingerly, but with a strength and a passion that suggested that he had also been holding this back. A need for her.

Initially Rose froze in response, but somehow, with all that had happened to them and between them in the months since Maggie had gone, it became clear that something had shifted.

Rose kissed him back, urgency flooding from his body into hers as she responded and wrapped her arms around him, pulling his whole body close to her. She ran her fingers through his thick hair and he almost growled at her, reacting to her fingers on his scalp. He kissed her neck, inhaling the scent of her, turning his breath ragged as lust swept through him. They had stopped thinking. They were reacting. Stephen stood up, pulling her up with him and he pressed against her before taking her hand and sitting down on the bed, pulling off their clothes as they went. Stephen moved to lie fully on her, his weight and heat pressing down on her chest, making her feel both safe and vulnerable at the same time. Rose looked at him, kissed his face once more and shifted to allow him to enter her. They moved together, connected as she came and then he did, fast and unexpectedly, as though the previous days and weeks had been an unacknowledged foreplay that meant this moment was always going to come.

Neither spoke afterwards, but as Rose lay there, she could not help but feel reassured. He wanted her. That was clear now. Not just as a mother for his children, but her for her own sake. If *he* wanted her, then *she* could have them all – him and the children. Stephen wouldn't stay alone forever, there *would* be another woman and she would become the children's stepmother. She would replace her, and Rose would be ousted back to her old life. She didn't want that life any more. She wanted this one – the children, Stephen, and the life he could offer her. She did not regret this. Stephen rolled beside her and pulled her close to him, nuzzling into her. He pulled the covers up over them both and drifted off to a sleep so deep that he seemed dead to the world.

Rose lay there, trying to feel as though she had done something wrong and yet finding that she could not. She could hear her own heartbeat in the silence of the house. Stephen gently breathing beside her, Emily and Elliot doing the same just across the hallway, and she thought, *I have brought this peace to this house*, and she smiled. This was all she had ever really wanted. She could see that she *could* have it. She could just *take* it. Her sister had rejected her wonderful family and they needed Rose, they wanted her. She fitted them in a way that Maggie had not. Rose had lost her sister, why should she lose everything else as well? How was that fair? She was already missing a sister and if she were to reject this, well, it wouldn't bring her back. She was gone, regardless of what Rose did or didn't do. This way, she would be able to heal the hole that her sister's actions had created and she herself would get the family that she had always craved. If Maggie didn't want this family, then wasn't it there for the taking? And wasn't it better that it was taken by someone who truly understood them? Rose tried to wrangle the situation in her head. She looked at Stephen, looked at the doorway towards the children's room and it was clear to her. This was hers now.

Rose breathed out slowly. This was what she wanted. She was used to getting her own way, and what was wrong with that? After all, doesn't everyone really want their own way?

But this? She knew that this would not sit well with people.

Stephen might wake in the morning full of guilt or remorse or anger and ruin what they had because he *should*. Oh, the lives destroyed by the word *should*.

Rose shifted to sit up in bed, her sister's bed. She closed her eyes and tried to imagine telling her parents that she and Stephen had decided to be together. Where would she start?

She pulled her knees up to her chest and hugged them close to her. Stephen shifted beside her as the duvet covers pulled up with her, letting in a draught of cooler air. Rose sighed. She was tired. She thought about Maggie and how exhausted she had clearly been. Sitting there, awake in the middle of the night, knowing that someone in the house would no doubt wake and need her soon enough, Rose felt that she understood. But then she corrected herself. Other people have children close together and don't run away. Hell, people have twins, or triplets! Or triplets when they have children already! They just get on with it, don't they? *When you have children, it stops being about just you. It can't be about just you*, she thought.

Rose turned and looked at Stephen, a peace on his face that she had not seen since Maggie's disappearance. He had been facing this alone until Rose had stepped up. His father didn't get involved and his mother had left a long time ago.

And she had stepped up. She had made everything all right again by becoming a replacement Maggie so efficiently. She would break them again if she left.

Children's brains are primaeval – they just need to know someone is going to keep them safe, love them, feed them and take care of them. They don't care what DNA runs through their veins and even if they did, Rose's was close enough to Maggie's to be as good as identical.

The children had accepted her. To solidify things, she needed to know that Stephen did too. There was clearly something between them. Rose looked at him, snoring gently. If she could just make sure...

She wriggled down underneath the covers, pressing herself against his back. He murmured but remained asleep. Rose reached over his waist and down until she reached his crotch. Then, slowly and gently, she began to touch him as she kissed his shoulders. As she felt him begin to respond, to wake up to the sensations she was causing, Rose quickly removed her hand, fixed her hair and draped herself deliberately, seductively across the bed and closed her eyes, pretending to be asleep herself.

Stephen woke up and turned to her, reaching out to touch her as she lay naked beside him. She knew that her body had not been ravaged by two pregnancies and she knew her appeal. She took a moment to enjoy knowing she was being looked at before she opened her eyes, pretended to be shaking off sleep and smiled at him innocently. He pulled her towards him. This time it was slower, less intense but more deliberate. This time Stephen had consciously chosen Rose.

This was all hers now.

13

'Hang on, let me just...' Rose reached out and adjusted the collar of Emily's immaculate shirt. Emily wriggled as she did so, unused to the restrictive feel of her new pre-school uniform.

'Muummm...' she complained as she jiggled from foot to foot.

'One second,' Rose said, as Emily grew impatient for her to take the photo. Rose wanted to preserve this moment. The first day of pre-school for her oldest child. A milestone moment for everyone. Emily was a mixture of excited and nervous, taking such a step towards being the 'big girl' she wanted to be. Standing on the doorstep in her slightly-too-big uniform made her look suddenly so small that Rose had to fight the urge to swoop her up in her arms, make her change back into her beloved sparkly dresses and call the school to say that she wasn't coming, they couldn't have her, she was a baby still and Rose wanted her to stay hers. But time had passed as it always does, whether you want it to or not, and the day was here. Elliot bounced about excitedly, with Stephen trying to keep the exuberance under control and failing. It was a pivotal family moment and Rose drank it in. She had made it all work.

That night barely a month ago had cemented things, just as

Rose had hoped that it would. When she and Stephen had woken the next morning, they had been entangled in each other. He had pushed her hair back from her face and smiled. He looked a little sheepish at first, as if not sure of how she would be feeling. She smiled back.

'This feels right, doesn't it?' she asked, her stomach in knots in the seconds it took him to respond. Had her charms worked? Was this all going to plan?

He nodded.

'Yes. It really does.'

Rose pulled him in for a kiss.

'I can't see everyone feeling that way, though,' he continued. 'People won't be happy.'

Rose waved her hand dismissively.

'People! Who cares what people say? We only get one life.'

She paused.

'Are you happy?' she asked.

'With this? Yes. Yes, very much so.'

'There then. So am I. We all are. Together – you, me and our children.'

And that had been that. At least within their own home.

They hadn't spoken about it again but continued as though this is how things had always been. He went to work; she stayed home and took care of the children and the house. The children were growing and thriving. They were happy. They no longer remembered the day that Maggie left. They had accepted that she was gone for now and they didn't feel the lack of their biological mother. They had a mummy. They had Rose. All it took was not looking too hard outside their bubble. It suited them both. The world as it was meant to be.

'Smile!' Rose cheered as Emily beamed from the doorstep. 'One with me too,' Rose said, crouching down to take a selfie with her daughter on her phone. One for the photo album. She wanted them to remember all the details of their childhoods with her when memories got blurry. Her family, with her at its centre. The matriarch.

But for all her bravado and confidence, on some days, she couldn't be wholly present because despite everything, a whisper of Maggie was still there, pushing Rose just a tiny bit out of centre. That middle-of-the-night worry – would Maggie come back? – just sneaking in to ruin the moment.

'Oh, what a special day!' their neighbour beamed at them as she came out to her car. 'You look so grown-up, Emily,' she smiled.

Rose had been relieved when their old neighbours had moved away. Understandably, not everyone had been happy with Rose moving in and taking Maggie's place. Even those who had been utterly supportive of her selfless behaviour in taking care of the babies and Stephen had been appalled when they reformed their family with Rose at its centre. The neighbours had stopped talking to them and the atmosphere had been icy.

Rose was furious with them.

'What a lot of hypocritical, sanctimonious shits!' she had yelled at Stephen after an altercation between her and the elderly woman next door had ended with her calling Rose a harlot.

'They did nothing to help when she left. Did anyone offer to help you, to help us? No. They left us to it, left it all to me and now that makes *me* the nasty one?'

They had settled into a stalemate of silence but it had been a wonderful day when not long after, a younger, friendlier family moved in, with children older than Rose's and with a mum who was willing to help guide a fellow parent through the uncharted waters of parenthood. It had been both the beginnings of a 'village' and a clean slate.

'Would you like me to take a photo of everyone?' the neighbour asked as she headed over to see them, glancing back through her own front door to ask her children to get their shoes on, please. Stephen paused for just a fraction of a second.

'Are you okay?' Rose asked.

'Yeah, yes. Fine.'

Rose knew what he was thinking, or rather who he was thinking of.

He hadn't mentioned Maggie to Rose since that night but Rose knew when he was thinking about her. They'd packed away her things, her photographs, but at times she was there all the same.

Whenever they disagreed on something, Rose would wonder whether Maggie would have behaved differently, or if Stephen was wishing his 'wife' was still the other sister. In rare moments of self-doubt, Rose would wonder if Maggie would do a better job of things, but then she would shake it off, reminding herself that Maggie left. It was hard competing with a ghost, but it's also hard to come out on top when your major contribution to the family is abandonment.

The four of them stood together on the doorstep. A beautiful family, one Rose was proud to call hers. Stephen, strong and handsome in his suit, Rose, beautifully radiant despite a make-up free face and pulled-back hair.

Emily was the spitting image of Rose, and she was clearly getting bored of being photographed but was persuaded to pose for just one more of the family. Elliot was still hopping about with the energy of a toddler awake and fuelled by breakfast.

'What a lovely photo.' Their neighbour smiled as she handed back the camera to Stephen. 'One for the grandparents' wall, I'm sure!' she said as she disappeared back into her house to wrangle her kids out of the door in time for school.

Rose scoffed at the comment. The four of them might have solidified into a new unit but it had shattered the rest of the family.

Rose's parents hadn't known what to do or say when they had told them they were together. It had gone as well as Rose had feared it might.

It was wrong, too soon, not fair on Maggie. It was confusing for the children, it was selfish, what would people say? Rose had stood her ground and refused to accept the criticisms. She knew that it was right for them all and her parents would have to come around to it. Yes, she knew that they were worried for Maggie, Rose was worried too if she was honest with herself, but she couldn't let that in. It ruined everything else. For this to work, Maggie had to be gone. And stay gone.

As they all got ready to leave, Rose's phone rang in her pocket.

'Mum. Morning,' Rose said as she answered Elizabeth's call. Her hackles were up as they always were when her mother called these days.

'Ah, good morning, dear,' Elizabeth replied in a deliberately breezy voice. 'How is everyone? Big day!'

Enforced jollity as usual. Rose felt it. With everything still so raw for her parents, she could feel the discomfort her mother felt. How she wished none of this had happened and Rose was living another life, one unconnected with the tragedy of her disappeared eldest child. It was hard not to take it personally, even though Rose could appreciate that she and Stephen had put Elizabeth in a very difficult position. Needing to be on both sides. Day-to-day life had settled into a new normal but any interaction with her parents reminded her of what a mess it was if you looked hard enough.

'Yes. Big day,' Rose echoed, neither one of them wanting to mention just how significant it was. Both of them wondering if, just perhaps, Maggie was thinking of it, thinking of them all. Or if... if she was no longer here to think of them. Big days always came with whispered anxieties and unsaid what ifs.

'Shall I get Emily on the phone for you?'

'Please.'

The stilted over-politeness of their chat was an unkind reminder of the closeness that they had once had. Rose knew that if she really *needed* Elizabeth, then she could still count on her and that she was still a wonderful and involved granny to the little ones, and yet something had been lost when Rose took Maggie's place.

It was all just too complicated and on days like today, it felt like a storm cloud lurking in an otherwise blue sky.

'Emily, love, it's time to go!' Rose called after a few minutes. 'Say bye to Granny and send her all our love!'

Relieved at the excuse, Rose ushered the family out of the door.

The pre-school playground was busy, full of new starters looking tiny in their uniforms, being fussed over by family members. Some children looking as unsure as their parents. Some eager to start the next stage of being grown up. Rose wasn't sure how she felt. She knew she was proud. She had got Emily here. Emily was a confident, kind and funny girl but she behaved so like Maggie sometimes that it worried Rose. Would she prove more resilient than Maggie had been? It made Rose ache when she saw glimpses of her sister peek out at her like tiny reminders of the lie she mostly forgot she was living.

Emily patiently stood for a few more photos and then ran off to play with some of her friends who were joining her at pre-school.

Stephen stepped next to Rose.

'Shall I stay, or shall I pop off to work now? She seems fine?' Always worried whenever he needed to have a life during work hours, Stephen had one foot metaphorically out of the gate already.

'It'll only be a few more minutes until she's in. You can wait,' Rose said kindly but pointedly. It was not a discussion. She loved Stephen but she wouldn't let his habits break her like they had Maggie.

Rose scanned the playground, nodding hellos to the families that she knew. She was grateful that none of these people who would be here for the next stage of parenting knew her from before. The only positive to Maggie being seemingly friendless. Rose had never been the aunt to these people; she was always the mother. Her sister had been lonely, and Rose was here, reaping the benefits of that. It wasn't nice. But it also wasn't Rose's fault.

A lady with an explosion of red curls walked over to her. Stephen was at the climbing frame, spotting Elliot who was proving he could do what his big sister could.

'You're Emily's mum?' the lady said, half statement, half question. 'I'm Sarah. I think your daughter and my son met at the induction day. He said they'd played together before, apparently? At a park maybe?' She smiled at Rose as she held out her hand to shake. 'Have we met before?'

It was an innocent, friendly question but it made Rose feel sick. She was looking forward to school as a fresh start. A chapter where Maggie had never been. Here, Rose could just be 'Emily's mum' and enjoy the semi-anonymity that it would bring. It seemed as though Rose had been wrong. She'd never met Sarah, so maybe Sarah had met Maggie.

'No, I don't think so,' Rose said, taking Sarah's hand to shake it. 'I have that sort of face – people say that to me all the time.'

It had been Laura who had last said it to her. Laura, who had been plastering flyers and posters with Maggie's face all over the place, trying to track her down.

'At least Maggie's face is unique, easy to remember. Yours always looks like it belongs. Do you know what I mean?' Laura had said.

Rose had been insulted by the insinuation that she was forgettable. She was anything but! Despite Rose's continued insistence that it was prudent to give Maggie the time and space that she so obviously wanted, Laura would not let it go. She kept coming round, making plans, reporting on the tiniest potential lead that she found. She was grasping at straws clearly, coming up short time and again. Maggie did not want to be found and that suited Rose.

'I really think you need to stop, Laura. All you're doing is dragging everyone back over the most painful part of our lives. And for what? For someone who walked away, who doesn't care enough to get in touch, for someone who seems to have forgotten us all.'

'No, no, I don't believe that. I will find her.'

'How?' Rose had retorted, to which Laura had no answer.

'Are you all right?' Sarah asked, breaking into Rose's thoughts.

Rose laughed and shook her head.

'No, yes. Sorry. Big day, I'm feeling all the feelings today! You know what it's like. You spend the first few years being their everything, and then, well, then the time for pre-school comes and they walk away from you. It's like you're holding their hands and one by one their fingers slip away from yours and they're gone. This is the first step of that, I guess,' Rose said, a sorrowful smile on her face. She had missed their really early years and she was losing part of them already. She wanted to hold them tight to her and never let go.

'God, don't!' Sarah laughed. 'You'll have me in floods! He's my only one, so this is *the* day for me. I'm mostly happy. He'll love it. I'll have more time. And yet.' She stopped, shrugged her shoulders as tears started to well in her eyes.

'Sorry,' Rose said. 'I've made you sad. You're right! He'll love it. So will Emily. By the end of the week, they'll be skipping off with barely a backwards glance and that's a good thing.'

Sarah blew her nose and nodded. 'You're right. Hey, do you want to go and get a coffee after this? We can share your little one.'

She gestured to Elliot, who had returned to Rose. His warm sticky little hand in hers a world of comfort to her.

'That'd be lovely,' Rose said, smiling.

'Shall we meet back here once they're in?' Sarah suggested. Rose nodded and turned to find Stephen and Emily, smiling to herself that this new chapter could be just what they all needed. Friends had struggled to accept her new situation and Rose had found herself more isolated than she would have expected.

A new friend was just what she needed.

A clean slate.

14

Maggie sat at the kitchen table with a selection of photos and small treasures that she had chosen for Emily and Elliot. A pressed flower that Maggie had thought pretty, a drawing of a duck that she thought Elliot would like, a small packet of chocolate buttons each. It was a carefully selected care package to accompany her latest letter, but Maggie was struggling with what to write.

'What's the matter?' Ailsa asked. She had been pottering in the kitchen, sorting out the pantry, keeping an eye on things.

'I've got nothing new to say! What *can* I say? Every week, I say that I'm resting, that I'm getting better. That I miss them more than I can say. That I hope they're well and that I'll be home soon. That's it! It all sounds so hollow.'

'But it is true, lovely. You're less depressed. You don't sleep for fifteen hours a day and spend the rest of the time staring into space. You were a shell when you arrived here. Now, you seem more yourself,' Ailsa encouraged.

Maggie sighed. Ailsa didn't know who Maggie's self was. She used to be vibrant and interesting and now she still felt permanently adrift. She was better than before, that's true. But she also felt lost. She didn't know where she was supposed to be and the anchor of her family felt so far away.

Ailsa came to the table, looking over the items that Maggie had selected.

'Oh.'

Maggie snapped her head up.

'What?'

'Oh, nothing. It's just... oh, it's just superstition really. Nothing. Forget I said anything.'

'No, tell me, what is it?' Maggie's voice was rising. She was tired of Ailsa treading so gently around her. She was getting better, she *was* stronger. Ailsa didn't need to treat her like a child.

Ailsa looked troubled but said, 'It's just that flower.'

Maggie carefully picked up the pressed flower, delicate lilac petals and a long green stem. 'What about it? I just thought Emily might like it. She always liked picking daisies.'

'It's a cuckoo flower. And it's supposedly bad luck to pick them.'

'Why?'

'I told you, it's a silly superstition, it's nothing,' Ailsa reassured Maggie. 'It's supposed to anger the fairies. See? I told you it was silly.'

Maggie's face fell. 'I can't get anything right,' she said morosely, defeated again.

'Forget I said anything. It's a lovely flower. I'm sure she'll like it,' Ailsa said, through slightly gritted teeth. Then, looking at Maggie, crestfallen and silent, she continued. 'You have to stop brooding, hen, you're not doing anyone any good.'

'Oh, I'm sorry? Is my grief too irritating for you?' Maggie shot back. 'Is it annoying you? That I don't know what to say to my own children? Should I write to them at all? Am I asking you to send too many letters now? Am I inconvenient?'

'No! Not at all. I like that you can be open with me. I *understand*, you know I do. I like having you here, I like the company and I'm happy to post the letters. I just said going to the city more than once a week was a lot to ask,' Ailsa said gingerly, despite a bite to her voice that Maggie had not heard before. 'You *are* getting better but you're not there yet. Can't you see? Little things like this still set you off. You're unpredictable. You need more time. You deserve more time. You matter too.'

'Why? Why do I matter more than the children?'

'Enough!' Ailsa shouted, shocking Maggie into silence. Ailsa took a deep breath before continuing more gently, putting a smile onto her face. 'Enough. Everyone is allowed a second chance. Don't fritter yours away.' Ailsa pushed her hair from her face and Maggie saw the tiredness in her eyes.

Maggie opened her mouth to speak but changed her mind. Ailsa had been so kind. She forgave all of Maggie's flaws and told her that she was family to her despite her being literally some random woman from the internet who had turned up on her doorstep. Ailsa understood everyone is flawed, that everyone is just trying to make their own way in this world. She did not judge Maggie as Maggie judged herself and Maggie tried hard to reciprocate.

'I'm sorry,' Maggie said, turning to look at Ailsa.

Ailsa kept her lips shut tight but nodded an acceptance.

'Look, I'll go out, get some air and try writing again when I get back. Can I get you anything while I'm out?'

'Thank you, hen, but no, I think I'm okay.'

Maggie forced a smile on her face and left the room, leaving her half-written letter and items scattered across the table. She picked up her bag and jacket and closed the front door behind her.

The day was bright but cold and Maggie crossed to the opposite side of the road to walk in the sunshine for added warmth. She took deep lungfuls of the fresh clean air and let it clear her mind. The air was one of her favourite things about this place. Back home, there had always been a taste of car fumes, here it was always crisp. This place had been good for her, giving her space to heal and rest and find her own mind again. To rediscover who she was before the steamroller of family life had come for her. But keeping her turmoil within her about staying away was exhausting. The only way she could carry the load was to try to put it to one side, but it was like she had put the bag down, only to find it waiting for her around the next corner, insisting she pick it up again. It was hard to find and grab hold of moments of lightness. Maggie was trying to find them here that morning as she reached the dockside café and sat down at an outside table. She looked at the sunlight dappling the water and breathed in the aroma of coffee and baking that wafted from inside the café building.

Maggie looked up and smiled at the waitress as she delivered her usual coffee to the table without Maggie needing to order it. One bonus of living somewhere so small was that even the local café felt like an extension of your friend's living room. A community. That was what she had needed back home but hadn't found. Here, if you were struggling, someone would notice.

A small wiry cat weaved its way around the table and round Maggie's legs, purring as it did so. A regular at the café, he was usually to be found at whichever table had the tastiest titbits. Maggie scratched his head behind the ears and then sat back in her seat. She took a sip of the strong black coffee and closed her eyes as she enjoyed the zinging of her tastebuds as she swallowed it. It had been a busy week, no wonder she had been cranky with Ailsa. She would apologise when she got home. Ailsa was right – she had come a long way in the months she had been here. She no longer woke in the mornings pained to find herself still alive. There was a purpose to her days. The seamstress work had really taken off. At first, she had accepted just one or two small jobs, encouraged by Ailsa to work with her hands, focus her mind and enjoy her own talents. A way to calm her soul. Word of her work had spread though, and she now had a ledger full of bookings and appointments. She was careful not to book up too far in advance, as she knew she wouldn't be staying here forever. Every day was a day closer to the day she went back to Emily and Elliot and when she did, she didn't want to let anyone down. She had let enough people down.

Maggie was just finishing up her coffee when a shadow fell over the table.

'Is this seat taken?' a familiar voice asked.

Maggie looked up to reply and found herself looking into the face of her once best friend.

Laura.

Maggie was open-mouthed and silent in shock. Laura sat down and looked at her.

'I found you,' she said, smiling while her eyes filled with tears. 'I knew I would if I just kept looking. I just knew it. I haven't stopped looking all this time, even though they told me to.'

'Who?' Maggie interrupted, but before Laura could answer, Maggie continued, 'How? How did you find me? I...' she said, looking wildly around in case Laura was not alone, hopeful and yet also fearful that she wasn't.

'It took some sleuthing, I can tell you that!' Laura laughed warmly, clearly happy to be back in Maggie's company. 'The only clue we had was that you got on a bus to Glasgow, then it was like you disappeared. There was nothing. I spent weeks, months, thinking through things you'd said, things you'd not said and then a spark came to me.'

'What?' Maggie asked, though not really listening as her mind raced with all the implications of what Laura arriving here meant. Was anyone else with her? Would they come to take her home? Was she ready? Part of her was over the moon, perhaps this was the sign that it was time to go home and yet part of her was terrified that she wasn't ready and being ambushed like this would undo all she had worked so hard on.

'Those mum groups you joined. You'd said how you felt at a loss at what to do sometimes and you'd joined these groups. And you said on one, there was this grandmother-type lady who was kind and supportive and you wished she lived nearer but she lived in Scotland. See? I *was* listening.'

'Oh... I – I don't remember,' Maggie said softly. To be honest, she barely remembered anything from the first years of motherhood, with her second pregnancy coming so fast on the heels of her first.

'So. I got online, saw which groups you were in and joined them all. I basically cyber-stalked a bunch of mothers relentlessly. And tried to track down this woman and eventually, finally, I found a thread where you and an Ailsa had chatted. And she lived, well, here.' Laura gestured around her. 'In Scotland. She was a lady who had helped you when you were struggling, had reached out. And well, as a minute chance as it was, it was the only lead I had. But here you are. You're alive and you're here!'

Laura's smile faded as her expression shifted.

'Look... I'm going to just say it right out. I fucked up. As a friend, I fucked up. I should have seen how hard you were struggling. I should have come around more often. I should have offered to have the kids so you could sleep. But we were young. I hadn't grown up and I was jealous. It had always been you and me against the world and suddenly you had all these people in your life – a husband, a daughter, a son. They all needed you. They had a higher claim to you than I did, and I felt pushed out.'

'It's okay...' Maggie began.

'No,' Laura continued. 'No, it's not. After you left, after I fell out with Rose and Stephen over... well, I took a long hard look at myself, at our friendship, and I realised I was as bad as everyone else. We all wanted you to be something for us. A wife, a mother, a daughter, a friend. None of us asked what you wanted from us or who you wanted to be. That's not okay. When I look back, it was obvious you weren't happy. I thought you'd stopped talking to me because I no longer fitted your life... but I'm here for you now.'

Laura reached out and squeezed Maggie's hand, smiling. Then, suddenly, a cloud passed over her face and she looked nervous. Maggie's stomach dropped.

'What? What is it?' she asked, petrified as to what possible answer Laura might give. 'The children? How are they? Are they okay? How are their scars? How have they been? How *are* they?' Maggie demanded, her rising voice causing other customers in the café to stare. Laura glanced around at them uncomfortably but Maggie was oblivious. How bad did it have to be at home that Laura tracked her down? They knew she was safe, she'd said as much in her letters. Why had Laura gone to so much trouble?

Laura looked nervous, chewing on her lip, and Maggie felt the core of her fall away. She had come here to tell her something terrible had happened to them. That's why she needed to be tracked down.

'They're fine. Emily and Elliot are fine,' Laura said, with a tone in her voice that Maggie couldn't place. Fine but not fine? Fine but with an edge of something?

'Did Stephen ask you to come here? Did he tell you to chase me down, that I was being melodramatic asking for time? That's why I didn't put a return address on. I didn't need him hounding me.'

Laura wrinkled her brow in confusion.

'What? I... I don't understand. What do you mean?'

'The letters. My letters. To Stephen, to Rose and the children. I told them I was taking space to recover. I wasn't well. I've not been well. I'm getting there but...'

Maggie stopped. Laura was looking at her, still confused, quizzical.

'What letters? No one ever mentioned any letters. We've... no one has heard from you since the day you *left*,' Laura said, with a look of concern.

Blood rushed to Maggie's head and it made her dizzy, as though she was suddenly under water. Laura was talking but she couldn't hear her, she was too far away, muffled. Maggie was struggling to breathe. 'No one has heard from you since the day you left...' But she'd *written*. Yet if no one had got her letters, then... then the children didn't know she was coming back. They'd... they'd think she'd abandoned them and walked away without another thought. Maggie's numb fingers tried to grasp onto the table's surface, needing something solid to cling to. She closed her eyes, shutting out the world while she tried to calm down.

'Is she okay?'

'I don't know, she was fine and now, I don't know!'

'Maggie, Maggie, are you all right?'

Maggie closed off the world. She knew that she had to focus on her breathing. That's all she needed to do in this moment. Breathe and the panic would pass. *It's just panic, you're not dying, you will be okay*, she told herself.

The world shrank further, and all Maggie could feel was her own pounding heartbeat and the sensation of her breath. Eventually her heart rate slowed, her breath became more even, and the world started to come back to her. She made herself focus; on the coolness of the metal table under her fingertips, on the aroma of coffee that permeated the air, the voices she could hear, voices that she recognised.

'Hen, hen, are you okay?' Ailsa said, sounding breathless. 'They called me. I came straight away. Can you hear me?'

Maggie opened her eyes, looked at Ailsa and Laura and mania replaced her panic. Adrenaline coursed through her body and all she could do was grab her things and growl at them both.

'I can't do this here. Home.' Maggie walked away from Ailsa and Laura, leaving them staring at each other in confusion.

'What on earth happened?' Ailsa shouted, looking at Laura for answers.

'I don't know!' Laura replied.

Ailsa said nothing but turned and followed Maggie up the hill. Laura followed.

The door slammed behind Maggie, but it didn't catch, and it banged in the wind, as anchorless as she was. Maggie tried to feel rational, to think logically but she couldn't do it. Her mind was jumping; trying to work out why no one had got her letters. Had they... had they not arrived? Had they not been posted in the first place? Had they been intercepted, and if so, by who? None of it made any sense! Why was Laura here, what did she want? Maggie had so many questions. All her sureties about being away or going home had collapsed.

She tried to settle, but she couldn't, so she wandered through the house like a poltergeist, moving things and banging them down without rhyme or reason to it.

She heard voices and then the sound of the front door being closed behind them. Footsteps on the hallway flagstones. Stilted conversation. Her hands were clammy, and she wiped them on her jeans. She was too hot and yet she felt cold. She was aware that she was in fight or flight mode, her body flooded with adrenaline.

Ailsa and Laura came into the kitchen and found her picking a teacup up and putting it down again. Maggie looked up at them both and saw the concern on their faces. She faced Laura.

'What did you mean when you said no one has heard anything from me?' She needed to hear it again, as much as she didn't want to, to be sure she understood.

Laura swallowed. She looked pained, like she knew she was the messenger and was hoping that she was not about to get shot.

'Shall we sit?' Ailsa asked, as everyone stood like toy soldiers, tense and rigid.

Maggie nodded and pulled out a kitchen chair, Laura the same.

'Just like I said at the café, nobody has heard anything from you since you left. No letters, nothing. At least, not that I know of. I can't imagine that things would... well, that things would have developed as they have done if we'd known you were alive and well.'

'I don't understand,' Maggie said, turning to look at Ailsa. 'I wrote every week. *Every week!* I wrote not long after I left, I... You – you *did* post them, didn't you?' Maggie asked, not wanting to accuse Ailsa and yet not understanding how this could have happened.

'Of course I did!' Ailsa retorted, insulted by the insinuation. 'It was my idea for you to write in the first place, why would I have done that if I didn't plan on posting them?'

'To keep me here? To keep me from calling, from going home?'

'Maggie,' Ailsa said gently. 'You are not a prisoner here, you can leave, and could have left whenever you wanted to, whenever you were ready to. It has been wonderful having you stay, having your company, but I have never made you stay against your will.'

Maggie slumped in her chair. Was Ailsa telling her the truth? All her certainty had gone but she could only take her at face value. What else could she do?

'You're right, I'm sorry. Just... none of this makes sense.'

She turned to Laura.

'They haven't moved? A postal strike, or...'

Laura shook her head. 'I'm sure there must be some explanation. I... I just don't know what it might be, unless...'

'Unless what? What else is there? What don't I know?' Maggie demanded, wanting for all this to make sense.

Laura's face drained of colour. She cleared her throat and looked as uncomfortable as Maggie could ever remember seeing her.

'What? What is it? Is it to do with the children? How are they? Their burns?'

'I promise you the children are okay. Their injuries were superficial. Right as rain in a month. No scars, nothing. It's not the children, well, not directly...'

'Just spit it out! My imagination is in overdrive. *Please* just tell me.'

'Okay.' Laura took a deep breath. 'Stephen and Rose are together, a couple. The children, well, they think Rose is their mother. They don't remember you. They were too young – it's been too long. They don't know you exist. Rose and Stephen haven't told them.'

Maggie stared open-mouthed. Her brain had stopped working. It wouldn't take in what Laura was saying. She said nothing. She blinked.

'Mags?' Laura asked, then turned to Ailsa. 'Is she okay?'

'I don't understand,' Ailsa said. 'Rose, Maggie's sister, is now with Stephen, Maggie's husband? And pretending to everyone, including the children, that Maggie never existed? That it's always been the four of them as the family unit?'

'That's pretty much it.' Laura nodded.

'But that's... that's appalling?'

'Yes. I agree. I'm not sure how it all happened, or when, or why. Some people seem to think that it's okay because Maggie left, left without a trace. But...' She turned to Maggie. 'Can you see, Maggie? You *have* to come home. You have to come home now.'

Maggie's mouth filled with saliva as she tried not to be sick. When she had first left, she thought that leaving the children with Rose was best for everyone. Those first few weeks when Maggie had not believed she could keep on living, the thought that Emily and Elliot would have Rose in her place had been a comfort. But not like *this*.

'No. No, you can't have this right, Laura. Stephen, Rose – they barely got on, they wouldn't... and Rose, she wouldn't just *take* my family. She's my sister. No, you must have made a mistake.'

'I wish I had. I saw them – at the beach, together as family. The children calling Rose "Mama", her and Stephen all loved up. You? Whitewashed out of the picture. We had a row right there. They told me it was none of my business, that you'd walked away, left them all and clearly didn't want anything to do with them any more and that what they did with that was none of my business. They didn't even want me saying your name in front of the children.'

'My parents? My friends? What about them?'

'Your parents are struggling with it, but they'd lost you. They didn't want to lose Rose and the children too. Your friends? Well, I'm here. You need to come home. Put all this right.'

'This isn't the Rose I know. I thought the children would be safe with her, but this is insane! She must be insane. I... I need to talk with her. And Stephen. Now. I need to get home. I need to go home now. This... I've been away a year – you can't erase someone in a *year*! I... I said I was coming back. I *wrote* that I was coming home!'

Maggie's eyes filled with tears, her past and her future crumbling in her mind, her hands shaking as everything she held dear slipped through her fingers. She had spent twelve months building herself back up, only to feel as though she were made of sand and the tide was coming in, washing her away again.

She turned to Ailsa, who said, 'I agree. I'm not sure you're emotionally ready but I think you need to go back all the same. You can come back here whenever you like, this is your home too. I've always said that.'

Maggie nodded. 'I have to go. For my family. Or whatever might be left of it.'

15

'Do you want anything from the café?' Stephen called out into the garden where the children were happily playing in the sandpit together despite the chill in the air. 'I'm popping out for my run and I'll swing past on my way home.'

'Biscuits!' shouted Emily enthusiastically as she tipped a bucket of sand over her brother's feet, making him giggle.

Stephen turned to Rose, who sat on a garden chair nearby, supervising. He tipped his head to say, 'Is that okay?'

She looked up at him in his running kit – part athlete, part PE student. She smiled and nodded. 'Why not, eh? Not for me though, thanks.'

'Mummy said yes!' Stephen shouted, to cheers from the happy children. He dipped, kissed Rose on the top of her head and she reached up and squeezed his hand with affection.

'I'll just do a shorter run today. Then I'll get the papers and the kids' treats. Anything else we need?' he asked.

Rose shook her head, smiling at him as he headed out.

He was an attentive husband and a happy father. He had blossomed as a parent since Rose had moved in and she felt that she had played no small part in that. She tucked her book away. She wasn't really concentrating anyway. She was enjoying the sort of Sunday morning that she had imagined family life would provide.

She was breathing in her contentment when the doorbell rang. She was annoyed at the intrusion. At this time of the weekend, it could only be a cold caller. A stranger wanting something that she didn't want to give and spoiling their peace in the process.

Sighing, she checked on the children, thinking it would be fine to leave them for five minutes while she despatched this irritation. She considered ignoring the door entirely, but it rang again, more insistently this time.

Rose reached the door and pulled it wide to stand in the doorway before the woman who stood in front of her.

She looked furious.

Everything slowed, apart from Rose's heartrate, which rocketed, and she swallowed hard as she faced the ghost on the doorstep.

'Maggie.'

Behind Rose, Emily had sneaked up to the doorway and hovered behind her, wanting to see who was visiting. She was an inquisitive child and Rose knew she'd have a million questions for the lady on the doorstep if Rose let her. She reached down and held Emily tightly to her. She felt sick. Would Emily remember Maggie? This is not how she should find out the truth if she did. Rose needed her away from this scene and fast.

'Are you okay, lovely?' Rose asked, her voice shaking.

'Yes, Mummy, I just wanted to say hello to...' she looked at Maggie, 'this lady. Hello!' Emily waved.

Without looking at her, Rose could feel the jolt of movement that indicated Maggie's shock. Rose felt relief flood her as she realised that Emily had no idea who Maggie was. Rose was her mummy. Her *only* mummy.

'Hi,' Maggie managed to whisper as the colour drained further from her face.

'Can I have a drink, please?' Emily asked.

'Yes, of course you can, my sweetheart, there's one on your little table in the kitchen.' Rose ruffled Emily's hair and ushered her back into the house. Emily scampered off but stopped at the end of the hallway and turned back to smile shyly at the lady on the doorstep and give her a polite wave before disappearing back into the house. Maggie smiled at her and waved back.

Rose was silent. She stared at Maggie, trying to get her words ready.

What could she say? Maggie was *gone* – except that clearly, she wasn't. Rose couldn't process this all fast enough to work out what to say. She was just trying to remember how to breathe.

Maggie was alive and well. And home! This was what Rose and her parents and Stephen and the children had longed for, but then had become what Rose had feared. What did this mean now for *her* family? Maggie was back. Why was she back now and what did she want?

Rose opened her mouth. 'I...' but nothing would come out.

The two stood facing each other.

Finally, Maggie broke the silence.

'Can I come in?' she asked.

Rose looked at her. What was Maggie thinking? She'd heard Emily call Rose mummy and yet her face gave away nothing. It was unnerving. Maggie was as much a mystery as she had been the day that she disappeared.

'I don't think that's a good idea, do you?' Rose said, her voice kind but with a territorial edge. Her maternal instinct and her own self-preservation kicked in. She looked back into the house, the sounds of the children playing in the garden floating in the quiet that followed her refusal to let Maggie in. She looked back at her sister, whose face showed that she had not expected her request to be denied.

'They don't *know* you. It isn't fair to them, or to *me*, to just turn up out of the blue and expect to walk back in!'

'They're my children. This is my house!' Maggie countered, anger rising in her voice.

'Oh, now they're your children. Where were you? It's been a year! We thought you were dead! Did Emily recognise you? No! Because when you walked out on her, she was barely out of babyhood.'

'She called *you* mummy. Why, Rose? Why did she do that?' Maggie narrowed her eyes accusingly.

Rose lowered her voice as she fixed a stare at Maggie.

'You got it wrong when you walked away, you got it wrong when you stayed away,' she paused, 'and now you've got it wrong by turning up unannounced. This is *not* how to handle this.'

Rose crossed her arms and stepped back into the house, indicating that she was done.

Maggie stepped forward but Rose swung the door into her, blocking her path, like a bouncer at a club denying entry to a troublemaker.

'No.'

Maggie's face dropped as her shock registered. This was clearly not how she had felt things would play out. Rose tried to ignore the pain in her chest that wanted to drag her sister to her and hug her so tightly and never let her out of her sight again.

But this wasn't just about Rose now.

It was about the children and Stephen, and she couldn't give that up. She wouldn't. Not for anyone.

'Yes,' Maggie insisted. 'I have clearly waited far too long to come home. I will not wait any longer. It might not be convenient but frankly I don't care. I need to talk with you, and it has to be now.'

Rose paused. She needed time to think this all through but to ask Maggie to wait too long could have damaging consequences. How stable was she? What did she want? Who knew what chaos she might decide to unleash if pushed? If she didn't let her in, she'd go to their parents and Rose feared that they'd side with her. No, she was *not* going to let this destroy everything. Rose had to control it. She couldn't do that through denial. This was happening. And happening now.

'Okay, come in and go to the front room. I'll get the children in front of some TV to give us some time. You *will not* talk with them right now. Do you understand?' Rose demanded.

Maggie chewed her lip as she considered this but finally, to Rose's relief, she nodded acceptance.

'Fine.'

She stepped through the door.

Rose gestured for Maggie to make her own way to the front room and hurried out to the garden, pausing on the way to compose herself. As much as she was happy that her sister was alive and well, she knew she couldn't let that affect things. She thought she had known Maggie but then she had walked away from her children. What sort of person was she really? Who was she now? The children needed protecting from her, that was all Rose could think of. She quietly ushered them into the playroom, put on their favourite TV show and gently pulled the door until it was almost closed. She wanted to be able to hear if they needed her, but she needed them to be oblivious to all but the brightly coloured cartoon in front of them.

Steadying her shaking breath, Rose pulled her shoulders back and walked into the living room. Maggie stood awkwardly, looking at the room around her. Rose wondered if it felt like home to her. Rose had changed it a lot, but was it still Maggie's home?

'Would you like a drink? Coffee? Tea?' Rose wanted Maggie to feel like the visitor she was. She needed her to feel as though this was Rose's domain – which it now was.

Maggie shook her head but said nothing, fury seeping from her every pore.

Rose could see her forming her words in her head before deciding against them. Always overthinking things, Rose scoffed internally.

The silence grew taut and unnerving.

'Yes?' Rose said, her voice hardening. She had so many questions that she wanted to ask; so much anger to let out. And joy – Maggie was alive, she looked okay. Yet she was also full of fear for what Maggie's return had the power to inflict on her. She needed to know what Maggie's intentions were before she gave anything away herself.

Finally, Maggie took a deep breath and began to speak.

'What have you *done*, Rose?' She shook her head in disgust.

Rose recoiled, shocked. Maggie was blaming *her*?

'What do you mean, what have I done?'

'You know exactly what I mean. *My* children don't know who I am. *My* children think that *you* are their mother. And why wouldn't they? You're sleeping with their father!' she spat out at her.

'You keep your damn voice down! Or you will leave. You know how to leave, don't you? Oh, that's right, sure you do. You turn your back and you walk away. You're good at that!'

Rose could see how this landed on Maggie as clearly as if she had reached out and slapped her. Good. That was what she felt like doing! How *dare* she? How *dare* she land on the doorstep, unannounced, a whole *year* after leaving and expect to be welcomed back with open arms, no explanation, no apology? Nothing!

'What have I done? I've done what was needed. I pulled this family back together. I gave the children back the mother they were missing. In all this time, you didn't get in touch. Not once!' Rose felt a glimmer of guilt as she said this. She did not know for sure that it was true. That phone call could have been Maggie. Still, she'd said it now. 'What hell of a parent does that make you? I'll tell you,' Rose spat, not stopping for Maggie to get a word in, 'a bad parent. A very bad one. You weren't meant to be their mother. You don't deserve them. Deep down, you knew that. And you still know that now.'

'What? So you just decided to pretend I don't exist? You can't just *take* someone else's children, Rose. What the hell? Do they even know about me at all?'

'I didn't take them, Maggie. You *gave* them to me.'

'I did no such thing!'

'What else would you call it?'

'I left them in your care! This is about you and your utter selfishness. You've always been like this.'

'What? *My* selfishness! *You're* the selfish one, you waltzed out the door and expected everyone to just fall in line to pick up what you left behind. What would you have had me do instead then?'

'You could have told them I was ill, told them about me, shown them photographs, told them I loved them, told them I'd be back.'

'How could we? We didn't know any of that! You walked away and left us floundering in the dark! We didn't know if you were still alive. To be honest, after a year, we assumed not.'

'Why would you assume that?'

'Why? Because you gave me nothing to show the opposite, and now you're back, complaining that I handled it badly. Well, tell me this – if it's so badly handled, how come everyone is happy? How come everyone is thriving? We both did what we thought was for the best.'

'How is stealing my children, cheating with my husband and then lying to everyone "the best"?' Maggie sneered.

Rose paused to swallow her anger for a moment. She would not let Maggie push her into reacting badly. She was better than that.

'I did not steal the children. I did not cheat with Stephen. *You* walked away. You left your burnt, injured children in hospital, walked away, got on a bus to Scotland and left us all. I nursed the children, supported Stephen and made us all a family in a way you never did, you never could because it wasn't right with you the way that it is right with me. And as for lying? Tell me this. Who takes care of Emily and Elliot? Who is there in the night when they're scared? Who kisses away the pain of scraped knees? Is it you? No. It's me. So I *am* their mother and I have been doing it just as long as you did. Only I haven't left. You did.'

Maggie slumped back into her chair, temporarily stunned into silence.

Rose couldn't read what she was thinking like she always used to be able to do. She was a different person to the one who left. How could she let this stranger near *her* children?

'Emily and Elliot,' Rose continued. 'I presume you want to know how they are. How they've been? Since you care so much?'

Maggie swallowed her pride and nodded.

Rose could see the desperation in her eyes, and it made her shudder. She recognised that steel. It was the same as hers.

'You brought them to hospital and then you walked away, knowing what a horrific experience they were going through. You didn't even say goodbye.'

Maggie looked at her feet, shame flooding her face.

'We waited for you to come back, and you didn't. The hospital had to ask us to go as they needed the beds for other patients once the children were discharged.'

'They let you out that evening?' Maggie asked, shocked. 'But their burns, they were so badly hurt, I...'

'No. The first aid that you administered helped a lot. They were burnt, yes, but not badly. Not deeply. They dressed their wounds and sent us home to recover. They were home in their beds that night, wondering where their mama had gone.' The memory of their sore, tired and confused faces broke Rose's heart all over again.

'I sat with them, the four of us wondering when you would be back. I was their aunt, I was good enough, but I was not who they wanted. Not who they needed, though neither left my side while we waited. I couldn't hold them tight for fear of hurting them. It was torture. For everyone. But we sat, like idiots, waiting for you, Maggie. Do you know how stupid you feel, sitting, waiting, reassuring two tiny children that their mother will be back soon as it becomes clear, moment by moment, that she isn't coming?' Rose's voice cracked.

'I'm sorry,' Maggie started, but she was shot down.

'They cried for you! "Mama, where Mama? Want Mama. Not you, no! Where Mama?" Do you know how hard that is to hear?' Rose accused.

Maggie visibly shrank, Rose's words cutting through her.

'I know that hurts to hear. Well, now imagine it's *their* voices, it's *them* clinging to you, asking where you are and you not knowing what to say to them. Yes? Now do that for days. Weeks. Now imagine the nightmares, the terrors, the tears, the crying, the questions that no one had any good answers for...'

'I understand, just...'

'I had to be not who they wanted while they struggled without you. They didn't understand where their mama had gone, why she had left. None of us did, so we couldn't fix it. You broke them. You broke their belief that they were safe, and I rebuilt that. We gave them back the family you broke. You understand? I made it better because I was *here*, I became Mama. Because they needed a mama and you?' Rose shook her head at Maggie. 'You were gone.'

Rose could feel a headache lurking behind her eyes and she rubbed at her temples to try to stave it off. Her hands trembled as she did so. Could her sister now see how she couldn't just pick up where she left off? How could she say that what Rose had done was wrong? She couldn't – Rose would refuse to let her.

Maggie was ashen-faced as she listened.

Rose tried to work out if she had convinced Maggie of her position. She scanned her face, looking for any clues, any tells as to what she was thinking. Nothing. Concerned, she glanced back towards the playroom. She could hear the sounds of another episode auto playing and relaxed a little. The children were fine. Her children.

'Our parents, are they? What about them? What's...?' Maggie started to ask. She was beginning to look rattled.

'I don't think you fully understand, Maggie. The children have a mother and a father. Me and Stephen. They are not aware of anything different. Our parents have come around to the situation. They agreed it was for the best for everyone if we carried on without you once you'd been gone so long without a word. We had to assume that you weren't coming back. I'm not saying it wasn't hard. It was. But we had to do what we had to do.'

Maggie looked as though she would pass out. Rose wanted this conversation to be over. She felt nausea rising in her throat.

'You abandoned us all, Maggie. As if we didn't matter. As if you wanted not to exist. Well, now you have it – you don't exist. Not any more.'

Maggie was breathing hard, her eyes on the floor.

'But... but my letters? I wrote. I wrote every week! I sent cards, and presents and... I phoned. Just that once but you, you answered. You thought it was me. You *knew* it was me.'

Rose breathed out to steady any shake in her voice. She couldn't let Maggie see any cracks in her confidence. That phone call. She hadn't told a soul about it. She wasn't about to admit to it now.

'What phone call? What letters? We didn't get any letters. We have heard nothing from you. Nothing! I haven't *heard* a single word from you since you left us in A&E. Nothing.'

Maggie looked furious.

'Don't *lie* to me! You can't lie to me like you're lying to everyone else, Rose. I *wrote*! You can't tell me I didn't.'

'I'm not the one lying,' Rose said, sneering in in annoyance. 'I'm not saying that you didn't write, although if you *did,* then why didn't I get anything? 'Cos I'm telling you – we haven't had a single thing from you in the year since you walked out.'

'So *I'm* lying to *you*? Is that what you're saying?' Maggie spat at Rose.

'Maybe. To make yourself look better. To make it seem like you didn't just walk away without so much of a thought for those you abandoned. You can say that you sent your letters all you like, it doesn't change the fact that we didn't ever receive any.'

Maggie looked as though Rose had slapped her.

'So Laura was right? You... you really never received any letters from me? None? None at all?' Maggie's voice wavered.

Rose crossed her arms in front of her defensively.

'If I had, I wouldn't have thought you were gone for good. If you'd given us any indication that you were coming back...'

'What?'

Rose stopped. She wouldn't say it, as she didn't know it to be true. Had she known that Maggie would come back, would she have done what she did? She didn't want to ask herself that. She didn't want to have to answer.

'You wouldn't have taken *my* family?' Maggie answered for her.

'They are mine. You *handed* them to me when you left. You were never meant to be their mother, like I said, that much is clear.' Rose shifted uncomfortably, not making full eye contact.

'How can you say that?'

'Because it's true. How can *you* justify what you did, Maggie? I can justify my decisions. Can you say the same?'

Maggie's shoulders slumped.

'I'm sorry,' she paused, 'for what I did, for what I've done. I'm... sorry.'

Rose faltered. She had expected more fighting.

'I don't know where to begin. How to explain,' Maggie continued. 'It wasn't just about that night. I wasn't coping. I was so busy trying to hide that fact that I lost sight of what I was supposed to be doing. I was supposed to be looking after *them*. My Emily and my Elliot.'

Rose shifted in her seat. *My Emily and my Elliot*, she thought but said nothing.

Maggie looked at the floor, unable to meet Rose's gaze as she kept talking.

'I hid it from everyone, from you, Stephen, Mum and Dad. But my days were... a flatness of caring for other people. I thought that this was how it was meant to be. No one talks about it. All the other parents I met seemed to have it so together. They were enjoying the chaos. I was drowning in it.' Maggie screwed her eyes shut.

Rose had to fight to ignore the instinct in her to reach out to comfort Maggie. She had to sit on her hands to stop herself. This woman in front of her, sister or not, was back to wreak havoc on her life.

'Just as I'd decided that I could cope with feeling nothing, so ong as it held back the fear,' her voice dwindled to a whisper, 'that night happened.'

'They were okay,' Rose replied quietly. 'They were going to be okay.'

'Oh, I know you and the social workers and the doctors were all so encouraging but you didn't *know*. You didn't know that I wouldn't do something like that again. How could you? I didn't know it!' Maggie's voice rose with her anger.

'The way that nurse protection lady looked at me. I could see her gauging doubt in her mind. "Will she harm them again?" After Elliot was born, everyone said it was all going to be okay and they were wrong. It wasn't okay. I could barely look at Elliot. I held him because you were supposed to, but I didn't *want* to. He was just another person *needing* me, judging me, finding me lacking!'

Rose flinched. Elliot was the least demanding of children, he was always ready with a smile or a cuddle and he always knew how to make you feel better. Rose put the difference down to her superior parenting. Another cross in Maggie's column, another tick in hers.

Rose looked at Maggie, her face etched with anger and disgust. It was not a version of her sister that she had ever seen.

'Maggie? What happened once you left the hospital?' she asked, quietly.

Maggie jiggled her knees, nervous energy coursing through her, clear to see. Her hands shook with it, her toes tapped and her voice wavered.

'I didn't plan it. Had I planned it, it would have been easier. I had no other clothes, barely any money on me. I left with nothing. I left my mind, my heart. I was a husk.'

The melodrama made Rose angry. She laughed a hollow laugh, 'All about you...'

'No! You don't *know*!' Maggie snapped. 'To feel like the only way to save what you love more than anything is to *leave* it. To feel that by staying with your babies you are *destroying* them. It twists you from the inside until you can't think straight. You're pulled inwards until there's nothing left.'

Rose pulled herself up. Her own fear reminded her that if she handled this badly, she could find out soon enough what it would feel like to lose everyone you love.

'Sorry,' she said, contrite.

'In all honesty, I can't remember. All I remember is the dread in my mind and the need to be gone. I loved you all, but I wanted to die so I couldn't hurt anyone any more and I wouldn't hurt either. There was only one place I could think of to go and so I went there. I knew I had to take myself far away and end it all.'

Rose looked at her in shock. Her sister had never tended to the dramatic. She was usually the most optimistic person in any room. This woman, she was different. Changed. She was her sister and yet not. The women sat side by side on the sofa were strangers to each other.

'Go on,' Rose said.

Maggie continued. 'It was in one way the easiest choice I had ever made. And in another, the hardest thing I have ever done. I loved them. I *love* them both so much that it hurts even to think about it. But I couldn't do it. I couldn't be their mother. Not then. Then I knew that I was not right for them.' Her voice dwindled to a whisper. 'By not being there, by wishing for it all to stop, I hurt them.' She looked ashamed.

Maggie got up and walked to the door so that she could see the kitchen from where she was standing. Rose could see the physical reaction in her as she did so. It was as if an invisible hand had slapped her.

'It wasn't your fault,' Rose whispered. 'I said it then and I meant it. I mean it now. It wasn't your fault.' Rose halted, she wanted to be consolatory and yet she knew she couldn't let Maggie back in like this. Not on these terms. 'But you left. You left them. Left us all and then... nothing.'

'I had to go!' Maggie shouted as she turned back into the room. 'I was going to do something stupid. I knew it! To keep them safe, same from me, I had to leave.'

Rose shook her head. 'No, I'm sorry. I can't feel compassion for how much you were struggling. You should have *told* me. I'd have helped, you know I would. That's why you left me the children, because I love them like you did. I can't even feel guilt for sleeping with your husband because your marriage was over. You didn't even want to marry him in the first place!' Rose said. 'But then you stayed away. Why are you back *now*? What do you want?'

Rose was anxious, angry, frustrated. She wasn't ready for Maggie's answer. She wouldn't give the children up. This was *her* family now. She had to be on the attack.

'Laura found me. That's when I realised that no one had got my letters, so you didn't know I was coming back. Or at least no one was admitting to getting my letters. And then she told me about *you* and about Stephen and your ridiculous set-up! About you sleeping with my husband. You cannot just take my family, my children, from me. I will not let you.'

'So even after all this time, it's still about you, isn't it? I see. You had to leave; you couldn't come back. It was only Laura dragging you back here that changed anything. You'd still be there otherwise?'

'That's not fair. I had to protect them. I wasn't well, I'm not well. And...' Maggie paused.

Rose knew what she was doing. All the fights they'd had as teenagers went this way, Rose saying whatever came into her head, Maggie pausing to think. Both ended up with vicious words being thrown and Rose could never work out which was worse – those from her, unedited and raw, or those from Maggie, thought out and deliberate. Which would win today?

'You aren't well. Exactly my point. You couldn't care for them then and you can't now, can you? When you left, the children needed a mother, and you weren't there. Emily and Elliot didn't understand where you had gone or why you had gone because they were babies. You *left* them, you *abandoned* them, and I was there. So I did my best for Emily and for Elliot. I stepped into the shoes you had left behind and I did it well.'

'And I am grateful for that,' Maggie said, apparently trying to appeal to Rose's sense of importance. 'You were a wonderful aunt to them. I knew they'd be safe with you. It's why I knew I could leave them with you.'

Rose could see Maggie clinging onto the last shred of hope that what had happened had not actually happened. She knew it was a sticking plaster moment – tear it off and be done with the pain, or eke it out.

'All very honourable, sister. What about all the days since? What about every single twenty-four hours since you walked away?' Rose gestured dramatically to the doorway. 'Why are you back now and how is that good for anyone but you? What exactly are you planning? Stepping back into your shoes as you left them? I don't suppose you noticed but time has passed, Maggie. You left a huge hole in this family when you didn't come back. And now? You think you can come back, step back in and pretend that no one can see the cracks?' she hissed at her, anger, guilt and defensiveness mixing explosively.

'No. It wasn't like that! I wasn't well! I *trusted* you with them. And... what did you do with that trust? What did...'

'I did what I had to do.'

'You had to lie to the children? You had to sleep with Stephen? Is that what you had to do?'

'He and you weren't working, you know that.'

'Maybe. I'm not back for him. You can have him. But the children? I'm better now, I'm getting better. I *can* be the mother they deserve.'

'You don't need to be. *I* am the mother they deserve and I have been that since the day you left.'

Rose stood her ground. Maggie was breathing hard, her eyes on the floor.

Rose stood up and ushered Maggie to the door. The love Rose had for her sister, the joy of discovering she was not dead, was struggling with the fear of a wife and mother fighting for ownership of her family.

She couldn't have it all and Rose had chosen. Maggie had gone then and now Maggie had to go.

'We're done here. You have to go now.' Rose ushered Maggie back out into the hallway. She handed Maggie her coat.

'What, I...? We need to talk. We can't leave things like this... I won't. How long do you think you can hide the truth? The truth always comes out, you know that, Rose.'

'I'm not hiding anything,' Rose said, despite knowing deep down that this wasn't true. 'The truth is that I am their mother, and you need to go.'

'No. No, we can't leave this here. I won't. When? When can we talk?'

'I don't know,' Rose said, stone-faced. 'I need time to think. Where are you staying? At Laura's?'

Maggie nodded.

'I'll call you. Don't come here again,' Rose insisted, and with that, she ushered her sister out of the door and closed it, leaving Maggie on the outside.

Rose leant against the wall, then slowly slid down it into a graceless heap on the floor. She allowed herself a moment. Her stomach flipped over and over as her mind ran through all the implications. What might happen, what she could stand to lose, what she was prepared to give and what she was not. She was dizzy with it all. It was too much. Too much by herself. She couldn't do this now. She had the children to care for. Rose closed her eyes and allowed the cool solidity of the wall behind her to soothe her, and began to pull herself back together and to think. She pulled her phone out of her pocket and called Stephen.

It rang briefly before he picked up.

'Darling,' Stephen said, out of breath from his run. 'Is everything okay?' he asked, concerned.

'No. The kids are fine but no, everything is not okay. I need you to come home. I need you to come home now.'

'What? What's going on? Are you all right?' The panic was rising in his voice. Rose was always so measured and the tremble in her voice as she spoke was unlike her.

'She... she's back. She's come back.'

'Who? Who's back?' Stephen asked, his wife apparently so far from his mind so as to not even register.

'Maggie. She's been here. She's gone for now – to Laura's. But she's come home, and she wants the children.' Rose almost shouted into the phone.

There was a pause, while the gravity of what Rose had said sunk in before he replied.

'Sure. Okay. I'm coming now.' He hung up.

Looking at her phone in her shaking hands, Rose felt tears well in her eyes. There were too many conflicting emotions to cope with.

'Come on!' she whispered to herself. 'Stop it!'

She knew she had to be clever. She knew she had to be calm. She knew that Maggie being back was sure, in one way or another, to destroy this life that she had made for herself. Rose couldn't let that happen.

Rose gathered herself off the floor and went to check on the children. She needed to see them and keep them close to her – safe with her, their mother.

16

Shaking with shock, Maggie walked away from the house, the street blurring into an alien place. She had thought that she was coming home for her family, but could it be that there was no family for her to come back to? She hadn't believed what Laura had told her, not really, but now, having seen the fire in Rose's eyes, she felt chilled. She had been stupid and naïve. How could she not have seen that staying away so long was a bad idea? Had she chosen to believe that staying away was the best thing because deep down that was what she really wanted? No, she had thought she was doing what was best for the children, getting herself better in order to be a better mother. But – couldn't she have done that closer to home? Closer to them?

A wave of loneliness washed over Maggie. She was isolated. Apart from Laura, who had tracked her down and brought her back. Maggie almost wished that she hadn't. Back in Scotland, had ignorance been bliss? She had felt safe there. Ailsa had supported her, reassured her that staying away was for the best, that writing her letters was enough. Maggie had believed her, and everything had felt like it would be okay.

Maggie couldn't direct any blame at Ailsa. She had rescued her, after all, but her advice had not been good, Maggie could see that now.

On the long drive back home, Maggie had convinced herself that Laura had got it wrong somehow. She had never really liked Rose, always jumping to the worst conclusions. She would have misunderstood somehow. Rose, with Stephen, taking everything Maggie once had, as her own?

Her sister and her husband.

Maggie stopped for a moment, and sat on someone's low garden wall. As she did so, a familiar figure turned the corner, running at speed down the road. As he got closer, Maggie saw him clearly. Stephen.

She felt sick. What would she say to him? All she really wanted to do was to hit him. Hard.

He got closer and Maggie could see that he was flustered. Had he seen her too? He ran right up to her, barely glanced in her direction and... ran right on past.

He had not recognised her. He had looked right through her.

Maggie gagged, and she tried to spit the sour taste from her mouth. She stood up but then doubled over for a moment while her body recovered from the nausea. She no longer existed for him. In all the scenarios she had played out in her head, when thinking about coming home, this had never once occurred to her. The closest she had come to it was when, one night, Maggie got up the courage to voice her deepest fear.

'What if they don't want me back? What if they don't remember me at all? They were babies, they won't remember me.'

'Aye,' Ailsa had replied gently, 'they were only babies when you left but you're their mother and nature never lies.'

Maggie had allowed herself to be reassured by this.

Yet Maggie had known it was possible, even likely, that Stephen had met someone new. She was prepared for their relationship to be unsalvageable. She didn't want him back in any case. They had been badly matched, Maggie knew that. They had let circumstance rather than decision guide them. Whether consciously or not, her marriage to him had diminished her, as he had tried to mould her into the wife he wanted. Maggie had lost sight of who she had been, who she was, and he had not tried to help her hold on to any of it.

But she had not been prepared for this.

For Rose. For her own sister to step into her shoes, her marriage, her bed.

'I'm sure Rose will do a grand job. The children will be safe with her, and their father,' Ailsa had said kindly.

Maggie had agreed. 'Yes, I know her. He won't cope but she'll be great. She's a natural with them and they adore her. She's my sister. I know she will do this for me,' Maggie said adamantly. 'People judge her for being the youngest, for being spoilt. But to me, that means she knows how to love, how to cherish because she has *been* cherished. I want that for my children. And while I'm gone, Rose can give it to them for me, I know it.'

Yes, Rose liked to get her own way, but this? Even from Rose, this was insane. And her parents? How could they be fine with all of this? Was Rose lying to her about that or did she mean so little to any of them that she was so easily forgotten? Did they blame her for leaving? The pain of it was physical. She couldn't stand up. Did anyone ever really love her at all?

Well, *she* loved the children. Everything she had done, she had done for her love of them. Leaving, staying away to work on being a better mother for them, coming back now to reclaim them from this insane situation. Everything was about them. To protect them. She would focus on that and only that. Once they knew the truth, once she had her children back, well, then she could deal with her manipulative sister and her spineless ex-husband to be.

She had to have it out with them all, no matter how much Rose would resist, she had to try. At the very least, the children would know that she had fought for them, that she regretted leaving, that she was just trying to do her best for them. She had to stay. If Rose could do this, then who was she even? Not the sister Maggie thought she was. Could she be trusted at all? How could someone who would *do* something like this be anything like a good mother? She couldn't allow Rose to push her out like this, even though she had handed her family to her and walked away.

Well, now she was back.

* * *

Back at Laura's flat, Maggie rang the buzzer relentlessly. Her initial shock had turned to anger and she was taking it out on the door. Laura came over the intercom and released the door to let her in. By the time Maggie had run up the stairs, Laura was standing at the door to her flat, holding it open. Her expression was serious.

'You were telling me the truth,' Maggie said grimly.

'Why would I make that up?'

'I know. I guess part of me had hoped you'd got it wrong somehow, but no. I saw Emily. She is fine, not a mark on her. I was so relieved. But she had no idea who I was. Not a clue.' Tears burned at the back of Maggie's throat. Emily. Her beautiful daughter. It had been wonderful to see her, despite the situation. She had grown up so much. Not much more than a baby when she'd left, now a confident little girl.

Laura brought Maggie a cup of tea and they sat at the kitchen table like they had done years ago, before children, putting the world to rights into the small hours.

'They have behaved appallingly. It's not even their being together but it's the lies. They have lied you out of existence. Your children don't even know your name!' Laura said in disgust.

'How could they?' Maggie asked as she slumped in her chair. 'I know I walked away. I know I left my children. I know I deserve some punishment – but this? Hearing my daughter, hearing Emily call *her* "Mummy". It felt like someone had stuck a knife through my chest.' Maggie closed her eyes. She thought the price she would have to pay would be the time that she had lost. She could not have imagined that it would be this. That her own family would have denied she ever existed. No one deserves that.

'I'm sorry. I'm so sorry,' Laura said. 'I told them it was wrong, I told them they shouldn't. I said it wasn't right. But so many months had passed and we hadn't heard from you.' Laura paused, struggling with how best to continue. 'They thought you weren't coming back. I guess they maybe even thought you were dead.'

Maggie put her head in her hands, her elbows on the table, looking at its surface.

'I still don't understand that.'

'What do you mean?'

'I told you – my letters? I wrote a letter to Stephen for the first time, about two weeks after I'd left. I told him that I was alive, that I wasn't well, and I was taking some time but that I would be home. I wrote *every week*. I sent birthday cards. I sent gifts. I even *called* on Emily's birthday – though I was too scared, too overwhelmed to say anything. But Rose knew, she *knew* it was me. She talked to me. Told me that everything was in hand, that I could take my time.'

'That little snake!' Laura slammed her fist on the table. 'Do you think she got your letters? Do you think she's lying about this? Like she's lying about everything else?'

Maggie shook her head. 'I don't know. I don't think so? She

denied outright that she knew anything about them when we talked. She did *seem* to be telling the truth. But, I mean, *because* she's lying about everything else, it doesn't make sense to lie about this? Or does it? I'm so confused I can't tell. She's unhinged, I know that.'

Maggie sipped at her tea.

'I've missed this,' Laura said. 'Not this exact situation, obviously, but us, working as a team, talking things out. I'm so sorry I let you down before. I won't do it again, I promise.'

Maggie smiled. 'I've missed you too. And I'm sorry I stopped talking to you about how things were.'

'God,' Laura laughed with relief. 'What were we doing?' She reached across the table and squeezed Maggie's hand. Maggie reciprocated.

'So,' Laura said, wiping tears from her face. 'What are we going to do?'

'I need to see them. Emily and Elliot. I need to know that they're okay because I'm really worried. Emily seemed fine but if Rose is prepared to lie to them about something this big, what else will she be prepared to do? I need to know they're actually safe with her. Once I know that, I can work out what I'm going to do. Rose was *cold*. When she's like that, it's because she's stubborn but also because she knows she's *wrong*. That's the problem with setting yourself up against your sister. I *know* her. Or at least I thought I did.'

'So we need to work out how she'll let you see them? And go from there?'

'Exactly. They don't know about me. Rose is their mother, and they don't know any different. I don't want to tear their lives apart.'

'What about applying for custody of them? Visitation rights?'

'I've thought about that, of course I have, but would I get it? I mean, I left. I have no home of my own, nowhere they could stay. I have diagnosed mental health issues. I have literally nothing solid to offer them.'

'You're their mother.'

'Yes, but as far as they are concerned, so is Rose. And she has Stephen, a house, security. I don't think a court would look kindly on me. Nor the children either, perhaps. And anyway, how long would that take? I need to know *now* what is really going on, how Rose and Stephen are treating them, if they're looking after them. I don't want this to be one of those cases where people look back and wished they'd acted sooner. I want to be part of their lives now. But I don't want to destroy the life they have. I'm so confused.'

Maggie stopped.

'Laura, are they happy? Does Rose really love them? Elliot always looked so much like me. Does he still? Can she love someone who reminds her daily that he's not hers just by looking her in the face? Is she a good mother? Should I even be doing this? Will I make things worse? What about them? Is this best for them?' Maggie scrunched up her face in pain, shaking her hands in front of her, trying hard not to cry.

'Calm, Maggie. Breathe. They seem happy now, yes. But they were distraught when you left, and these things always come out eventually. Isn't it better to do it now, on your terms? Let Rose think she has the upper hand and then...'

Maggie took a shaky breath but then nodded. 'Yes. Maybe. Yes, you're right. But I have to make sure I'm there for them when they find out the truth. They will need me. I will do whatever Rose says, whatever she wants. I need a safe way back to my children and I will do what's necessary to make that happen.'

'What about Stephen?'

Maggie scoffed.

'Rose is welcome to him. In fact, if they're happy with each other, fine. I don't really begrudge them that. Maybe my leaving brought them together. They can have each other. But they can't have my children. They're mine and I want them back.'

17

Rose felt queasy as she closed the door to the playroom behind her, the children placated with more cartoons and snacks. They must have thought all their birthdays and Christmases had come at once with this much TV.

Rose had to fight the urge to take them and run, somewhere, anywhere that Maggie couldn't reach them. The house felt ominous, like a reminder of all she had taken from her sister and all that her sister could take back. She walked into the kitchen and Stephen jumped up from his chair.

'We need our ducks in a row,' Stephen said, business-like.

'We haven't done anything wrong,' Rose insisted. 'But you're right. We still need our story straight. We need to know what, if anything, we are going to tell the children about her. Do we need to warn the pre-school, friends? Will she try and tell them? Will she try and *take* them? What does she want with us? Why is she back, why is she back *now*?' Rose's voice started to tremble, petrified that her sister was about to destroy all she loved.

'Steady. You're shaking,' Stephen said as he pulled her to him.

'I feel sick. I'm *scared*, Stephen. What we have – us, the children. It's perfect. It's everything I've ever wanted. I'm happy.'

'I'm happy too,' Stephen agreed, trying to reassure Rose, but she wasn't listening.

'I had to lose my sister to get it. My sister, who I love. It tore me to pieces when she left. Until I saw, really saw, what she had left me with. It felt like a gift, like she had given me the life I wanted, like she always looked out for me. And now? Does she want her gift back?'

'She can't have it,' Stephen said, before pausing. 'She can't have me. I refused to admit it at the time, but she and I were a mistake.'

Rose smiled at his attempts to reassure her, clumsy though they were.

'But can she have the children? She's their biological mother. Would a court give them to her even after she abandoned them?' Rose felt cold. Legally she hadn't a leg to stand on. 'And even if a court wouldn't, would we have to tell them that we lied, that I'm not their mother? Which breaks my heart because *I am*!'

Stephen opened his mouth to talk and then stopped. He furrowed his brow as he considered this. 'I know. I haven't caught up with the fact that she's back. That she's alive even. I thought...' He paused, choosing his words carefully.

Rose could see he was struggling and her heart melted. He had found this so hard to deal with the first time around and even with her help, talking about emotion still didn't come easily to him.

He shook his head. 'Knowing what state she was in when she left, hearing nothing from her... I thought she'd killed herself. I felt awful. Guilty.' He looked pained and Rose squeezed his hand.

'I spent, well, you know, you know how it was for me, once it was clear she wasn't coming back. And now? It turns out that she'd just had enough of us all? She walked out on us. She decided she didn't want us but now she's changed her mind?' The line of his jaw tightened, his anger coursing through him.

Rose shivered. Was it even possible to fix things now? Maggie's disappearance had caused fault lines to develop in the family. It was a constant regret of Rose's that her actions had allowed them to grow enough to shatter things apart.

Her own parents tried, were still involved in the children's lives, but it was always odd and uncomfortable. Her dad, in particular, refused to let go of his eldest without any firm evidence that she was gone. Said it was too soon to make any assumptions without proof, that everyone just needed to wait. Her mum tried her best, not wanting to lose any more than she had already, whilst it was obvious she agreed with her husband. The inner family had healed and was happy but the wider network that Rose felt the children deserved was fractured and she despaired of it ever recovering. She had refused to live in a state of paralysis but found that in doing so, she had left some people behind.

Now that Maggie was back, was she being wildly optimistic to think that they might, possibly, just possibly find some sort of resolution for everyone? Or would it push them all apart, with her on the opposing side from the rest of her family? Would her parents disown her now that Maggie was back? There *had* to be a way of making this work, of getting everyone on board with her, before she lost everything.

'But...' Rose started, her voice lighter somehow, as an idea, as hope made its way into her mind.

'What?' Stephen said. He was clearly still angry, but Rose knew him well enough to know that part of that was his guilt. He was a good man and the idea that he had been a bad husband to Maggie niggled at him.

Rose knew that from the outside his actions could look appalling. Some people had whispered that Maggie's disappearance might have been his doing, as though they'd find her in the cellar or underneath the patio if they looked. He had endured sideways glances and muttered insults. At one point, he and Rose had considered moving but decided that the children had gone through enough without uprooting them. The gossips would eventually find someone else to gossip about. And they had. But it had shaken Stephen's confidence and guilt was the emotion he went to most often.

'Well, it's just...' Rose paused, trying to form the thoughts in her mind before speaking them out loud. It was ridiculous, she didn't know if anyone would even consider it, but she was desperate. She refused to give in without trying absolutely everything. Perhaps Maggie was just as desperate as she was. It might be preposterous, but it might work. 'Just – it's *Maggie*. My sister. Your... wife. Neither of us fell out with her. We both loved her. And she loves the children, doesn't she? They lost an aunt when I moved in. Your family is mostly absent, and my parents – well, they try their best, but it's hardly bedtime stories and hot chocolate when they visit, is it? I just... if... is there a solution that we're not seeing?' Rose said, rubbing the back of her neck. She was tense and her muscles were starting to ache.

'What are you suggesting?'

'Well... We're all family. Isn't there a way we can be a family again? For the children's sakes?'

'I still don't understand.'

'I was their aunt before I was their mother. Now that I'm their mother, who is their aunt? Who *could* be their aunt?'

Rose knew it was a long shot and that there was a chance that some sort of reconciliation was not on the cards as far as Maggie was concerned. She was beyond angry with them. Rose didn't know if she would listen. The problem was that while Rose loved her sister, she wouldn't give the children up for her. She wanted them all. This could give that to her. Was that so unreasonable?

Stephen looked at her incredulously. He clearly thought she was mad. But he wasn't saying no either.

'The children are ours. She can't have them back. Not after how she abandoned us all. I won't let her ruin their lives all over again. I won't,' he said.

'No. I agree.' Rose took his arm and hugged him. 'We just have to find a way to be sure she doesn't even get to try. And this could just work, couldn't it?'

She knew that whatever Maggie wanted, if she had come back for the children, she and Stephen weren't going to let her have them, no matter what it took. They were *hers*, just as they always should have been.

18

The doorbell rang and Rose jumped up. It had been a long day waiting for this moment, but they needed the children to be out of the way, and so after their bedtime was the only option. Thankfully, Rose's heightened anxiety had led to a day full of activities and both had fallen fast asleep with little encouragement needed.

'No, let me,' Stephen insisted, straightening his clothes as he stood. Rose thought he had the look of someone about to face a jury, unsure of how it would go. She stayed in the living room, wanting as much time as possible to gather herself before Maggie came in and they had to try to find some solution to this mess. She knew that she had to be strong, to stay calm for the good of the children but something about being faced with her big sister, especially if she was going to be angry, made her feel like a child again. Usually, a debate was something Rose enjoyed. She liked to be right, liked to get her own way. But too much was at stake here and all she could feel was dread.

She could hear the strained conversation from the hallway. How had they ever been man and wife? Rose had thought, when she'd first met Stephen all those years ago, that they seemed far too much like strangers to each other, and now, it was clear that she had been right. He had married the wrong sister.

Rose rolled her shoulders to try to loosen the tension that had settled there and felt the band of pressure around her chest lighten. She was in the *right*. She had picked up the pieces that Maggie had left and put them back together. She had Stephen, the children and the upper hand. This would be okay. They were all adults. They would be able to talk like it, to find a way forward for everyone.

Despite her internal pep talk, Rose still felt her stomach drop when Maggie walked into the room. It felt like an echo of the past, a ghost from a life that no one lived any more.

Stephen followed her into the living room to join them. He stood looking uncomfortable. He adjusted his shirt and cleared his throat. He ran his hands through his hair. It was obvious to everyone that he was on edge and unhappy.

'Stephen,' Rose reprimanded, 'stop fidgeting. No one here is enjoying this, but it has to be done. Stop making everyone jittery.'

Stephen looked at her. The effect of her stern but affectionate smile noticeably calmed him. Rose knew they needed to present a united front.

Rose smoothed her dress over her lap, the only movement that betrayed her own nerves. She caught Maggie noting it, knowing that it was what their mother did whenever she was nervous.

'Have you spoken to anyone else yet?' Rose asked. She wondered whether Maggie had already been in touch with their parents. They had not called her, but was that a sign that they didn't know, or that they had chosen sides and had not chosen her? The very idea made her feel ill.

'No,' Maggie replied. 'Just you, Stephen and, of course, Laura. I wasn't sure what Mum and Dad... what they felt about all this.' She gestured towards Rose and Stephen, clearly trying to keep disgust from her voice. 'I haven't been able to face calling them yet.'

Rose wondered if that was a veiled threat. The 'yet'.

'They could see it was for the best,' Stephen said, matter-of-factly.

'I see.' Maggie nodded grimly, looking grey.

Rose was silent, knowing Stephen was not telling the whole truth. Rose was terrified that Maggie being back would shift her parents' allegiance to their eldest child. She had lost enough of them already, to lose more was too much. She had to lead the situation, to be the one with the steering wheel.

'Okay. I'm going to cut to the chase here, Maggie.' Rose turned to face her sister and felt her throat go dry. She pictured Emily and Elliot in her mind on her last birthday when they had made her a birthday card, hand drawn and absolutely covered in glitter. They had both drawn pictures for her on stones they had carefully chosen themselves. Tiny important gifts, giving all that they had to her. Their faces, full of love for their mother, wanting her approval, had melted her heart. Rose fixed that moment, and what it represented, in her mind as she tried to block out all that she felt for her sister. She loved Maggie. But she loved the children more.

'What do you want?' Rose asked, her face stony. Stephen stood next to her and the effect on Maggie was intimidating.

'I...' Maggie stammered. She was shaking, and Rose had to harden her heart to it. *No one who gives in first gets what they want.*

'Why are you back now? You abandoned us, so why are you back? What do you want?' Rose shot at her.

'That's not fair, that's not what...' Maggie stopped.

'It is!'

'I think that's how we felt, Maggie, if we're being honest,' Stephen said, placing his hand on Rose's shoulder. Rose placed hers over his, thankful for his intervention, and for stopping it

deteriorating into sibling bickering at the first instance. She took a
deep breath and started again.

'Okay. How about we let it all out, shall we? You have no idea
the impact your leaving had on us, so shall we enlighten you and
then you can tell us if that wasn't abandonment?' Rose said,
shocked at the anger spilling out of her. She had to rein it in. She
knew that she had to keep the upper hand without pushing so
hard that her sister snapped.

'Okay,' Maggie said, crossing her arms in front of her like
armour against the oncoming attack.

Rose tucked a strand of hair behind her ear and adjusted her
earrings. She knew she had to explain things rationally, in a way
that wouldn't provoke the anger she could see was simmering just
beneath Maggie's surface. Maggie had always been a peacekeeper,
that much was true, but it didn't mean that she was a pushover.

'You left,' Rose said, facing Maggie directly. 'Even now, I don't
understand how you could. But there is no argument with that. You
left your injured children in A&E and you walked away from them.
That was bad enough, but then you let us sit here waiting for you
and you let that drag out. Minute by minute, hour by hour, then
days, months, a year ticked round. We had no idea if you were all
right, if you'd had an accident or been murdered.' Rose sniffed and
blew air out of her cheeks. *Keep your cool, don't lose it.* 'When you
called me, I came to you and the children, no questions, no delays,
I dropped everything for you.' Rose couldn't keep the petulance
from her voice. *I let my life go for you, why won't you do the same
for me?*

Rose deliberately avoided looking at Stephen. She knew the
guilt he felt for prioritising work the way he had, for leaving family
life wholly to Maggie and for how desperately unhappy she had
been as a result.

'And you know how the children suffered without you and you

know how I made it all right again. Now you want to undo that? Is that your idea?'

'Can I speak?' Maggie asked, an aggressive tightness in her jaw.

Stephen glanced at Rose. Rose looked from him to Maggie and nodded.

Maggie bit her lip, then started to speak.

'I told myself that I wouldn't try to justify what I did. I have spent all this time blaming myself. There is not an insult under the sun you can throw at me that I haven't already thrown at myself. It took me a long time to understand, to accept that I didn't get to the point that I did by myself. I needed help but I was too far down to see that.'

Something shifted across her face that Rose couldn't place. Was it sadness? Was it rage? Rose had to repress her instinct to talk, to take over. She wanted to know what Maggie's intentions were.

'When I hurt them, when I hurt Emily and Elliot...' Maggie's voice choked. 'Rose, I left them with you because I thought you could do a better job than me. I knew you loved them like I did.'

Maggie smiled at Rose.

Rose smiled back, caught off-guard by such gentle words.

Maggie's smile dropped instantly. Rose felt as though she was suddenly coated in ice. Fear rose the hairs on the back of her neck.

'I asked you, indirectly, to care for them for me and I knew that you would. I wrote to you, every week, I told you how ill I was, how I was getting help, how I was getting better and that I would *be back*. That I would come *back* for them, but I needed your help in the meantime. But. I didn't think, I never imagined, that you would just *erase* me entirely,' she scoffed. 'I suppose I shouldn't be surprised. You were always efficient. How could you make sure I couldn't take them back from you? By making sure that I didn't exist for them in the first place. As far as they know, I was never here.'

'You *weren't* here!' Rose said, frustration in her voice. 'And these letters. You keep saying that you wrote, you wrote every week, but I don't know what you are talking about! We never *got* any letters from you! We had absolutely no idea where you were or if you were even still alive. Silence. Nothing.'

Rose looked from Maggie to Stephen, exasperated.

'You say that you weren't well. How do you know you didn't *imagine* sending the letters? How sure are you that it wasn't some detached reality thing? Did they ever really exist?'

Rose looked at Stephen for support. He raised his eyebrows in a 'perhaps?' response.

'Don't patronise me! I know perfectly well the letters were real things. I wrote them, Ailsa posted them for me.'

'Who? Who's Ailsa and why was *she* posting these *alleged* letters?'

Maggie paused.

'That's where I went after... she is the one who stopped me from... ending it. I knew her from, well, we'd met online. She'd been helping me, and she was the only person I could think to go to. That's where I've been. With Ailsa.'

'Some random woman from the internet?' Stephen scoffed, almost laughing, before Rose shot him a look that suggested he stop it immediately.

Rose was affronted. That Maggie would talk to a complete stranger over her. She took a moment to process this new information, to work out what it meant and to allow her own ego to settle, before deciding what angle she needed to take next.

'So this Ailsa?' Rose said, arching her eyebrow. 'How well do you really know her? Some woman from the internet? And you trusted her to post these vitally important letters that you wrote? The only way in which you were willing to let us, let your *family* know that you were safe?'

'Yes,' Maggie said resolutely. 'I trust her.'

'Do you? We know how well people from the internet are known for their trustworthiness? Their reliability. You can't say for *sure* that these letters ever made it to a post box, can you? As you didn't post them yourself but handed the job to someone you barely know.'

She let the accusation hang in the air. Maggie was silenced.

Point made.

If she could get Maggie questioning everything she believed, then Rose could manoeuvre her to where she needed her to be. It wasn't pretty, she might not be proud of it but sometimes you had to do what it took.

Maggie pursed her lips. Rose couldn't tell if she was coming around or if she was about to burst with rage. She was unpredictable.

'Letters or not,' Maggie said, hesitantly, 'I don't think it's unreasonable for me to be shocked that you failed to tell them that I existed. Did you even try?'

'We... we didn't plan that. It just happened and then, well, to undo it was also to undo all the recovery that the children needed. It seemed best to just let things lie. I see how it looks but it wasn't deliberate. If you'd have come back, if you'd got in touch, things might be different. But we work – the four of us – we work as a family, and we are happy.'

Maggie's face lit up.

'I called.'

Stephen snapped his head towards Rose. 'What? When?'

Rose flushed red at this. She'd never told him.

'Did you?' Rose asked, trying to sound innocent.

'You know I did, on Emily's birthday.'

'I'm sorry – what phone call, when?' Stephen asked.

Rose turned to Stephen, flustered. 'There was a phone call, on

Emily's birthday. A ghost call. I – I presumed... I didn't say anything because there was nothing to say. It could have been anyone. Sorry – I – things were so busy that day and...' She tailed off. She knew that if she kept talking, she'd dig herself into a hole. So she stopped.

Stephen looked at Rose, an odd expression, almost relief, on his face. 'It's... it's okay.'

The room was silent for what felt like an age. The atmosphere was thick with the heaviness of memories, each trying to wrangle them into some sort of order.

'You know why I stayed away, Rose. *You* know what made me think it was okay,' Maggie said quietly, not looking up from the floor.

Rose was insulted. *Even if I did tell her to stay away, that was still the choice that she made for herself. She's an adult. Her decisions aren't my fault.*

'I left because I wasn't well. I know that now. I couldn't see it at the time. I *stayed* away because I believed that you, that *both* of you were looking after things for me until I was well again, until I could manage again. I stayed away because *you told me* that you were taking care of it all, Rose. I believed you because I thought that you both loved me and loved me enough to do that for me.' Maggie shook her head as if she couldn't believe her own naivety.

'No. No I have to say something,' Stephen said, his face a picture of disgust. 'Firstly, Rose *has* taken care of everything, and I for one am grateful for that,' he said, coldly, 'and secondly, you don't get to scold her for it. You rejected your responsibilities; and you did so without a word to us. I don't believe you called and I know *we* did not get your letters.'

Rose shot Stephen a grateful look. He was standing firmly on her side.

'You say you didn't get the letters, but I *know* I sent them! I told you every week how grateful I was for this time, how relieved I was knowing that you were keeping my family safe for me until I could come home again. Only... now I find that you weren't. You replaced me almost the minute I left. Their own mother.'

'Actually,' Rose said, ignoring the detail about that phone call, 'actually, I'm their mother.' She was calm. This wasn't an argument. This wasn't up for discussion. This was fact. 'You can't just walk back in after all this time and pick up where you left off. You know that, Maggie,' Rose said, looking at her. 'The children don't know you. They haven't missed you, not since those early days. They are no longer yours to come back to. We're the picture-perfect family and I won't let you spoil that!"

Stephen nodded in agreement.

'Spoil the picture? What is this? We're not in an Instagram story here!' Maggie sneered. 'And you and Stephen? Did you just step right in there too?'

'That's not fair, Maggie,' Rose said, keeping her cool in face of her sister's fury. 'It's not as though you left the bed warm and I hopped right in. Don't think we didn't try to find you, because we *did*. The pain at losing you was what brought us together in the first place. And then it became clear that we fitted each other in a way that you and Stephen never did. It felt as though all the pieces had fallen into place. Sometimes in life you have to take what is meant to be yours before you lose it.'

Rose was resolute. She had defended herself enough to her family and friends and to herself. The only person hurting was the one who had walked away in the first place. Maggie would have to live with that. 'You're my sister and I love you, but I won't allow you to destroy this family a second time. I don't think you want to, either. You didn't know what you were doing back then, that's fair enough. I know you love them, that's true. But I am their mother now and I won't give that up. Not for you. Not for anyone, and I'm not sorry for that.'

Rose crossed her arms. The matter was closed. Her stomach was tying itself in knots while she waited for Maggie's reaction.

Finally, Maggie spoke.

'I won't force myself back. I can't. I was wrong to trust you, Rose, and that hurts too. I've lost my children, my husband *and* my sister.'

Rose exhaled a breath she hadn't been aware she had been holding in. Maggie was going to back down.

'But.'

Rose tensed.

'But. I will not let you cut me out. I want to do what is best for the children and I believe that me being back is part of that. I *have* to see them. I *have* to see that they are okay. You lied to them about me, about you. What else have you lied to them about? What sort of parents are you?'

'Now just hold on a minute!' Stephen snapped. 'What exactly are you accusing us...'

'Stop!' said Rose. 'Just wait. Let me think.'

This was starting to go awry. Maggie was not rolling over like Rose had assumed she would do. She needed to keep hold of things and flinging blame about would not achieve that.

Rose stood and paced the room as she always did when she was thinking. Passing the mantlepiece, she picked up a family photo that had been lovingly framed and placed in full view of the room. Her perfect family. Gently, she traced her fingers over the faces in the picture, feeling satisfaction as she did so, and then she turned to Maggie and Stephen. Her face was calm as she chose how best to suggest this to Maggie. It was a way for Rose to keep everything, to keep the children and keep Maggie on a short leash – she had to convince Maggie of its merit.

'I think we're overthinking things. I think we're getting mixed up in semantics. What we have in this room is three people who love and care for Emily and Elliot very much and who all want the best for them. Yes? This is not about us, it's about them. Correct?' She raised her eyebrows in expectation of agreement from the room.

The other two remained silent but nodded, waiting to see what Rose had come up with.

'They don't *need* their mother back, Maggie. I *am* their mother. I am who they have known since their very early days. This is the truth. What they lost, however, when I stepped up, was an aunt. They know that I had a sister. I have told them of memories from my own childhood about her.'

She looked up at Maggie, catching a flicker of understanding in her expression. Maybe her sister could see where she was going with this.

'I don't want *my* children to miss out. I don't want them to lose family because of bad decisions their parents made.' Rose, very deliberately, did not confirm which parent she was referring to.

'Could they not have an aunt again? An Aunt Maggie.' Rose turned to Stephen, an imploring look on her face, hoping he was still on board after their earlier conversation. She put out her hand and Stephen went to her. He unfurled for Rose in a way that he had never done with Maggie. He nodded his agreement.

Rose turned to Maggie. 'Well? What do you think? We'd have to lay strict ground rules, of course, but this could work. We just have to keep the children at the heart of it.'

Rose's heart was fluttering like a butterfly trapped in a glass jar. Everyone's future happiness depended on this moment, and she could not control which way it would go. This way, she got everything she wanted. Emily and Elliot would have her as their mother, Stephen as their father, an aunt and surely then, her parents would come back into the fold. The family, reunited, just in a slightly different alignment. It was the only thing that made sense to her. In Rose's mind, it was the only way that didn't lead to a future built on uncertain ground.

'I don't understand,' Maggie said, confused. 'Are you asking me to lie about who I am?' The distaste clear in her voice.

'No,' Rose said coldly in response. *Why wouldn't Maggie see that what she was offering was the best solution for them all?* 'I am asking you to be my sister. You cannot be their mother. You are not their mother. The only thing I am offering you is to be their aunt.'

'What?' Maggie scoffed. 'Are you insane?' She looked at Stephen, but he looked away. 'Are you actually insane? You want to feed the children more and more lies? Why? To cement the lies that you've already told them?'

'Don't push me,' Rose threatened. 'You are not in a position to argue. We could send you away, back to Scotland.'

'I don't have to go anywhere. I could just tell the children, tell our parents, tell the world, the police, everyone,' Maggie spat back.

Rose hesitated. The destruction that Maggie could render was unthinkable. It seemed if Maggie was going down, she was taking Rose down with her. Rose's mind scrambled. She had to convince Maggie, to get her on board.

'That's true, you could,' Rose replied, as measured and calm as a politician trying to prevent a rebellion. 'But what would that get you? Everyone would hate you. You destroy everyone; you destroy yourself. You forget, I know you, *sister*...' Rose implored. She had to reel Maggie back in, to get her somewhere that Rose could control. Rose could see Maggie's mind working through the implications. She looked worried. She looked beaten.

'Sister...' Maggie said, as some sort of understanding settled on her face.

Had Rose done enough to convince her? What could she offer to sweeten the deal?

'You can be their aunt. My sister, who has been in Scotland. We don't need to say anything more right now. That's enough. And it's easy on the children. They've been through a lot, and we have to put them first. You'll be in their lives again; you'll get to love them and be loved *by* them. You can be Aunt Maggie – fun, loved Aunt Maggie. Part of the family again.' Rose looked at her, hoping to see the moment that she surrendered.

Maggie closed her eyes, thinking.

Rose watched her, desperate for her response. She needed to win this.

Maggie opened her eyes again.

'Aunt Maggie. I am Aunt Maggie,' she said, trying the words out on her tongue, despite a tone that suggested that they disgusted her. 'If you will let me see them, if you will let me in, I can do that. For them.'

Rose smiled with relief. They could work out the details later, but this way she could make sure that Maggie wasn't the wrecking ball that destroyed the home she and Stephen had built. She would know where she was and what she was doing. She could keep her on side. She had found a way of keeping her children. Of keeping it all.

19

'They want you to do what?' Laura exploded as she handed a cup of tea to a shell-shocked Maggie. Maggie took it and curled up on the sofa. She stared into the tea, as though an answer could be found at the bottom of the cup.

'I know,' she said quietly. She was exhausted. Meeting with Rose and Stephen had taken every ounce of her energy and now all she wanted to do was sleep. Trying to stay calm when she had wanted to scream, to get across her point of view against the solid wall that was her sister and once husband had taken all she had. They clearly worked well together and in different circumstances, in a different time, she might have been happy for them both. But they had both betrayed her trust utterly and it was hard to separate her feelings about that from what they had offered, from how she was feeling about seeing her children again, from everything.

'You told them to get stuffed, right? Didn't you?' Laura asked, looking at Maggie.

'No. I said I would do it.' She was flat, like a wrung-out dish rag.

Laura looked appalled. 'You said you were going there to work out what was going on but this... it's insane. You can't just swap!'

'I know, I know. It's ridiculous. I mean, how can we build a future based on more lies? Emily and Elliot deserve to know the truth. And yet...'

'And yet what? Don't tell me that you're actually going to go through with it?' Laura said, a hard edge to the compassion in her voice.

'What choice do I have? Really? What other option is there?'

'The truth?' Laura said exasperatingly. 'The children deserve to know the truth.'

'Do they?' Maggie said, pointedly. 'What? They deserve to know that their birth mother abandoned them, their aunt stole her place and all they've known their whole lives is a lie?'

Laura paused, then said quietly, 'You have to start with the truth somewhere.'

'They're too young to understand it all. Maybe when they're older?'

'Can you hear yourself?' Laura scoffed. 'I left my children, now I'm back and I'm going to lie to them for a few years until I can explain why I left and why I lied? You think that's gonna end well, do you?'

Maggie sighed. 'I know. You're right. I'm just scared that if I go in, all guns blazing, insisting on my own way or nothing, that they will just close the door entirely and then what? What are my options then? Go through the authorities to get custody? How long would that take? I have no money, how would I fund it? Would they even give me the children, or even let me near them?'

'You're their mother – they'd have to give them to you.'

'Would they? Like I said before, I left of my own free will. I have no home, no job, no income. I have nowhere for them to visit me, I'm not wholly stable. Versus Rose and Stephen. Two solid parents, in a happy relationship, all living in the family home. Why would anyone give them to me? And I'm scared, Laura. Because you're right – this is insane. I don't even recognise Rose. How safe are the children with her really? What lengths would she be willing to go to? You hear those stories of spurned parents and they think "if I can't have them, no one will". I can't risk that. I just can't.'

'She wouldn't. He wouldn't.'

'How can you be sure? I never dreamed in a million years that Rose would steal my own children from me and yet... here we are. I *have* to get back inside the family so that I can make sure Emily and Elliot are okay.'

Maggie chewed her lip.

'What about your letters? Have you called Ailsa to talk about it yet? To try to work out what on earth happened?'

Maggie shook her head.

'No. I... I can't work out what to say. She insisted when we were there that she posted them. I have no reason not to trust what she says. She took me in, a complete stranger, and asked for nothing. Why would she lie?'

'Maybe she wanted you to stay? Maybe she was lonely?'

'I suppose that is possible. Though... I... I don't know.'

'What happened then? Do you think Rose is lying? Or Stephen? Or both?'

Maggie sighed. 'I don't know! They've lied about so much. I kept looking at them, trying to see if their masks would slip and I'd see behind their words. But I saw nothing. I honestly don't know. Maybe they really *did* get lost. There used to be an address that the postman got mixed up with ours all the time. I'd take their post over and pick up ours – it got me out of the house. Maybe there's a pile of my letters waiting to be collected and no one ever went?'

Laura said nothing but looked sceptical. She obviously thought the answer was less innocent.

'I need you on my side, Laura. I haven't even called my parents yet. I'm too angry with them for being okay with this all. Or scared to have them turn their backs as well. You are all I have.'

'I *am* on your side, which is why I'm being honest with you. You haven't made the best decisions, especially when under stress.' She looked at Maggie as she winced at this truth. 'I'm sorry, I don't want to hurt you. I just want to be truthful with you, that's all.'

'Officially, the best I will get is supervised visits, if I'm lucky. And children who might hate me and a sister who definitely will. How is that the better option? It could drag on for years. Rose might use the children as pawns against me. I can't risk that for them. I left because I thought I was keeping them safe. I'm back now and doing this because I want them to be safe. It's all that matters to me.'

'Hmm,' Laura said disapprovingly. 'This is nuts. I can't see how this ends well. I *really* don't think it's a good idea, Maggie.'

'I don't think it is either, but it may be my only chance. You weren't there, Laura. You didn't hear them. I ruined everything when I left. I honestly thought I had disfigured them and leaving was the best thing I could do, for everyone. But I was wrong. The children were broken, and Rose was there.' Doubt wormed its way into Maggie's mind. 'Maybe she does deserve to be their mother…'

'But she isn't! You are!'

'Am I?' Maggie asked sadly.

'Yes!' Laura yelled at her. 'Come on! What happened to the "I'll do whatever it takes"? Are you just going to roll over and take it? That's not a mother fighting for her kids. That's not enough, Maggie!'

'You're right. I will. I am. But – if I do what they ask, I can fight without them knowing. I can get close, keep an eye on the children, get to know them again and work out from inside what the hell I'm going to do. If I fight in a way that Rose knows I am fighting her, she will tear me to pieces. I know it. I've seen Rose when someone is standing between her and what she wants, and it isn't pretty.'

Just then, the phone rang, and Laura went to answer it. She returned, holding it in her hand, the caller on hold.

'It's Stephen,' she said. 'He wants to come around to talk, just him. What do you want to do?'

Maggie stood up to her full height, as though Stephen could see her.

'Tell him yes. We need to talk.'

'Fine,' Laura said as she walked back to the hallway. 'Come here. I'll go out,' she said into the phone.

Maggie took a gulp of breath and felt her spirit harden. If they wanted a battle, Maggie would give it to them. They just wouldn't be aware of it.

* * *

Half an hour later, the doorbell rang. Laura looked at Maggie and picked up her coat. Maggie felt sick but also ready. This was a conversation that had waited too long to happen and she was ready to finally get her point across. She was stronger now. She was getting better. Stephen was going to listen, whether he liked it or not.

'Good luck. Give me a call when you want me to come back. I'll stay out as long as you need, okay?' Laura said, hugging Maggie as she went to answer the door.

That she and Laura had picked up where they'd left off gave Maggie such faith. It *was* possible to start again; it *was* possible to make amends and move on. She *could* get her children back.

'Stephen...' Laura's voice said, coldly, from the hallway. 'She's through there.' And she closed the door behind her.

Stephen walked into the living room. He took off his coat. He somehow managed to look both angry and sheepish and Maggie couldn't tell whether he was about to rage at her or not.

'Maggie,' he said in greeting, more business-like than she was expecting. She nodded at him but said nothing, taking him in. His hair was speckled with greys, his face had aged. He looked tired, but he also had more laughter lines than she remembered. Somewhere, deep down, Maggie felt both a frisson of relief that he was okay and then a jolt of rage that she was the one who lost so badly when they had both failed at being a family.

'Aren't you going to say anything?' he asked.

Maggie had been staring at him in silence and the effect had clearly unnerved him. *Good*, Maggie thought, *get him off-guard.*

'What is there to say? You've got the kids, you've got a new wife, a new life together. What can I say to that?' Maggie snapped. All the pent-up anger she had kept in until now was bubbling up to the surface. If she so much as let the tiniest crack open, she would surely explode with it.

Stephen shifted his weight and started fidgeting, uncomfortable in his wife's presence. At least he wasn't bastard enough to be okay with sleeping with his wife's sister, lying to his kids and still being able to look her in the eye. Maggie let a laugh escape her lips and Stephen's head snapped up to look at her. She swallowed the rest of the giggle and looked straight at him until he looked away again. *You won't squash me this time*, she thought defiantly.

'We need to talk. About the idea, about Rose's suggestion,' he said, looking at the floor.

'About my being their long-lost aunt? That one? Or the one where you all wish I'd go back to wherever I've been and leave you to play happy families without me? Which? Which idea do you mean, *darling*?' Maggie spat.

'You can be as angry as you like,' Stephen said pointedly. 'I understand. But none of this was deliberate. And none of it would have happened if you hadn't turned your back and run away leaving me to handle our hurt, scared and exhausted children by myself.'

'I *didn't* leave you by yourself.'

'No. No, you left me with Rose. And now you're angry that I'm *with* Rose. That's not fair.'

'I didn't leave *you* with Rose, I left the *children* with Rose. I did not expect my husband to shack up with my sister and then pretend to *our* children that I never existed! For Christ's sakes, can't you see why I'm so angry? You left me to it, while you forged ahead in your career, never mind my own lying in tatters on the maternity suite floor, and when I couldn't cope, you replaced me with my own bloody sister!'

Maggie slammed her palm down so hard on the living room table, the vase of flowers jumped, wobbling noisily as it righted itself. She looked at Stephen to see his response.

Maggie had seen anger rising in him many times. His jaw line would start to pop, the muscles in his face tighten and relax as he tried to control it, tried to swallow it. She wondered if Rose had ever seen this side of him.

'I think it's time I had a say, don't you think?' he replied more calmly than his face suggested. 'I won't make this about me, but I do want to say my bit. I won't be painted as the villain here. I haven't done anything wrong.'

Maggie held her tongue and gestured for him to go on.

'From our time at university, Mags, to when you left, it was a conveyor belt and we just went along with it, didn't we? Emily, as much as we love her, was a surprise. Elliot the same. I felt so stupid, a fully-grown educated man being caught out twice. Unexpected pregnancies. Not part of the plan. I knew where I wanted to go and how I wanted to get there and then you, you turned up and turned that all upside down...'

He waved away Maggie's incredulous gasp.

'No, I am not saying that I had no input, obviously I did. But you were pregnant and suddenly there was a wedding and we were a family of four and I had to make sure I could support us all. My father said I shouldn't have married you. Did you know that?' he asked.

Maggie looked at him. A thin smile on her face as she acknowledged what her father-in-law had never *quite* said to her but intimated almost every time they'd met.

'I can believe it,' she laughed harshly.

'He thought you would derail my career, a career that he had invested his time, money and contacts in. I worked all hours to try to show him that you weren't a bad decision, to prove to myself that I wasn't a failure who'd knocked up his university girlfriend and screwed up his life.'

'What about *my* career? I loved what I did, and it was just expected that once the kids were here, I'd put it aside. Like it was the 1950s or something. Married? Kids? No career for you – it's housework time!'

'God, it certainly wasn't 1950 at home! It was always chaos. Always mess and clutter all over the place. You never looked happy to see me. Relieved, yes, but not happy. Work was precarious. I was relatively new in my company and I had to establish myself. If I lost my job, what would we do? Live on your dressmaking money?'

'How *dare* you!' said Maggie. 'Don't belittle what I do. I was establishing my career too and just because what I do doesn't necessarily make as much money, doesn't make it worth less.'

'Not in itself, no, but tell that to the mortgage repayments. Tell that to the gas bill. We had outgoings and I had to meet them. For all of us. There was a time when people were being laid off and I needed it not to be me. We'd just had Elliot and...'

'What? You never told me that,' Maggie interrupted.

'No.' Stephen looked abashed. 'No. I didn't. You were struggling just after he was born, I could see that. And I didn't want to add to it.'

'You should have said. It might have helped me understand,' Maggie said, her anger deflating. There was so much that they should have done differently. So much they ought to have shared but didn't. Where would they all be now if they had? 'I should have gone back to work after Emily. It was what I wanted, but then Elliot followed so hot on her heels, there wasn't time. I was blindsided.'

'Me too. It became easier to stay at work. I admit that. I wanted a wife who was happy to be at home, happy to be a wife and mother and you clearly were not. I had to do my job, even when I hated it. I had to turn down a secondment that would have been great, because of the financial implications. I had to stay in my lane and keep going. For us.'

Stephen stared at the floor. It was clearly hard for him to talk like this.

Maggie slumped onto a chair. Her mind was spinning. All these years, she had been convinced that Stephen was working so much because he wanted to, because he found home too awful a place to be, that she was not enough of a wife for him.

'It hadn't occurred to me that you felt the pressure of being the sole breadwinner,' Maggie said quietly, apologetically. 'I was so angry at you wanting me to put my own career aside, maybe I didn't stop to consider that you weren't doing what you wanted either.'

'No, well... exactly,' Stephen tailed off.

They'd trapped each other without either meaning to.

Their words hung in the air. For a moment, they stopped. Maggie's long-held anger started to break down. Surely they could be grown up and find some solution? There was love there once, they could find respect now, couldn't they? This whole aunt scenario could let her in enough to find some way to move forward. A strange, roundabout way of getting towards honesty with each other.

'We can try this Aunt idea. If you think it might work.' Maggie said, trying to hold out an olive branch, whilst also testing how much of the scenario was being driven by Rose. If Stephen wasn't sure, maybe there would be an opening there that she would be able to use somehow.

'I came to say that I wasn't sure if it was a good idea,' he started, but now I think perhaps it is the best way forward.' He cleared his throat. He still seemed unsure.

Maggie looked at him. Maybe he could be brought round to her way of thinking, if she appeared to be toeing the line.

'I really did write, you know,' Maggie said, still smarting from Rose's suggestion that her letters were all in her mind. 'I wouldn't just leave you all hanging like that.'

Stephen's mouth flattened into a line, but he said nothing. Maggie wasn't surprised, he wasn't going to take her side over Rose's, no matter their history.

Maggie needed to see the children, needed to know they were okay and then, surely, three adults who loved them could work out how best to fix this mess.

Surely they could do that?

20

Maggie's throat was dry, her hands were clammy and her body would not stop fidgeting.

'Come on!' she said to herself. *This is not how you want to meet your children for the first time.* The oddity of that sentence sat with her as she stood on the doorstep, adjusting her jacket, trying to work out how to behave. Who was Auntie Maggie? Could she be this new person? She wanted to be on her best behaviour, to show them her best side. She wanted to be able to show them that she loved them and have them love her back. She was aware that she couldn't push this and that she needed to do what was best for them, however much it hurt to keep herself at arm's length.

Trying to ignore the shake in her hands, Maggie rang the doorbell and stepped back. She picked up the bags that she had with her, scooping up all the presents that she had chosen. She knew that affection couldn't be bought, but Laura had pointed out that a few gifts wouldn't go amiss and had given Maggie some money to buy some. She had said they could be in lieu of presents missed; a way to break the ice with the children.

The door opened. Stephen stood there, a strange, forced smile on his face. This new layer of deception obviously sat hard on him. *Good*, Maggie thought to herself, *some of this has to be difficult for him*. Trying to remember their agreement, she threw him a wide and generous smile, handing him her coat as she swept excitedly into the living room, like an out-of-season Father Christmas.

Emily sat on the sofa with her head in a picture book and Maggie's heart soared at the sight of her. She had loved books from an early age too.

Maggie had to try desperately hard not to swoop down next to her and ask her all the questions that leapt to her lips as she looked at her baby girl. Emily was interested in their visitor, but shy this time, and so she hid her face behind the book with furtive glances upwards. Elliot was driving a toy car around the living room floor. It felt strange to see this small male version of her. Maggie gazed at him, taking in as much as she could.

Then it hit her again. They really *were* fine. Perfect. Not a mark on them. Laura had been telling the truth, not sugar coating at all. There was not a single sign that she had hurt them, as she had spent so long fearing she had. She looked again, trying to see if there was any sign that Rose was anything but a good mother to them, any indicator that they were in harm's way. Could she really love Elliot, who looked so much like Maggie? Could she love Emily, who at this moment was behaving so much like Maggie, instead of the outgoing child Rose had been? She had to be sure.

Maggie told herself that this was the reason for her deception. That she needed to keep an eye on things, for the children's own sakes. It was an awful thing to do and yet it did seem that it was for the best.

Rose walked into the room from the kitchen, her eyes shining.

'Maggie!' Rose called, embracing her wholeheartedly. 'I've missed you,' she told her.

Maggie felt the truth of this as her sister squashed her, like she used to do when they were kids. Awkwardly, she dropped the bag she was holding as Rose's hug pinned her arms to her sides. Maggie picked her hands up and returned the gesture, wanting to and yet not wanting to relax. She had missed Rose, she loved Rose. But she couldn't let her guard down, not now, there was too much at stake and Rose was not to be trusted. This could just be Rose luring her into a false sense of security. She had to stay focused, but her heart was softening. Then Rose whispered into her ear. 'It's all going to be okay from here. We have each other. We have the children. It is going be fine.'

Suddenly rage churned inside Maggie, and she held her fist together so tightly that her nails bedded into her palms. The pain kept her calm. How *dare* Rose suggest that anything about this situation was *fine*! Being so close to her children but not being able to tell them everything was not *fine*, her own flesh and blood looking at her like a stranger was not *fine* and watching her own sister live her life *for* her was anything but *fine*. And the children, was their being lied to again *fine*? As always, Rose was only thinking of what worked for her. Typical. Well, Maggie would toe the line so long as it got her where she needed to be, where she could be sure of how Emily and Elliot really were and then, then she would take back what was hers. She could be patient. She knew how long time could be.

'Kids?'

The children immediately turned to their mother, clearly keen to know who Maggie was.

'This is your Aunt Maggie. My sister.' Rose turned, beaming with happiness at Maggie, taking her hand before turning back to the children. 'She's been away, up in Scotland, for a long time since you were tiny, but she's back now and she's really keen to meet you again so come and say hello.'

Emily put her book down and looked at her. Maggie hoped that her nerves wouldn't betray her, but she couldn't help hoping that there might be something about her, a memory that Emily might recognise. She knew it was foolish, but she wanted her daughter to remember her. Did she still sigh in the same way she used to when she fell asleep? Would she still wiggle her toes when she concentrated?

Maggie opened her mouth, but no words came. She laughed nervously and cleared her throat.

'Sorry. I'm excited to meet you, but I'm nervous too. I always am when meeting someone important,' she smiled shyly. Within this lie, this lie of monumental proportions, she wanted to be as truthful as possible, as though somehow it would help balance things out.

Emily laughed a little and smiled back.

'Me too,' she said, and looked up, making brief eye contact with Maggie.

Maggie's heart melted. Emily was still her baby but also, she was now a proper little person.

'Does your mummy help you?' Maggie needed to know what sort of parent Rose was. Was she kind? Was she cold?

Emily nodded.

'Mumma helps. She holds my hand. A squeeze means "I love you" and I feel braver.'

Maggie was torn. That was exactly what she wanted for her daughter but the jealousy inside her burned. She tried to push it away.

'That's nice.'

Emily nodded and Maggie took the chance to sit alongside her.

'What do you like doing?'

'I love drawing. And colouring.'

'That's lovely. What do you like to draw?'

'Dresses. And hats! And silly shoes!' Emily said excitedl looking up at Rose for assurance.

Rose nodded, a tight smile on her face. 'Yes, you're our artis They're really good.'

'Mummy and Daddy can't draw. But I can!' Emily laughed.

Rose looked grim and said nothing.

Maggie beamed at this smaller version of herself. 'I draw,' sh said encouragingly. 'Maybe you get it from me?'

Had it made Rose and Stephen uncomfortable to see Emil develop the same skill as her, Maggie wondered? Did it remin them with each lovingly presented drawing that Emily was n wholly theirs?

'Presents?' Elliot interrupted, with all the grace of an excite toddler. He had been observing silently from behind his game bu the lure of a bag of parcels wrapped in enticingly bright paper wa too strong. He launched himself across the room and stood, soli and expectantly, at Maggie's feet.

'Eli!' Rose laughed kindly. 'You know that's not polite. The might not be for you,' she teased gently. Elliot's face droppec Clearly this possibility had not occurred to him.

'Don't worry, Elliot,' Maggie said, wanting to scoop him up int her arms and pepper him with kisses. He looked so young an bereft in those seconds before she had spoken that her hear swelled. It brought back those nights when she had been the onl one able to console him, to make him feel safe and loved. She fel sick when she thought of her leaving him to cry without her, ever though the little boy who stood in front of her seemed to show n ill effects. Was Rose really a good mother? How could she be whe she was wrapped in so many lies?

'There are things in here for both of you, I wanted to...' Sh

ailed off. *Make up for missed birthdays and Christmas.* Reminding
veryone of her absence was helpful for no one and she did not
ant to shatter the happy atmosphere. Even with Stephen
rooding in the corner and Rose, trying to be happy but being
trained with it, the open joy of the children was infectious.

'Is this one mine?' Elliot said, jumping up and down like an
verexcited puppy, holding the largest parcel from the pile.

Maggie laughed happily. 'Yes, my poppet, that one is for you.'
nd before she could even gesture for him to open it, he started
earing at the paper with great enthusiasm.

'Ooooh!' he shouted happily as he revealed a new shape set.
rightly coloured interlocking plastic pieces which glimmered in
he light.

'It's a bit grown-up for him,' Rose said, not hiding her
nnoyance.

'I thought we could maybe build some things together?' Maggie
aid, not looking at her but reaching out to hug Elliot before
hinking better of it. Her arm hung in the air briefly, while her
rain scrambled to think of how to move it naturally. How did she
ome to be so awkward with her own children? She was in the
niddle of berating herself for it when Elliot barrelled into her
rms and hugged her tightly.

'Thanks you!' he beamed at her, before sitting back on the sofa
vith her, his new gift shining up at him from his lap. Maggie
elaxed her arm around him and leant her head sideways to rest on
is, briefly, gently. She breathed in the scent of him, and it immedi-
tely recalled intense memories of his babyhood. Maggie's
tomach contracted hard. She felt pulled inwards. Her throat
urned and she had to close her eyes to keep the tears from form-
ng. Trying to swallow her emotions, remembering to be this aunt
haracter was painful. Images played in her mind of the children

as babies, intercut with that night, their screams, their tears, as th boiling water hit. Maggie shuddered.

'Aunt Maggie?' Emily asked timidly.

'Yes, my lovely?' Maggie said, opening her eyes and blinkin away the dark thoughts that had started to spiral in her min drinking in instead the sweetness of Emily's face. She had spen many hours gazing happily at that face when she was a baby sh realised, looking back. She had missed it.

'Is there a present for me?' Emily inquired, trying to be polit but also not wanting to be left out.

'Of course. Of course, Emily. I wouldn't miss you out!' Maggi said, aware that her brightness was forced, but also aware that th only other option was tears. She had forced them away for years now was not the time to let them go.

Maggie handed Emily her gift, suddenly nervous that it woul be too young for her. Or too old. She couldn't tell.

Emily opened the package. It was a book. A journal with a dar soft cover, with threads of sparkle running through it, tied with golden ribbon. The front cover had a crescent moon and stars tha twinkled with sequins at the top, and on the bottom, a grass hilltop with a rabbit and its mother, staring up the night sk together.

Maggie had drawn her breath in when she had seen i Emily's favourite book as a toddler had been about a bunn and her mummy telling stories by moonlight, and Maggi hoped that the hundreds of times she had cuddled down wit her and read her the story, sometimes over and over, woul have ingrained the image onto Emily's brain, as it had don hers.

There was silence in the room, apart from the sound of a card board box being slowly torn by Elliot, impatient to get started wit his new toy. Emily turned the journal over in her hands, feeling th

uxurious softness of the fabric cover and tracing her fingers over
he sparkly sky.

'Do you like it?' Maggie whispered.

Emily turned her face to Maggie, with a curious expression. A
question, almost.

Rose's smile had dropped, Maggie noticed. Was this too much?
She needed to be subtle, she had to convince Rose she wasn't
trying to steamroller her way back in. She knew anger in her sister
when she saw it. Had she ruined things before she'd even started?
Would the children pay for Maggie's misstep?

'It's pretty! And...' Emily stopped, forming the sentence in her
mind before speaking, in a way that reminded Maggie so sharply
of herself that again she had to stop her lips from trembling. Rose
never paused, what she thought came out of her mouth at first try.

'Yes...?' Maggie asked, gently, encouragingly.

'The bunnies! I love bunnies. I want a real live one. Mumma
read me a book... and... wait...' and Emily leapt from the sofa and
ran upstairs.

Rose exhaled and Maggie deflated. Emily remembered the
book. She did remember something of those years, but in her
memory, it had been Rose who read it to her. It was hard to take.
Even the tiniest flicker of a memory of Maggie had been success-
fully obliterated from her daughter's mind. If Maggie had thought
that the time away from her children had been her punishment for
leaving in the first place, then she had been wrong. The years away
had been her purgatory. This, now, this was her hell.

'Elliot, darling?' Rose said gently.

'Yes?'

'Where are your slippers? Don't you have cold feet?'

'No?'

'Go get them, lovely. You left them in the playroom, okay?'

'Okay!' Elliot sang and jumped out of the room. Stephen

followed, clearly wanting to be anywhere but in the room with the two sisters.

Rose whipped back to Maggie. Her face was furious.

'What are you doing? How would you know about that book? Don't push it.'

'I wasn't! I just thought she'd like it. She *does* like it. Don't you want the kids to like their new *auntie*?' Maggie struggled to keep sarcasm from her voice. These were her kids and Rose was trying to keep them distant from her.

'We want you back, we do. But it's best this way. If you push your luck, I will shut the door on all of this so fast...'

'Slippers, Mummy. Can I play now?'

Rose's smile snapped back on her face. Maggie realised how much hiding Rose had needed to do and how much pretence she would have practised over the years. It was now clearly second nature.

Maggie smiled warmly at Elliot.

'Sure,' Maggie said, then bit her lip. She hadn't meant to respond to 'Mummy'. Thankfully Elliot hadn't noticed, he was too focused on his toys. Rose, however, was obviously seething.

Emily bounded back into the living room, just at the right time holding an obviously well-loved and battered book.

'Look!' Emily beamed, holding the two books side by side.

'It's the same! How did you know?' Emily smiled, looking pleased with herself for connecting the two.

'Perhaps it's auntie intuition,' Rose interrupted. 'You loved that book, my darling. I read it to you over and over again. When you woke in the night, scared or upset...' Rose glanced at Maggie. 'I would read it to you to calm you and settle you back to sleep. Bunnies and cuddles, we used to call it, do you remember? "Mama – want bunnies and cuddles pease," you used to ask. And we'd cuddle up, just you and me, and read it until you couldn't keep your eyes open any more.'

'Mummy,' Emily groaned self-consciously. Rose kissed the top of her head in reply.

'What lovely gifts. Say thank you to your auntie, children.'

'Thank you,' they intoned.

'There's more...' Maggie started but was cut off immediately by Rose.

'Shall we have drinks? Who's thirsty?' she trilled. 'We can do more gifts later. Really, you're too generous. You don't need to *buy* them,' Rose said firmly. There could be no tussle for primacy here. Rose was staking her ground. Maggie needed to be careful.

'Coffee...' Stephen announced quietly as he walked into the room, holding a tray with mugs, a steaming cafetière and a small jug of milk. Elliot jumped out of the room again and returned almost immediately, wobbling slightly as he walked, trying to keep a plate of biscuits level. His face a picture of total concentration. He placed them, proudly, on the table alongside the tray of drinks. They were somewhat misshapen and with tell-tale fingerprints of a child chef on the surface.

'Biscuits!' he shouted as he took one and stuffed it into his mouth before any of the three adults in the room would have time to stop him. With crumbs tumbling from his lips, he picked another up and proffered it to Maggie.

'Yug wan un?' he mumbled.

Maggie chuckled at him and took the offering. 'I'd love one. What flavour are they?' she asked good-naturedly, happy again to be having a conversation that flowed.

'Chocolate chip,' Emily answered for her brother, who had accepted that despite all best intentions, it wasn't possible to talk and eat at the same time.

Maggie took a bite. 'Oh that's tasty. Your mother taught you well,' she said, smiling up at Rose, acknowledging her status to keep her on side.

'Actually, I cook with them,' Stephen said, a little too curtly.

Maggie spun round to face her him, somewhat shocked. He was clearly more hands-on than he used to be. Had he learnt from his mistakes? Was it having a different wife?

'They're good.' Maggie tried to smile. The children weren' idiots, they'd pick up on any animosity.

'Actually, I'm just going for a quick jog or something,' Stephen said, clearly in need of a break. The atmosphere in the room with him was stilted. The children noticed it too – eyes downcast, obviously working to 'behave'.

Rose nodded at him.

He needed to be on board if this was going to work, if Maggie was going to be let back into the fold. They couldn't do it without him, and Maggie could see that his agreement was wavering as the doubt crept in behind his eyes. Maybe they needed to work out the baby steps without him.

With Stephen gone, Maggie felt some of the strain drift away from her. She loved Emily, she loved Elliot, deep down she even loved Rose, despite what she had done and what she was proposing now. But Stephen? She doubted that she had ever really loved him. Maggie rose from the sofa and went to sit with Elliot.

'Can I join in?' she asked. 'Emily? Rose?'

The four of them got to work on the building shape set that she had brought for Elliot. There was companionable silence and Maggie breathed it in. Her children were relaxed in her presence. They liked her. She glanced at her little sister and felt a wave of love for her, immediately followed by anger. She might have walked away from her children, but at least she wasn't the one who stole people's children from them.

Lying on the floor, she glanced over to Rose, who met her gaze and smiled back.

'When they were babies, this is what I imagined for us. This,' Rose said, as though this were a perfectly normal situation.

Maggie nodded. If she opened her mouth to speak, she would not be able to keep her rage inside. This was never what she had imagined. *She* was their mother. Rose was not in her right mind to imagine that she could just *take* them from her. What on earth was going on here? What had Maggie allowed to happen?

21

She could hear voices from outside Laura's apartment door. Rose hadn't rung the doorbell yet; a man at the main entrance had let her in as he was leaving. Rose hated apartments; complete strangers being let in by your neighbours, just for smiling. Rose knew that a big smile and acting as though you were supposed to be somewhere was often enough. She tried not to think too much about whether it was the same with the children – hers just because that was what she wanted. No. They were hers because she had loved them and cared for them and put them first, especially when they needed her most.

She was grateful that Maggie seemed to have acknowledged and accepted how things were and Rose was excited to be invited over to spend time with her. It meant that her plan was working, that she was keeping things in the direction she had intended. But now, hearing multiple voices inside the flat, her palms felt clammy and there was a fluttering in her chest as she knocked on the door.

'Rose! I didn't hear the buzzer go! Come in,' Laura said as she stepped back from the door and gestured to let Rose pass. The hallway was dark and narrow and Rose could feel animosity pouring from Laura as she squeezed past her. Would she ever feel not on trial with her? Laura obviously felt guilty at her part in Maggie leaving and Rose resented her focusing her anger on Rose rather than just accepting her share in the blame. *It's really none of your business*, Rose thought as she smiled and handed Laura her coat. Laura grimaced a smile in return and opened a cupboard to hang it up.

'You've made the place really nice,' Rose said, trying to lift the mood, but it came out flat and sarcastic. Laura didn't reply. Rose caught the wave of voices, clearer now, and her heart sank. She knew exactly who they were. It was her parents. Feeling ambushed, she turned to look at Laura accusingly. But Laura was looking at the floor and ushered her into the living room where three pairs of eyes looked up at her.

'Rose,' Maggie said, a look in her eye that Rose couldn't decipher. Was it triumph? Was it an apology? Damn her for getting to their parents first! Rose had intended to be the one to announce their plan. A done deal. No need for parental interference. Now, Rose didn't know what she was walking into.

She tried to gauge the feeling in the room, to work out what Maggie might or might not have told their parents, trying to see in her parents' faces whether she was about to get the scolding of her life or whether they were angry with Maggie for walking away. What was it about being back with your parents and siblings that seemed to make you regress? Rose was a grown woman, a mother of two and yet she felt like she was about to get grounded.

'Rose, darling,' her mother said as she got up and gave her a hug. That was a good sign. Her dad couldn't look at her. That was not. He had struggled with things being how they had been.

'Mum, Dad.' Rose smiled, trying her best to looked pleased to see them. 'I didn't know you were going to be here. I...'

'When were you going to tell us Maggie was home? Was safe?' Bill said, looking at her reproachfully.

Rose stiffened. 'When *she* was ready to tell you, Dad?' Her face stuck in a rictus grin. 'It wasn't my news to tell. I didn't want to rush her into anything. I didn't want her to...'

'Leave again?' Maggie asked defensively.

'Well. Exactly,' Rose said, biting her tongue to keep from further comment.

There was an awkward cough in the corner of the room and everyone turned to see Laura in the door to the kitchen.

'I've made a pot of coffee. I'll head out now and give you some space. You've all got a lot of talking to do and catching up. So, yeah. Okay,' she said, placing a tray on the side table and trailing off as she put on her coat.

Rose was glad that Laura was leaving. She didn't want an audience. She was clearly going to have to stand her ground again and she was tired of defending herself to Laura. It never changed her mind and it was exhausting. Some people just didn't know when they were beaten.

The door clicked as it closed behind Laura, and Rose stood still in the middle of the room, not sure what best to do. What had Maggie said? What did they know? How on earth did she get here, trying to work out what version of what truths were known by who? These were her family, those who had known her all her life. They were supposed to be her support, her allies. Not pieces in an overly complicated chess game. Rose's chest ached. Was it all supposed to be this hard?

'Are you going to sit down? Or stand there all day like a lemon?' Bill said, still gruff but smiling.

Rose sat, noting that Maggie was on the smart grey sofa, next to their father, and he had one of her hands in his. Their mother sat in a bright orange high-backed chair, with her legs to one side, her knees facing away from Maggie, ankles crossed. So – it would be her father who needed most convincing. She could do that. Rose deliberately took a place next to her mother, on a purple velvet cube chair, creating a subliminal split of daughters and parents.

'So, I've told Mum and Dad everything,' Maggie announced.

'Everything?' Rose questioned, wanting to make sure that she knew what she would need to deal with. She looked hard at Maggie, who, under the scrutiny of the sister who had once known her better than anyone, began shifting in her chair uncomfortably. The high, defiant chin had dropped, the hard line of her lips had softened. Maggie was lying – she had not told them the whole picture. What was she hiding?

'Yes.' Maggie paused. 'Yes, everything.'

'Darling...' Elizabeth started.

'Yes – she's told us where she went, why she went. She's told us about how she nearly...' Bill's voice broke, 'about how she kept in touch, though goodness knows what happened there, as *we* never heard anything.'

Maggie stared at Rose while Bill talked. Rose pretended not to notice.

'She's told us about this insane idea to keep lying to the little ones and about being an *aunt* now. What the hell do you think you're playing at?' he roared.

'Bill...' Elizabeth admonished him. She took Rose's hand. Rose forced tears into her eyes, so that when she looked up, it was like they would be looking at Bambi. She knew that her father could never cope with his girls crying. It melted him every time.

'Sorry, love, sorry. But you know that I wasn't happy when you and Stephen got together but at the time, well... It felt like too soon, if it should have happened at all, but none of us knew what to do for the best. I've told Maggie as much. The dishonesty that followed, the deception that developed into much more than a white lie. It never sat well with me; you know that. I said so at the time, *we* said so at the time,' he gestured towards his wife, 'now we have a chance for everyone to come clean, to start again, and you don't want to take it? I don't understand.'

Rose sighed, trying to keep the impatience from her face. Really? They didn't get it?

'Because we can't start again, Dad. We can't undo time. She wasn't here, so Emily and Elliot don't know who she is. Even if we had shown photographs and talked about her, Maggie would still be an abstract. They know *me* as their actual mother because I did the *actual* mothering.'

'We know, love, you did a good thing stepping in like that. But...' Elizabeth said, gently.

'But what? I know that *maybe* we didn't necessarily make the best choices, but we made them under stress at a very difficult time. The children are settled now. They are happy now. They know they are loved. Think of them – think of what you are *actually* asking me to do to your own grandchildren?'

Maggie looked pale. She could see where Rose was going with this.

'How do you mean?' asked Bill.

'You're asking me to tear their mother from them. Again. To tell them that the stable family foundation they rely on isn't true. That the people they depend on to keep them safe aren't dependable. Like their original mother wasn't dependable.'

'I wasn't well!'

'So you say. Mental health matters, doesn't it? So...' Rose was thinking fast now. What could she say to convince them, without a shadow of a doubt, that her way was right? 'What would you say if I told you that children exposed to trauma in their early years have stunted brain development? That children who have prolonged exposure to upset have identifiable negative effects on their neural pathways. Did you know that?' Rose said calmly, looking at her audience, their faces in shock. 'I know that because when Maggie abandoned them and I had to take over, I did my homework. I did the work and I knew that it was *vital* that I got them to feel safe and loved again. Before the whole terrible situation caused irreparable damage to them. I made it so that my family were going to be okay.'

'They're not your family, Rose,' Bill said, with quiet firmness.

Ignoring this unhelpful comment, Rose continued.

'Can't you see? If you all insist on telling them the truth now, you are going to expose them to more trauma. Who knows what damage that could do?' Her voice wavered, to make sure her point hit home. 'They're so young, so delicate. They need stability and surety and to be able to *trust* those who look after them. Right now, that is what they have. And you want me to take that away?' she implored.

'Rose, lovely, let's not get overly emotional...' Elizabeth interjected.

'I don't think I am. I'm being rational. *Scientific.* Yes, I can see how in retrospect Stephen and I may not have handled this well. Yes, Mum, I know that you warned me, worried that I was overstepping the mark. But can't you see? I did it for the children. For their wellbeing. This is where we are, and I am sorry for my part in this mess. I really am. This is not how I wanted things to be either...'

Rose looked over at Maggie, trying to see if she could read the double meaning in Rose's words. No, this is *not* where she wanted to be. She wanted everyone to stop arguing with her and just see that her way was for the best.

'But for the children, for them, can't we do what's best? Do you really want to see them crying every day like they did when Maggie left? Dad? Do you remember – Emily had sore eyes from all her tears. Elliot's voice was torn to shreds from all the crying. I can't make them go through that again. Can you? Or you?' Rose looked at them, one then the other, and then she sat down and looked away from them all, out of the window. This wasn't *fair*. She and Maggie and Stephen had come to an agreement, an arrangement for what was best for everyone, and now Maggie and her parents were trying to undermine that. Maggie made bad choices time and time again and Rose was supposed to step aside and let her? No! What guarantee was there that she wouldn't make bad choices again? And destroy the children again? No. They deserved better, someone who wanted them, someone who had been there and would be there when they needed them always. They deserved *her*.

The room fell silent. The atmosphere was thick with thoughts unsaid and the only sound was the tick from the clock and the slight squeak of the springs in the sofa as Bill fidgeted on it. The air was scented with the aroma of coffee, cooling untouched on the table. Maggie chewed her lip. Elizabeth played with her wedding ring, twisting it anxiously, looking from Bill to Maggie to Rose. It was she who broke the silence.

'Now, love.' She looked at Rose, who glanced up at her sulkily and then away again. 'You too.' She looked at Maggie, whose jaw was set in a hard line. 'Rose. You are a wonderful mother to the children, that's true. And you and Stephen, you work well together, I can see that, however unsure I was at first,' Elizabeth said conciliatorily. 'No one is saying that you can't continue to be one of their parents, to look after them and live as a family with Stephen, in some way. We're just asking – is *this* the right way to continue now that Maggie is back?'

Maggie opened her mouth to speak but thought better of it.

'We've had a long talk with Maggie,' Elizabeth continued, 'about how she was feeling back then, why she left and how things have been here since. She knows that we didn't approve of how things went after she left but accepts that we were all in freefall. We thought we'd lost her. Every day was filled with uncertainty and fear that the phone would ring and that would be it. Every time there was a knock at the door, my first thought was always, *is this it?* We couldn't lose you, Rose, and the grandchildren as well. We just couldn't. We'd already lost too much.'

'Grandparents don't have rights over and above the parents either,' Bill said. 'If we'd gone against Stephen, we wouldn't have been able to see the kids and that, we couldn't do that.' His eyes grew watery and he coughed to clear away tears before they fell.

'I'm sorry,' Maggie whispered.

'We all are, love, we all are.' Bill squeezed her hand harder.

'You're *both* our daughters and we love you equally,' Elizabeth said. 'We may not agree with what either of you have done, or the choices either of you have made or what we ourselves did or didn't do, but it doesn't change that we love you. Both of you. As parents, we have to do the best we can for our children.'

'That is my exact point,' Rose said with a calm that belied her inner fury. 'That's what we need to for Emily and Elliot now. Telling them the whole truth would destroy them. Maggie, you and Dad, you don't get what you want because it isn't about *you*, it's about *them*. And I know that you all love Emily and Elliot, and that you love them enough not to do this to them.' Rose nodded, smiling gently as she hammered her point home.

Rose went to the window and looked out, blocking out the room behind her. She ran her hands over the leaves of the huge plant by the window, giving the others time, unobserved, to come round to her way of thinking. They would, Rose knew it.

'She's right,' Maggie said suddenly, as everyone turned to look at her in shock.

'Love, you don't have to do this,' Bill said.

'I do,' Maggie said sagely.

Rose turned to face her, trying to work out what game, if any, Maggie was playing. It was exhausting trying to second guess her all the time. They had never been like this as children, they were always each other's shadows, always supporting one another. Rose was unused to her sister being her enemy. Everything felt wrong, but any other way meant the destruction of the rest of her life and she was not going to let that happen.

'Rose has earned the title of mother. She has. I accept that. I know that I cannot come back in and pick up where I left off. That isn't fair on anyone. Especially the children. If Stephen and Rose feel that this aunt suggestion is the best way to go, then we have to give that a chance.'

Maggie walked to Rose and stood next to her. They looked like chalk and cheese, the only similarity the grim expression on their faces.

'More lies?' Bill said.

'Perhaps,' Maggie said quietly, 'but Rose is right. I don't want to upset Emily and Elliot's lives. I don't want them to associate me with sadness. I just want them to know me. I want to be part of their lives and know that they are safe and loved.'

'Exactly, thank you,' Rose said, hope beginning to spark in her once more. She had convinced them that she was right, that this was right. They could do this. It was the only way that would work. She knew it, Stephen knew it and now, finally, her parents would see it too. How could they continue to reject it if Maggie herself agreed?

Bill sighed and said no more.

Elizabeth stood. 'Come here, you two,' she called.

She wrapped her arms around them, and the trio stood, holding each other. Elizabeth and Maggie closed their eyes. They looked peaceful, content. Rose looked at them. Did Maggie really agree? She seemed... guarded? Rose couldn't be sure. She was going to have to take a leap in the dark and hope beyond hope that her sister wasn't planning to stab her in the back.

22

The high street was crowded as they tried to navigate their way to the shops, people Christmas shopping already. They had to swerve around people who were ambling slowly, gazing in the store windows. Rose nearly tripped over someone who had got too far away from their dog but had its lead stretched across the width of the pavement. The woman looked at Rose with disdain as they passed. Rose worked hard to bite her tongue. She had not slept well in recent days, the stress and worry of the tightrope she felt they were all walking on had been getting to her and she found it hard to switch off at night. She was not in the best of moods. Emily and Elliot both needed new shoes and Rose was already annoyed about that.

'We'd only *just* bought your pre-school shoes and now they don't fit!' Rose said exasperatedly.

'Shopping is boring,' Emily sulked.

Rose sighed. 'Yes, I know, it's boring for me too, darling. And expensive. That's why I don't really want to do it twice!' She forced a laugh.

Maggie didn't comment. They were struggling to find who

Maggie could be around the children. Any way she tried to reach out to them made Rose feel threatened and it spoiled the atmosphere. Rose knew that she had to try to let Maggie in, but she couldn't relax enough to do it. She had asked her to come along on the trip, partly as she knew the kids would be better behaved with another adult there but also to show that she *did* want this to work. Maggie *could* be a part of the family under Rose's scrutiny.

'Let's just get this done and then maybe we can go somewhere fun afterwards, hmm?' Rose suggested, trying to lighten everyone's mood. If the kids were grumpy before they even set foot in the shoe shop, then this was sure to be a disaster and Rose wasn't sure her nerves could take any more.

'Yes – perhaps I could treat you all, a little fun afterwards,' Maggie said, brightening. She looked at Rose, perhaps hoping for some nod of approval, but Rose couldn't find it in herself to comply. She was trying too hard to squash down the feeling of resentment that Maggie had set Rose up as the dull parent vs herself as the fun one. This wouldn't work if it was always going to be a competition. Competitions had losers and Rose wasn't prepared to be one of those.

'I don't like them,' Emily said, turning up her nose, surrounded by boxes of previously rejected shoes.

'Why not?' Rose asked a little too sharply. 'They seem fine to me, and they fit well. What's wrong with them?' Rose could feel her patience wearing thin. She didn't want to have to do this and especially not in front of Maggie.

'They hurt.'

'Where?' Rose enquired, then added, 'So we can work out what we need to change.'

'And they feel too big, no, too small,' Emily whined. Clearly fit was not the issue.

'Do you just not like them?' Rose asked, exasperated.

'No.' Emily crossed her arms.

Rose tried to keep her patience. She had planned a lovely family day together. After shoes, they would have lunch in a local café and then Elliot could nap in his pushchair while Emily let off some steam in the park. Arguing with Emily over four pairs of as-good-as-identical black leather shoes was not what she had in mind.

'I've got an idea,' Maggie said, finally joining in, having given no input or opinions until now.

Everyone, including the exhausted-looking shop assistant, looked at her with hope on their faces.

'Why don't you get your sensible shoes and then you can each pick a pair of fun shoes as a gift from me?' Maggie suggested, beaming at them all. 'I did some sewing repair work for Laura's neighbour, he paid me in cash,' she explained to Rose, who was surprised at Maggie's sudden ability to be generous. She obviously had no idea just how much shoes cost.

'Yay! You're the best!' Emily shouted, running towards the wall of overly decorated, mostly pink, shoes. Elliot picked up some trainers that lit up when you walked. Shoes that Rose would never have agreed to buying.

Rose sucked in air through her nose and let out a breath.

Maggie's faced dropped.

'Well,' Rose said, nodding her head slowly, trying to calm the resentment that was surging in her. *Maggie is trying to help. She is trying to find her feet. I have to let her in somehow if I want to keep her onside. Aunts spoil their niblings. That's what I did when they were little. Let. It. Go.* She closed her eyes for a moment. Then she opened them again, determined to be positive.

'What a lovely idea! Thank you, Maggie. You've saved the day!' Rose said, deciding to be grateful that the battle of the shoes was over. Being rescued from hell by her sister getting her children gifts was not the worst outcome. She would be reasonable. This was not strange behaviour from an aunt, nor from a sister. This was normal. They all needed some normal.

'I don't know about you, Maggie,' Rose said as they walked out of the shop, 'but after all that, I could do with a drink!' She smiled and took Maggie's arm in hers, like old times. Rose's heart lifted. She *had* missed Maggie.

'Great idea,' Maggie agreed, flinching at first and then taking Rose's arm as well. 'Kids, do you fancy a drink? I thought I could treat us all.' She looked nervously at Rose, aware that deference to her was necessary.

Rose smiled. 'That'd be lovely, thank you. Then I'll get us lunch. Did you have anywhere in mind?'

'I did, actually,' Maggie said almost sheepishly. 'Is that café still here? The one we went to as kids. The one with the insanely good milkshakes. They could try one maybe?'

Rose wrinkled her nose while she tried to recall. 'Hmmm... Carrington's? I think so. Did you want to go there? It's a bit scruffy.'

'But we loved it, didn't we?' Maggie pressed.

Rose had to admit that they did. She had fond memories of being told off for blowing milkshake through her straw at her sister, especially the time that she had missed, and it had landed in the hair of the lady sitting behind her. There could be times like that again, memories for the children of happy days with their mum and auntie. She wanted that for them, for herself. This *could* work, it *was* working. Stephen and his reticence, her parents and their concerns, they were wrong. Everyone was wrong. Weren't they?

'Okay, let's go there,' Rose said with a smile. As they walked, Rose felt herself relax. She was being paranoid. Maggie wanted this to work as much as she did.

They found the café eventually, after both of them remembered it being in a different street, having to walk from the first one to the next before finding it. The kids got impatient and grumpy, only just being placated with snacks.

Manoeuvring the buggy down the steep steps to the café, which was below street level, they had just sat down at their table with its sticky oilcloth table cover held down with metal clips, when Maggie noticed another customer, paused, and then waved. A lady with greying hair pinned up in a messy bun and wearing a warm tweed coat buttoned up, waved back and came over to them all.

'Mrs Murray!' Maggie exclaimed happily and she turned to the others. 'This is my old art teacher, from school!'

'Less of the old, please!' Mrs Murray laughed. 'Goodness, is that you? Maggie Richardson? And Rose? Gosh, you haven't changed a bit, have you? You barely look a day older than when I saw you at school!' the lady said, looking misty-eyed at the sisters.

Rose tensed immediately, a rictus grin on her face. What was Maggie doing? They didn't associate with people who knew them from *before*. What if someone said something?

Rose smiled politely, trying to place the woman in her mind. She did look familiar, but art was not a subject she excelled at in school and she had dropped it as soon as she had the chance.

'Ah, it's no wonder you don't remember me, I've aged more than you two, that's for sure,' she said. 'I never forget my students! You always had such talent, Maggie. And Rose, your flair for colour was wonderful!'

'I like drawing!' Emily piped up, wanting to join in the grown-up conversation.

'Do you, dear?' Mrs Murray said kindly. 'You know, I haven't seen you since you were a tiny wee thing!' she cooed.

Rose's heart froze. Her breath stuck in her throat. She knew Maggie from when the children were still *hers*? Had Maggie called her over on purpose, knowing that? Was everything going to go up in flames in the middle of a shabby old café that she hadn't wanted to come to in the first place? Rose felt on the edge of tears as her hands gripped the table tightly. She had to keep it together. If she was to keep this conversation light-hearted and brief, then she couldn't let her emotions slip, especially in front of the children.

'You were tiny, and your brother here was a tiny new baby. You were! You were wrapped up in one of those baby sling things on your mummy here.' She gestured to Maggie.

'You made such a lovely mother,' she continued, oblivious to the terror on Rose's face and the confusion on the faces of the children.

'Thank you,' Maggie said, hesitantly.

Rose looked at Maggie, her eyes indicating that she needed to shut this conversation down and now, but Maggie just smiled triumphantly. She was enjoying this.

'You had your hands full, that's for sure, but you were handling it beautifully, I remember that.'

'That's too kind of you, Mrs Murray, very kind,' Maggie said, nodding.

Rose knocked over a glass of water that had been left on the table. She had to do something. She couldn't let Maggie go on.

'Oh, gosh, so sorry, what a klutz I am!' Rose said shakily. She wanted to stand but her legs wouldn't work, and the cold water dripped onto her lap.

'Mummy, you're getting wet!' Emily said, jumping up.

'I'll get paper. Elliot, come on!' Emily said, keen to help as always, now her mood over shoes had dissipated, and she dragged her little brother with her before either shell-shocked sister could argue. Rose shifted to keep them firmly in her line of sight.

Mrs Murray looked from one sister to the other, confused, as Emily and Elliot headed towards the counter. Neither Rose nor

Maggie said anything and the silence that developed turned awkward.

'Well, sorry to interrupt your lunch,' Mrs Murray said. 'It was lovely to see you both and see your lovely children again.' She smiled and waved as she went back to her table and, from there, to the door.

As soon as she was out of sight, Rose whipped to face her sister.

'What the hell was that? What are you doing? I should have known you were up to something. You couldn't let me have this, could you? But even if you *do* want to ruin this all and tell the kids, *that's* how you want to do it? Using our old art teacher? Are you literally out of your mind?'

Maggie said nothing. Her mouth was shut. Her face blank. Rose could get nothing from her, no idea as to what she was thinking.

'This is not about you, Maggie. This is not about game playing or point scoring. You don't *win* by blurting out the truth. It's too complicated for that. Either you are on board with this, or you are not. Either you stay and deal with this or you go, somewhere, anywhere, and you never come back. Don't mess us about, don't mess me about and absolutely *never* play with the kids like that.'

'I can't help it if people remember the truth,' Maggie said, initially defensive, arms crossed. 'But no, I hadn't thought about how that might have been for the children.' Her shoulders sagged. 'I'm sorry. It felt good to be acknowledged, I admit that. I know that wasn't a good idea now. I won't do it again. It's just...' She paused, checking that the children were still out of earshot. 'It's a slap in the face every time I am reminded what I am not any more. It's harder than I thought it would be.'

'Do you want out? Do you want call it all off?' Rose said. Not sure whether that was what she herself wanted or not.

'No,' Maggie said quietly. 'I will fall in line, I promise. I won't let you down, I won't let the children down.'

'Again,' Rose said curtly, her point made. 'You pull a stunt like that again and I will kick you out of our lives faster than you can blink. This *is* the truth now.'

Her face brightened back into a smile as Emily and Elliot arrived back at the table with a roll of blue catering paper towels and started mopping up the spilt water.

'Who was that lady? Aunt Maggie isn't Mummy?' Emily asked, confused.

'She was our big school art teacher. She couldn't remember our names *then* and she's clearly got no better since!' Maggie laughed nervously. 'I mean, look at us, how could she have got us mixed up like that? Hey, Rose?'

Rose nodded. She wasn't capable of talking. Fear was still sitting on her chest, making it hard to breathe. She had thought that Maggie was about to ruin everything, right in the middle of the café, despite everything Rose had said to her. *Maggie still didn't get it. How on earth was this ever going to work?*

23

'Hello, darlings!' Elizabeth called to the kids, as she hurried into the room, her arms wide for her grandchildren to run into, as they always did.

'Granny! Grandpa! Auntie Maggie!' Elliot called as Bill arrived, followed by Maggie, who was nervous as to what her reception might be after the debacle in the café.

Was she welcome still? Rose had been so furious with her, had she taken it out on the children later? She hadn't seen any indication that Rose was anything other than a kind, dedicated parent. But she was lying through her teeth to them. Could both of those things be true side by side? God, this was such a mess.

Rose looked at her coldly but said nothing. Maggie was relieved that by not wanting to make a scene, Rose would by default give her a chance to make amends.

Bill affectionately ruffled the children's hair and handed them a chocolate lollipop, then made an exaggerated gesture of 'sshhh' as he smiled at Rose. She stood, arms crossed, a smile playing on her lips. Bill winked at her and she laughed.

'Thank you, Grandpa. Not until after lunch, kids, but then, yes, you may have them.'

'Yay! Thanks, Grandpa!' the children trilled and hurried back to a shape construction they were working on and Maggie noted happily that her gift had been a good one. She hung back, nervous. She had gone back to Laura's in tears and drowned her sorrows in a bottle of wine. Waking up with a monster hangover and full of regret, she had spent much of the morning in tears, which had left her feeling wrung out and exhausted. She didn't know if she could find the energy to be who she needed to be today.

'What if this is all a terrible idea?' she'd asked Laura as she handed her the box of tissues. Maggie took one, then another, to dab at her tears and blow her nose. Her face was red from all the crying, and she looked as crumpled as the tissue she dropped beside her.

'Which part?' Laura had asked, concerned but nursing too much a hangover of her own to be subtle.

'All of it. The plan to lie about everything – who I really am, what I want. What even is the truth now? There are so many lies all tangled up, I honestly don't know which way is up. Rose doesn't trust me, I don't trust her and the children aren't getting to know me as I'm not being myself. What's the point?'

'You agreed to this so you could keep tabs on Rose, remember?' Laura replied.

Maggie was grateful that the 'I told you so' that she was sure Laura was thinking remained unsaid.

'That's true. To keep an eye on Rose and work out how I can get my children back.'

'And?'

'Well, I still think that Rose's suggestion is insane and yet... she's a good parent. The children are settled, happy, confident. And Rose is in her element with them. I don't remember her being so happy with her life before. Stephen is obviously happy too. It's working for everyone.'

'Everyone but you,' Laura reminded her.

Maggie sighed.

She picked at the skin around her nails, which was torn and red and sore-looking.

'You want your kids, don't you?'

'I do, yes. But at what cost? And to who? Maybe I *should* go with this bizarre scenario, try to enjoy it, try to get to know the children again.' Maggie pulled her arms around her and curled up. This was not sustainable. Something was going to give. Maggie could feel it.

'Or maybe it's time to tell the truth?' Laura suggested.

'Maybe,' Maggie nodded. 'Maybe it is.'

Maggie dragged her attention back to the present as they sat at the long dining table, which was beautifully set for a family Sunday lunch. It would be the first time they had spent the whole day together since Maggie's return. They were all trying to be relaxed, but there was a smudge of tension in the otherwise perfect picture. Sitting around the table, they could have almost been in a TV advert. Three generations of a beautiful family – and an odd one out.

'I got a sss-tif-kit at school, Granny,' Emily chimed. 'For being kind!'

'Here it is – see?' Rose said as she brought another dish to the table, handing a brightly coloured cardboard certificate to her mother.

'Well done, Emily,' Bill said. 'Proud of you. And you too, Elliot. You are super kids.'

'They are that,' Stephen said, smiling at his children.

Maggie tried to smile too, but the relentless breeziness and positive conversation made it feel like only the canned applause from a studio audience was missing. It felt scripted. Rehearsed. Fake.

Maggie sat, quiet and removed. Being Auntie Maggie was exhausting. It took all her strength at times not to make comments that might give her away. She had to think through every word out of her mouth in advance, to check them, and that often meant that by the time she was ready to speak, the conversation had moved on without her. She was there but not there at all.

Rose glanced at her, a jangle of nerves only noticeable if you were really paying attention. Maggie could see the hard set of her jawline and she knew that the café debacle had not been forgotten. She looked at her sister, trying desperately to convey how much she regretted what she had done. Rose was unmoved.

'Can I get you a refill, Maggie?' Rose asked pointedly. Maggie had been absentmindedly sipping at her wine whilst the conversation carried on around her, and now she could see that she had drained her glass and realised that her head was starting to spin. Rose stared at her and Maggie could read her thoughts. *Don't mess this up. Don't get this wrong. Don't you dare.*

'Just water, thanks,' Maggie replied, trying to smile. She wanted to say to Rose, 'I'm trying, I really am.' They always used to be able to read each other. Before. Surely that part of the past could be regained. Maggie was realising that perhaps they really both wanted the best for the children, they were united in that, weren't they?

'Probably a good idea,' Rose said, pouring some water into a glass.

'Oh, Auntie Maggie, I did a drawing in my book,' Emily said. 'Do you want to see? Oh, is that okay?' she asked, suddenly concerned that she had got it wrong.

'It's your journal, my love, you can use it however you want. And yes, I'd love to see it. Please,' Maggie said, smiling.

When she had chosen it, she thought that it was exactly what she would have loved when she was Emily's age, and her heart lifted now at the knowledge that Emily loved it too. She was a good mother. She *could* be a good mother.

Emily came bounding back into the room, proudly holding the book with the rabbit and her mother on it, showing it for all those seated.

'Oh!' Elizabeth said unthinkingly. 'Your favourite book was just like that when you were a baby! Maggie read it to you over and over and over. We'd joke that you'd be a bunny if you could!' she laughed. Then she gasped and slammed her lips shut as though she could unsay the words that had already escaped.

The room fell quiet. Rose looked furious. Bill looked at his feet. Maggie tensed. The children looked around, nonplussed as to why the grown-ups were behaving so strangely.

'You mean Mummy?' Emily asked.

'Yes, yes, she does,' said Stephen briskly. 'You know how I get you and Elliot mixed up sometimes. Granny does the same with her children, I'm sure.'

'But that teacher lady said Auntie Maggie was Elliot's mummy too. He does look like her. I look like Mummy, but Elliot, he looks like Maggie, doesn't he? But he is my brother, isn't he?' Emily said, an edge of upset in her voice that made Maggie's heart break. What other questions might she be asking herself? What upset might they be causing?

'Yes, he's your brother,' Bill said, taking over as Elizabeth said nothing. 'He looks like his old granddad, that's why, and his old grandad is Maggie's dad too, aren't I?' He reached over and ruffled Elliot's hair as Rose gave Emily a hug.

Maggie didn't know what to do, where to look. She had to put her tongue between her teeth to stop herself clenching so hard that her teeth hurt. She tasted blood as she bit down on it.

'Funny Granny!' giggled Elliot and everyone laughed, grateful for the break in the tension.

'I just need to get some more drinks from the garage, back in a minute,' Rose said, a touch too sprightly as she disappeared out of the kitchen door.

'I'll help.'

Maggie pushed her chair back abruptly, following her.

Out in the garden, Rose stood by the flower bed, clenching and unclenching her fists. Maggie went to stand with her. Neither sister spoke.

A single jackdaw hopped across the grass, hopeful that scraps were about to be laid out for it. It moved in impatient little circles, until Rose kicked the grass nearby and hissed at it, sending it fluttering for the safety of the trees overhead.

'Greedy things, they are, pushing their way in. They frighten off all the little pretty birds,' Rose said. 'God, I sound about ninety.'

'You do.'

'I feel about ninety,' Rose sighed, shaking her head. 'I can't do this any more. I can't.' Her voice cracked.

Maggie had been expecting rage, but this quiet sorrow was somehow worse.

'Don't say that,' Maggie implored. 'Look, I'm sorry about the café. It won't happen again.'

'How can you guarantee that? I can't. *You* can't. You're unpredictable and it's too much. You clearly aren't okay with this and I cannot live my life on eggshells. It's not fair on anyone.'

Maggie felt fear creep over the back of her neck.

'Maybe... maybe we should just tell them the truth. Like a plaster – just tear it off quickly?' Maggie looked at Rose to try to gauge her reaction. The idea that she could be about to reveal her identity to her children made her sick with nerves and sick with excitement. They would be hers again.

'No,' Rose said quietly, shaking her head. 'You don't understand. This "plaster" is what helped heal the wound you left. Tear it off and you'll poke at it. No. I thought that you could be okay with things. That it might work for the children to have us both. But it's *not* working, is it?' Rose asked.

Maggie's stomach dropped as she began to understand what Rose meant. The truth of what she was saying. She would not be getting the children back. Not now, not ever.

'Everyone is on edge, nervous,' Rose continued, looking at her sister with defeat on her face. This was not what she wanted either. 'The kids are picking up on it. They know something's up, something to do with you, but they don't know what. Emily had an almighty meltdown when I mentioned you the other day. She's not done that since she was a toddler. Her pre-school called me. Did I tell you that? Her behaviour has deteriorated. This situation is obviously affecting her.'

Maggie's mouth flooded with saliva. It was bitter and had the acrid tang of wine behind it. She was full of shame, and she was afraid. She couldn't speak. Rose wasn't done anyway.

'I thought it would be better for them, for all of us, for you to be here. They'd have an aunt back, more people to love them. But it's *not* better. Not at all. They like you, that's true. But they're nervous too, confused. You and I are playing tug of war with them under the surface and it's not fair. I thought we could make it work but...'

'But what? What are you saying?' Maggie's eyes filled with tears. She blinked them away.

'I don't want you to go. Despite all this shit, it has been good to have you, my sister, back. But this doesn't work. It's not going to work. You have to go, Maggie. You have to go and not come back. I'm sorry. Stephen was right. You need to go.' Rose's voice broke as she finished.

Maggie looked at her – was this play-acting? Was Rose manipulating her like she manipulated her parents and anyone else who got in her way? A wave of cold washed over Maggie. Whether Rose was genuinely sad about this or not, Maggie knew that she meant it. She was telling her to go.

Maggie was going to lose them all, all over again. She had been naïve to think that she could just step back into their lives and not cause a catastrophe. Yet how was this fair? She had left, yes, but she had kept in touch, she had just needed some time.

She needed to play Rose at her own game, had to show remorse instead of fury in order to convince her. She'd be more careful with the children than before to ensure they weren't upset.

'Please,' Maggie finally managed to whisper. 'I can't lose you all again, not when I can see how I should never have left in the first place. I know I made a mistake. And I'm sorry for that. I will forever be sorry for that. But I didn't make this mess all by myself. If you and Stephen hadn't lied to them in the first place, lied all this time, then there would be no untruth to try to keep going, would there? They would know about me, I could get to know them as me, as their mother.'

'Don't accuse me...'

'I'm not.' Maggie held her hands up appeasingly. 'I'm not, Rose. But that is the truth, isn't it? I made one bad choice to leave and stay away. You made one bad decision to pretend to be their mother when you weren't. Small lies, enormous lies. Everyone makes mistakes. Good people make bad choices sometimes. We've both made them. Haven't we?'

She had to convince her. She knew that even if Rose told them the truth, in *her* way, that there wouldn't be a chance in hell that the children would choose her over Rose and Stephen. She was on the back foot and had to play it that way. Rose wanted her to go. She had to stay.

'Please. Let us try once more. Give me one last chance. Neither of us are in the right here, not wholly, so let's not make it me versus you. We don't want that, do we?' Maggie begged.

'Isn't it me or you, though? Isn't that the point?' Rose said.

'I thought it was us *both*. For *them*.'

She had to make them let her stay. Then the decision about what best to do from here would be hers. Maggie closed her eyes. She told herself that she wasn't being deceptive, or manipulative. She just wanted some control. There had to be some way out of this mess, but Maggie was no longer sure what that might be.

Rose looked at her, uncertain and then looked warily back towards the house. Maggie saw the moment that the fight dropped out of her. She looked deflated, shrunken. For the first time, Maggie thought Rose looked old.

'I don't know. Every time, you promise, and every time you do something else.'

'I didn't say *anything*,' Maggie reminded her.

'Perhaps not today, no...' Rose crossed her arms.

'I've said I'm sorry,' Maggie said quietly. 'This is not my ideal situation either, but here we are. Mum and Dad are trying, but it is hard. It's going to take some time to settle.' She spoke calmly, all the practice she'd had in their childhood, persisting until her little sister gave in, staying forcefully calm against her rages, was paying off. She could see how much Rose wanted this crazy scenario to work, she just had to hope that her desire for that won out.

'I know, I know,' Rose said, her shoulders drooping. She looked exhausted.

Maggie held her breath. She really didn't want to create chaos, she didn't, not consciously.

'Fine,' Rose said. 'You have today to convince me. If you do as much as breathe in a way that I think isn't right, then I will personally pay for your taxi all the way back to Scotland. Don't think I won't, because I will. This is your very last chance. Think of Emily, of Elliot. Don't mess about with them. Do you understand?'

Maggie nodded. She exhaled in relief. She had come close to closing the door in her own face. She had to be better than this. She couldn't slip up.

Elizabeth popped her head around the door, looking sheepish.

'Girls? Lunch is going cold. Can I help?' she asked, a remorseful look on her face as she leaned out towards them. 'Sorry,' she mouthed at them silently.

'Coming,' Rose called and started back towards the door.

'Uh, Rose?' Maggie asked and her sister swung back round to face her.

'Yes?'

'The drinks? You can't go back without them. They'll wonder what on earth we've been doing out here.'

'Oh. Yes. Sorry,' Rose said, getting some bottles from the garage and handing one to Maggie to carry.

As they went back inside, Maggie could see how tired and thinly stretched Rose was. She recognised it because she felt the same. The only question was – who was going to break first?

24

Maggie sprawled on the carpet in the living room with Emily and Elliot. They were surrounded by books that had been read, Playdoh that had been squished, drawings that had been scribbled. After that Sunday where Rose had told her to go, Maggie had decided to take a step back. She was in this for the long haul after all, and pushing at Rose to get to the children had not worked, for anyone. It had been an upsetting shock to Maggie that her presence had been unsettling the children. This was about them, after all, and she had decided to remind herself daily of that. She had relaxed a little in Rose's company, no longer so worried that Rose was a danger to the children. The issue was no longer their safety, but their security. Maggie would have to choose her time wisely, if she wanted to re-stake her claim as their mother. A month had passed by without any slip-ups or drama and Maggie was beginning to feel that she had more solid ground to stand on.

It was still often tense, however, as neither Rose nor Maggie could wholly relax with each other. They still both wanted the children and they each had the knowledge required to tear them from the other, should they choose. It was a delicate balance, each hovering their finger over a big red button, in case the other looked as though they would be tempted to push it first and blow everything up.

Rose had left Maggie to it with the children, grateful for the chance to get things done in the house. She was in a cranky mood, having argued with Stephen that morning. Stephen had suggested they let Maggie babysit while he and Rose went out for lunch. Maggie had jumped at the chance, but Rose had felt it was too much.

'It's too soon. I won't be able to relax. I'm sorry, Maggie, but no.'

Maggie had been disappointed, but she bit her tongue. The idea had been raised, and not by her. If Stephen wanted to use her as free childcare, then she was fine with it – she'd have unsupervised time with her own children again. It would be wonderful. If she refused to take sides now, Rose might come round to the idea.

'Why not? She *is* their...'

'What? She is their *what*, Stephen?' Rose had demanded, her face turning an unflattering shade of puce.

'Their aunt.'

'Exactly. Who they don't know that well, and who doesn't know them well enough to look after them alone.'

'I disagree. I think you're being overly protective.'

'I think you're being careless!'

'I think you're...'

'Enough, Stephen. Look, go for your run, we can talk about it when you get back.'

As usual, Stephen conceded, and Rose went to the kitchen to cool down.

Maggie and the children returned to building a bridge with magnetic tiles. They'd been at it over half an hour when the children began bickering over how best to do it.

'Your way is rubbish!' Emily said, nudging her brother hard on he shoulder.

'Ow!' Elliot complained, before throwing a tile at his sister in esponse.

'Come on you two, that's not what I want to see,' Maggie replied kindly. She knew she was supposed to tell them off for fighting, but t was such a slice of normal family life, exactly what she had eared she would never experience, that it gave her a frisson of happiness just to be in the midst of it. Aware of being watched, she glanced up to see Rose in the doorway. Rose smiled at her, then ooked down at her watch.

'He's been a long time. Where has he got to?' Rose said, nnoyed but with concern creeping in at the edges. 'It's starting to get dark.'

'I'm sure that it's just busy in town,' Maggie assured her. 'Isn't here a football match on today or something?'

Rose agreed absentmindedly, not looking at Maggie, only half-listening what she said. 'I'll call him anyway. He could pick up ome more milk while he's out.' She took her phone out of her pocket, scrolled away a few notifications, then held it to her ear.

'Oh,' Rose replied as her call was answered. She pulled the phone from her cheek in order to check the screen.

Maggie caught the confusion on Rose's face. She mouthed, 'You okay?' at her.

Rose nodded though clearly unsure.

'I'm sorry, this must have misconnected. I, um... I was looking or Stephen. He...'

Maggie saw Rose's face as a possibility entered her mind. Her voice suddenly tinged with possessiveness as she demanded, 'I'm sorry, but who are you?'

Maggie got up from the children and went to stand next to her sister. Suddenly, all the colour drained from Rose's face. She looked deathly pale. Maggie went cold, something was clearly very wrong.

'Is this some sort of a sick joke?' Rose yelled into the receiver her hands now shaking.

'What's the matter?' Maggie asked.

Rose shook her head, not listening to her.

'No. No, this isn't funny. You put him on the phone now, please Now,' Rose insisted.

Maggie took Rose by the shoulders.

'Let me?' she said, taking the phone from Rose, who offered no resistance. Rose stood still, ashen-faced and shivering.

'Hi. This is Maggie, I'm Stephen's... I'm his sister-in-law. Can you tell me what's going on, please?' she said, the calm in her voice belying the tremor in her hands.

She listened to the chaos from the other end of the line. Wherever Stephen or his phone was, something dramatic was clearly going on. It was difficult to hear the woman talking, she seemed traumatised.

'I'm sorry, I didn't catch that. Could you say it again?' Maggie asked, trying to keep calm despite the dread spreading through her veins.

'Oh, God,' the woman on the phone said, sounding shaken 'God, I'm so sorry. I'm sorry. There's been an accident. A car, he ran out, I think... God, it's... the ambulance is on its way. I just... I just answered this because it was ringing... I think. Sorry... I think he might be dead. I think, I think he's dead.'

Maggie's heart stopped. She gasped in a breath and held her hand out for Rose. Rose took it. Her hand was frozen. Emily and Elliot stopped what they were doing, and looked up at them both wondering what was going on.

The woman shakily explained what she had witnessed, the distant siren becoming louder as the ambulance approached and then the noise of radios and paramedics and police as help came to the scene. It wasn't entirely clear what was going on, but it was clear that it wasn't good. That even the best outcome was going to be bad.

A different voice came on the line.

'Hello? This is Dave. I'm a paramedic. We're going to be taking...'

'Stephen... Stephen Fairfax,' Maggie repeated into the receiver.

'... Stephen to A&E now. Can you come there immediately?' Dave asked.

'Yes. Yes, we're on our way now. Thank you,' Maggie agreed before hanging up and taking Rose's elbow, guiding her out of the room and away from the children.

Rose was breathing erratically. She held onto the kitchen table to keep herself upright when her legs suddenly crumpled beneath her. Maggie reached out and held her up.

'Rose... Rose, look at me. There's been an accident. It seems Stephen didn't see a car and he stepped out into the road. He's been hit, and from what I can understand, he's been hurt quite badly. We have to go to the hospital, and we have to go now. Do you understand what I'm saying to you? We have to go *now*. Gather up your things, I will round up the children and call us a taxi. We have to go to him now.' *While we still can.*

Maggie paused, trying to find the balance between keeping her sister calm and impressing on her the seriousness of the situation.

'Go... go!' Maggie urged as she went back to Emily and Elliot.

There wasn't time to concoct a story and the children needed some truth in their lives. Now was not the time for fairy tales.

'Kids?' she said, and they turned to look at her, innocent faces expectant. Maggie's calm wobbled. She took a breath.

'Your daddy has been in an accident and we need to go now and see him at the hospital. Emily, put your shoes on, please. You too, Elliot, I'll help. We have to go as soon as we can.' Maggie nodded at Emily, who nodded back gravely, immediately understanding that now was not the time for questions. The fear on both of their faces made Maggie want to retch. She swallowed the feeling and went to get her things.

By the time the taxi arrived, everyone was ready and waiting to step into it. Everyone was silent, too caught in their own worries to speak.

'A&E, please. It's urgent,' Maggie instructed the driver.

'You all right?' he asked, concerned either for their welfare or for that of his upholstery.

'We're fine,' Rose snapped.

'It's her husband,' Maggie replied, hoping that the driver would accept this and just get going. He turned back to the wheel, started the engine and pulled away from the house.

Rose was pallid and muttering under her breath. The children were scared. It felt as though no one dared as much as breathe. How badly was he hurt? Was he going to be okay?

Maggie smiled at Emily, and Emily smiled a doleful smile back. 'We will be all right. Together,' Maggie said, and Emily cuddled up to her, holding around her arm and bringing it tight next to her. She was old enough to be perceptive but still young, too young, to carry the fear that resonated inside the thin walls of the car. *I will carry it for you, for all of you*, Maggie promised herself. *I will not fail my children again. Not ever.*

The car pulled up outside A&E and they stumbled out. Maggie stood, immobilised, as she recalled the last time she was here. That night. That awful night, when she had set in motion the events that had ended up with them here, *now*. Had she caused all this? Was even Stephen's accident her fault? The row between him and Rose before he left had been about her. Had his mind been elsewhere when he stepped off the kerb?

Rose took Maggie's arm and pulled her and the children into the reception area. She was desperate for confirmation that everything was all right. Maggie wanted to pause, for fear that all was far from it.

Inside the hospital, it was eerily quiet. There were only a few people waiting to be seen. A few were milling around, and the reception area had one member of staff catching up on paperwork, surrounded by files, manila-coloured folders, and piles of paper. The space smelt clinical. Chemically clean, mixed with the scent of fear.

Maggie ushered Rose and the children to the seated waiting area and approached the desk. The lady looked up and removed her reading glasses.

'Can I help?' she asked.

Maggie hesitated, unsure of what to say.

'Hi. Yes. My... brother-in-law was brought here this evening. He's been in a car accident, a road traffic accident. We were told to meet the ambulance here by the paramedic. Dave? Oh, his name is Stephen Fairfax,' Maggie explained, scanning the woman's face for any clue as to how he might be doing, but her face was expressionless.

The woman placed her glasses on her face and slowly, calmly, checked the records on her screen. Maggie's mind wandered briefly. Was detachment a skill that you brought to the job or did working amongst life-changing situations de-sensitise you to it, like working in a strongly scented shop? Eventually, your brain stops registering it.

'Hmm... yes, here he is.' She looked up at Maggie, a kind expression on her face. 'I will get a colleague to come to you as soon as they are able. They took your brother-in-law straight through. Let me see if we can find you a room to wait in.'

She motioned to a passing colleague and they conferred briefly, before the cheerful-looking nurse in spotless scrubs, hair pulled back off her face, ushered them all to a private room to the side of the main waiting area.

Maggie's heart sank.

These were the rooms used to give people news that they did not want to hear. No one got the all-clear in rooms like these and you could practically smell the grief lingering in the airless space. Emily sat between Rose and Maggie; Elliot sat on Rose's lap. The fear on everyone's faces had registered with him and he crawled up as far as he could onto his mummy's lap, trying to ignore the trembling of her body as she held him tightly to her. Maggie reached out, squeezed Rose's arm and took Emily's hand into hers. They sat like this, a chain of fear and hope, when a doctor in white shirt and grey skirt, stethoscope draped around her neck, entered the room followed by a kind-looking nurse.

'Hello. I'm Dr Greenwood. I've been looking after Stephen, your...' She scanned from Rose to Maggie, trying to discern who to focus her conversation on.

'My brother-in-law. This is his wife, Rose, and his children, Emily and Elliot.' The lies slipped from Maggie's lips with an ease that shocked even herself.

'Hi, Rose,' Dr Greenwood smiled politely. She turned and gestured to the nurse, 'This is Nurse Michelle, if you wanted the children to go and have a play while we talk, I hear she knows where the best toys are,' she said in a way by which the adults in the room knew what she really meant.

Emily clung on tighter to Rose and shook her head.

'No,' Rose said, her mouth in a flat line, 'no, they can stay here. Thank you, though.'

'Are you sure?' Nurse Michelle said in a concerned tone.

'Yes.'

Nurse Michelle nodded sympathetically, met eyes with Dr

Greenwood and walked from the room, closing the door quietly behind her.

Dr Greenwood turned back to them all. Despite her practised attempt to hide it, Maggie saw the moment when she steeled herself for what she was about to say.

'As you know, Stephen was in an accident with a car. Witnesses say that the collision took place at a high speed and I'm afraid he was very badly injured. He presented with severe internal bleeding on arrival at the hospital. He was seen straight away...'

Maggie immediately noted the past tense the doctor was using, and she felt the core of herself fall away.

This couldn't be happening.

Rose was shaking so badly now that Elliot got off her lap and moved across to Maggie. She scooped him up and held him close. She then did not let go of Rose, nor Emily, nor Elliot. Not for one second.

'We worked on him for a long time, trying to stem the bleeding, but I'm afraid his injuries were too severe. I'm so sorry, but I'm afraid that Stephen has died.'

There was a moment of shocked silence and then, quietly at first, there came a whimper that grew into a keening sound, a howl that burst from Rose, her face white and her body shuddering. She turned and was violently sick into the wastepaper bin beside her.

The children cowered into Maggie, who was calm despite her shock. She hugged the children to her, tight as she could, not wanting them to feel the panic that was clear in Rose. They needed reassurance now. Stephen was gone. Stephen was dead.

'You will be okay. I'm here. You're safe,' she whispered to them, kissing their heads and rocking them slightly as she had done when they were babies.

'So...' Emily managed to squeak out. 'Daddy is dead?' she asked, looking from the doctor to Maggie and Elliot and glancing

at Rose before snatching her eyes away, scared. 'He's... not alive an
more?' she said, not really asking a question.

'I'm afraid so,' Dr Greenwood said kindly, practised at givin
such news but still clearly moved by having to do so. 'He was to
badly hurt in the accident, and we couldn't fix him. I'm so sorry.'

Emily buried her head into Maggie's shoulder as her tear
came, her little body racked by her sobs.

'Daddy, I want my daddy!' she cried.

'I know, my lovely, I know,' Maggie said gently, stroking her hai
to try to offer some crumb of comfort. She felt her own hear
breaking as she watched Emily's heart crack.

Elliot was quiet and motionless, as if he didn't understand full
but was scared all the same.

The doctor looked up at Maggie and added, 'We will nee
someone to formally identify him.'

'I can do that,' Maggie said.

The doctor nodded. 'Thank you. Someone will come to get yo
for that in due course. I will come back to answer any question
unless you have any now?' she asked.

Maggie shook her head.

'Thanks.'

'Take as much time as you need,' Dr Greenwood said, as sh
discreetly picked up the bin and left the room, closing the doo
gently behind her.

The room was heavy with grief. Rose had stopped crying. Sh
was rocking gently in her chair.

'No, no, no. No! No, no,' Rose whispered angrily, as though b
denying it she could somehow make it not true.

What should they do now? What were you supposed to do? N
one knew. No one moved.

Maggie sat with her own thoughts for a moment. Her husband
the father of her children, a man she had loved then hated, wa

dead. The children had lost their father. Their family would never be the same again.

Maggie realised, with horror, that this was what she had been planning on wreaking on Emily and Elliot, albeit not in quite the same way. But still tearing their mother away from them. Looking at them now, feeling their pain as if it were her own and wishing beyond anything that she could take it away from them, she did not know how she had ever thought her plan had been a good one.

Maybe some lies are just too big to undo.

'Rose?' Maggie whispered.

Rose had fallen silent, slumped in her chair staring at the floor. She was breathing deliberately trying to calm her ragged breaths. Maggie reached out to touch her.

'Rose?' she asked again, gently.

Rose started at the touch, then looked up. The distress on her face was palpable. She looked like a shattered mirror, like she would never be quite whole again. Seeing her baby sister in such profound agony was like a punch to the guts. Rose stared back at Maggie, lost, angry, defensive. She needed someone to blame and, at that moment, Maggie wasn't sure that she hadn't chosen her as the target.

Wordlessly, Rose opened her arms and Emily and Elliot rushed to her. Rose encircled them, creating a family bundle where their tears came freely.

'I love you. I love you two,' Rose said, again and again, as though she was trying to cover them in so much love that they were somehow protected from the pain.

Maggie sat and watched, feeling on the outskirts once again, whereas she had been part of them only moments earlier. She could never quite be in that innermost circle. She had forfeited her place in it and she had done it to herself. Her own grief flared up – *I am not family yet. Not who they want* – before Maggie pushed it away again. The children had Rose, and Maggie found herself grateful that they had that, even if it couldn't be her.

Suddenly, without looking up from the circle, Rose opened her arms again and waved her hands to indicate that Maggie should join them. Maggie knelt on the floor in front of them and wrapped her arms around them all, bringing the four of them together.

'I'm so sorry,' Maggie whispered as she rested her head gently on Rose's shoulder. Maggie knew that she shouldn't have felt her heart lift at this moment, only minutes after learning of the death of her husband, of her children's father, and yet, despite the grief and sorrow, Maggie couldn't help but feel happy at being included with all those she loved.

After a long time, Rose pulled away. She wiped tears from her face and from the faces of Emily and Elliot. Then, red-eyed and broken, she turned to Maggie.

'So, what do we do now?' Rose asked.

25

Rose wasn't asleep when she heard a gentle knock on the door, before someone pushed it open and came in. In the darkened room, she was curled in a ball under the duvet, one hand on the space where Stephen should have been. She had tried getting up earlier but hadn't been able to find the energy. Once she had heard Maggie get up with the children, she couldn't bring herself to move. Despite worrying about what Maggie might be saying to them, Rose knew they were being cared for, as Maggie had done in the few days since Stephen's death.

'Rose?' Maggie said quietly. She placed the breakfast tray she was carrying to one side and sat down on the bed. 'Are you awake?'

Rose was aware of a hand gently resting on her shoulder, giving her the smallest of nudges. She didn't move. Her brain was telling her to sit up, but her heart asked: what was the point?

Maggie got up from the bed and went to the curtains. She pushed them aside and opened the window a little. The morning was breezy, and the cool air wafted into the room, giving it a life that it had been missing before.

'Come on, Rose, you need to eat. I've brought you tea, toast, fruit, juice. Just try something. Please.'

From the warm and safe cocoon of the bedclothes, Rose could smell the inviting aroma of hot buttered toast. Her stomach growled at her. She tried to remember when she had last eaten but nothing came to her. Her stomach growled again. She wriggled out from under the duvet and sat up, pushing her wild bed hair away from her puffy face and clearing her throat, dry from hours of silence and raw from crying.

'Thanks.'

Rose allowed Maggie to place the breakfast tray on her lap. She then watched her as Rose took one bite of toast, and then another.

'That's better. I was starting to think you'd waste away.' Her bedside manner slipped a little, reminding Rose that she still didn't really trust her.

Rose shifted and took a sip of tea. She wasn't sure whether to speak or not. She had so much bottled up inside, so much she wanted to say, but was *this* Maggie, the one sitting in a room that was once hers, her sister or her rival? Rose couldn't decide. She took another sip of tea and decided to risk it.

'I'm scared,' she said. She could feel the hot stab of tears at the back of her throat. 'I'm so scared, Maggie. How do I do this without him? How do I help the children through this grief? Again.'

Maggie winced. 'I'm here this time.'

'I keep forgetting. I forget he's gone, and then I remember, and it punches me so hard in the stomach I can't breathe. I wake up and remember. I go to tell him something and then I remember I can't.' Rose fell silent.

'It doesn't seem real. I get that.'

'What if this was my fault?' Rose whispered.

This fear had plagued Rose time and time again in the days since the doctor walked into that room in the hospital. She had tried to rationalise it, to explain away the guilt, but found that she could not. There was a reason. Someone had to be to blame.

Maggie sat up straight and turned to Rose. 'What do you mean? Your fault?'

'Karma,' Rose replied, as though this was obvious. She hadn't said a word to anyone about how she felt, how she tortured herself in the small hours of the morning, when she was awake and alone. To say it out loud now made it real. *How would Maggie react*? She was terrified that if she spoke the words that she wanted to, that Maggie would leave her, if not the children.

Rose looked at her and saw glimpses of her sister looking back at her. She could see that Maggie wanted to believe her but was struggling to do so. Rose had to speak the truth, aware that it had been a long time since she had done so.

'Karma. You left. You left me holding everything together for you and it felt like you did it without a backwards glance.' Rose held up a hand at Maggie, who had opened her mouth to deny this. 'Wait. Please. Let me. Please.'

Maggie nodded, acquiescing.

'I struggled. Stephen, he struggled. We had no idea what had happened and yet over weeks, months, it all started to feel like it was meant to be. It felt awful to admit it, but things worked without you there. I felt that you had left them *for* me, not that I was taking them *from* you. And when Emily, then Elliot, started calling me Mummy and Stephen and I, we... we became husband and wife, it all slotted into place. It felt like there had been a mix-up and the wrong sister had been in the wrong place and now, everyone was where they should have been. And yet.'

Rose stopped. She was still lying to herself. She knew it had not been the right thing.

'And yet,' she continued, 'there were glimpses, especially in the early days, when I would think I'd see you somewhere, before you slipped into the crowds, or a wrong number called, and my mind would automatically think it was you. Times when you were very much here despite being gone. From how difficult Mum and Dad found it, from how some friends walked away, I knew. It wasn't right. The universe, if you want to call it that, was not happy. And now? Now, this is my payback. I sent him on that run, I...' She broke down. 'I loved him, I love him, Maggie, and he's gone.'

'Oh, Rose...' Maggie said, pulling Rose to her.

'I know he was yours first, but he was *mine* and we were *right* together, our family was perfect. What the hell am I going to do now?' Rose broke away and curled right up on herself. The rawness of the grief rippling through her body hurt so much that she felt like her sinews were tearing apart from her bones, as if she were literally falling apart.

'Stephen's death is not your fault, Rose,' Maggie said firmly. 'I can say that because I had the same thought. What if I'd caused this somehow? But then I realised that no, bad things just happen sometimes. Not because we deserve it but because that's *life*.'

'Are you not going to pay me back, then?' Rose asked, a hint of bitterness in her voice.

'What do you mean?' Maggie asked, confused.

The implications ran through Rose's mind as sickness rose from her stomach, sitting sharply at the back of her throat, sour and painful.

'You could take everything from me,' Rose said, almost defiantly.

'What?'

'The kids, the house. Stephen and I talked many times about the practicalities, but it always felt wrong to do anything. His Will still names you as his sole heir. He was not my husband. He was yours. This house is not legally mine. It's yours. The children are not legally mine either. I gave up my job to become a full-time parent, I left my flat. I have nothing. I am entitled to nothing. It's *all* yours.'

Maggie looked shocked. Clearly none of this had occurred to her yet.

Rose closed her eyes and tried to still her racing heartbeat. She was now entirely at the mercy of Maggie, who, as Stephen's wife, estranged or not, would inherit everything. And when she did, she could choose how to explain this to the children. Rose had taken everything from her. Would Maggie now take it all back?

'And?' Maggie finally said.

'And are you going to take it from me?'

Maggie paused.

'Let's see what the solicitors say.'

Rose felt cold. *That isn't an answer.*

26

Maggie stood at the kitchen sink, allowing her mind to wander through all Rose had just told her as she cleared away the breakfast dishes and finished the washing up. The morning outside was sunny and beams of sunlight flooded through the windows into the kitchen, specks of dust dancing in its rays. Her grandma had once told her that they were the souls of lost loved ones, only seen in the sunlight because of all the joy that they held. Maggie smiled at the thought.

The shock of Stephen's death had made one thing crystal clear to her. She did not want to break up the family again. She couldn't cause any more hurt. Despite Rose telling her that legally she had every right to do so, she did not want to oust her sister and reassert herself as Emily and Elliot's mother any more. It was not what they needed from her.

She had been angry beyond words with both of them, but she'd never wished for this. Stephen dead and Rose broken. Never in a million years. If she insisted on the truth now, she would break everyone all over again and she couldn't do that. She loved them. That was all that mattered now.

Life is so full of *ifs* and *buts* and *what ifs* and *maybes*. If you allowed every possible scenario to play out differently in your head, you would surely drive yourself mad. Life happens – how you deal with it is the only thing you *can* control. Maggie knew that she couldn't undo the past, she couldn't bring Stephen back or reclaim the time that she had lost. But she could control what she did from here.

Rose came downstairs and into the kitchen. She had got dressed and brushed her hair, but despite looking more put together than she had done since Stephen's death, her face held the expression of someone walking to the gallows.

'I need to find all the paperwork. I need to start getting things in order,' Rose said, with barely any energy behind her words.

'Would you like me to look for you?' Maggie offered. After all, the legalities affected her as much as they did Rose. She dried her hands and came to stand next to Rose.

'Would you? I can't bear to be rifling through his things, I just can't.'

Maggie nodded and made her way to Stephen's study.

It felt strange to be in there by herself. This had always been his domain. It reflected him – spotlessly tidy, everything in its place. The room smelt of him too, of the cologne he had always worn after Rose gave it to him one Christmas. Maggie had hated it, as her pregnancy hormones had made her retch when she smelt it, and still he had refused to stop using it. 'You'll get used to it,' he had said. She hadn't, and the hint of it still in this space made her feel nauseous.

Where would he keep his Will? The children's birth certificates and their marriage certificate, Maggie had kept in a hat box in their bedroom. Domestic. But all the household things, the deeds, the mortgage statements, he had insisted on dealing with. Business. Even these elements of his life he had kept separate.

Maggie shifted a few of the boxes on the shelves and flicked through their contents. Lots of documents about energy suppliers, bills neatly filed in date order. A whole folder dedicated to work done on the house, trades quotes and invoices. She understood why people went paperless – there could have been half a forest of paper here and no search engine to help pull out the document she needed.

As she moved one of the boxes placed further back on the upper shelf, something caught her eye. A scruffy-looking brown envelope stuffed behind it. Far back out of her reach. Hidden. It was out of place in the immaculate room. Maggie stood on the desk chair to reach it, stretching out and hoping not to lose her balance as she closed her hands around it. She sat down on the chair, opened it and looked inside.

Letters.

It felt as though someone had punched her, hard, in the stomach, knocking all the air out of her. She couldn't breathe.

Her letters.

Maggie flicked through them, checking the postmark for the date. They were all here, in date order. Some opened, some not.

Clutching the packet to her, she walked more calmly than she would have expected back out to the kitchen, where Rose sat at the table. She turned to her as Maggie came in.

'Did you find anything? Maggie... are you okay? What's the matter?'

Maggie, wanting to catch Rose's true reaction, simply stood over her and emptied the contents of the envelope onto the kitchen table. Letter after letter fluttered to the surface, settling like drifted snow.

When the package was empty, Maggie crossed her arms and looked at Rose, demanding an answer.

Rose looked up at her, bemused.

'What are you doing? What are all these?' she asked, nonplussed.

'Look at them.'

Rose did as Maggie asked, picking up one and then another, reading the address, clocking the postmark and then, as her hands began to shake, she opened one that had been read, and scanned its pages to see for herself. Her eyes widened as she did so. When the recognition fully hit, she turned and looked at her sister.

'Your letters...'

'My letters. All of them. Each and *every* week. Just as I'd said.'

Maggie looked at Rose, reading her reactions, seeing what she was thinking as it etched itself on her face.

'You didn't know? You didn't know,' Maggie said. First a question and then, on seeing Rose's face, a confirmation. She really had not known.

The lie had been Stephen's alone.

'How did you not know about these? Every single week, how did you never see any of them?'

'No... I... no. Stephen, he used to get the post from the outside post box on his way in every day. It was just one of his jobs. The bins, the post. I had no reason to...' She stopped. 'Why? Why would he *do* that?'

'To get what he wanted? A wife and mother for the children.'

Maggie first wanted to be cruel, to say that it didn't matter to Stephen who it was, her or Rose, but having seen them together, she wasn't wholly sure that was true. Besides, kindness was what they all needed now. He was gone, he couldn't explain himself and Maggie had her proof that she had stayed in touch. What else was to be gained? Everyone had lost so much, what was the point of losing any more?

'And specifically you. He wanted you. And if I was coming back, then he might not have got you.'

'We were supposed to be a team. Us. Together. And he kept this from me?' Rose said, her eyes still red from crying over him, filling with tears of a different sorrow.

Maggie kept silent, wanting to allow Rose the chance to speak.

'I'm... I'm so sorry, Maggie. I... I thought you were lying about the letters. I thought it was just so convenient that you'd written and yet we'd never received anything. Like a get out of jail free card you were using. It... it never even occurred to me to question Stephen about it, despite questioning you and Ailsa. I'm sorry.'

Rose looked like a child again, like the little sister that Maggie had grown up wanting to protect. Her heart opened up to her.

Maggie nodded. 'It's okay. I didn't trust you either. I assumed someone was lying but I didn't know who. I couldn't trust either of you.'

'What have we done?' Rose whispered. 'I'm so sorry.'

Maggie sat next to Rose and took her hand. It was cold. Knowing now that Rose really had no idea that Maggie was alive and planning on coming home cemented a decision that had been growing in Maggie's mind since the day Stephen died.

'We need to talk,' Maggie said.

'Okay,' Rose replied, as the remaining light drained from her eyes.

'The kids are in the garden with Mum. They're planting some flowers. I think she's planning on talking about new life and things enduring. She thinks it might help. She's found some information on grief counselling for children we could arrange for them. I think that's a good idea, don't you?'

'Hmm,' Rose nodded.

I have to get this out. If I don't say it now, I'll lose my nerve. This is for the best. For them. For all of us. I know it is, Maggie thought.

'The children are yours, Rose,' she said sincerely.

Rose opened her mouth to speak but then paused. She looked

shocked. This was obviously not what she had expected to hear and she needed time for her brain to catch up.

'Really?' Rose whispered, bewildered.

Clearly, she had not believed Maggie all those times that she had promised she would step aside, not really. Well, this time, she meant it.

'They're yours. I can't and won't take another parent from them. Not now. I can't. I love them and I want what's best for them.' Maggie's voice wavered as she swallowed down the pain she felt. 'And that's you, as their mother. I won't take the house or the money either. It's all yours. I want nothing from Stephen. It should go to you and the children.'

Maggie felt heavy, and yet, as though a weight had been lifted.

'You don't know... this means... I...' Rose stammered before bursting into tears.

'It's okay. It's okay,' Maggie said, going to her sister and wrapping her in a hug. For the first time since coming back, it felt normal between them. Maggie was where she was supposed to be. Rose, too.

It felt right, honest somehow.

'The kids have lost too much already. They have gone through too much trauma in their lives. I can't knowingly add to that, not if I really love them, and I do. I do love them.' Maggie paused in order to give weight to what she was about to say. 'I love them enough to give them away to you.'

She took a breath. She had to be done with it and stop fighting. She could fight for them in other ways than this.

'Maybe I wasn't meant to be a mother. It never suited me. I was always fighting against it. I love them with all that I am but part of me was always trying to run away. One foot in the past, one in a potential future. *You* don't do that. Like you said, maybe this is how things were always meant to be.'

'Do you really mean it?'

'If I can still be important in their lives, then yes. I mean it. I will be their aunt,' Maggie said decisively.

Perhaps in order to keep my children, I have to give them away.

Rose said nothing and walked to the door, looking out at the children playing with their grandmother. She seemed unsure. This was not the reaction Maggie had expected. What was Rose thinking? How could she convince her she was genuine this time?

'Can we really do this? We've been trying but it hasn't been working, has it? Like we said, neither of us trusted each other,' Rose said hesitantly, looking at Maggie.

Maggie felt ashamed.

'It hasn't been working because I wasn't on board, not really.' She saw Rose wince at this confession. 'I wanted to be, but I couldn't. I couldn't see past my own pain. I was pulling in a different direction. I'm sorry. Now I know that you didn't hide my letters, now I know that Stephen was controlling the narrative? Now I trust you. I believe that you want the best for the children. And so do I. I mean it. They're yours.'

'God, we're both paying for our choices, aren't we? We're both losing something for making them.' Rose's voice wavered as she played with her not-wedding ring. 'But,' her voice lifted, 'I do think we can do this. If we pull together, you, me, our parents,' she sighed. 'You'll have to talk to Laura. I can't imagine she'll be pleased.'

'She will be if she knows I'm okay with it.'

'Do you mean this, Maggie? Really? Because I can't hold the children up again, support their grief again, without Stephen, even knowing what he did, and cope with all this. So if you are playing with me, then please, for whatever love you once had for me, please don't.'

Maggie hesitated before replying. She knew that it wouldn't be easy in the coming weeks. Yet she felt released. Her family would not abandon her as she had once abandoned them. The children loved her for herself, as their aunt. Rose knew and had accepted that Maggie leaving was a mistake, a mistake made for love. A mistake that she would willingly spend the rest of her days making right. Maggie would not fail them again. She would be better this time.

'They may never know the whole truth, but they will know that we love them. And isn't that enough?' Maggie said.

Maggie had to hope that it would be. It was all they had.

27

The mid-morning sun streamed through the living room window as Rose sat in quiet contemplation, drinking coffee. The children were enjoying cartoons, still in their pyjamas. Maggie was trying to read. It had been Stephen's funeral the day before and everybody was exhausted. The whole process had been drawn out by Christmas happening in the middle of it all and they'd had to cope with trying to create some festive magic for the children when no one had really felt like it. Again. It was all too much. The funeral had been a day to celebrate his life but with everyone trying so hard not to say the wrong thing, it was a million times harder than it could have been. Rose had seen how Maggie had struggled. Laura managed to keep her opinions to herself, though Rose knew that she was in disbelief over Maggie's decision to let the children go. Maggie had defended her choice when they'd rowed, and Rose had felt the balance shift. From Laura to her. Maggie was now on her team again. Blood was thicker than water and Laura would just have to accept that.

Rose still felt like a dandelion clock, as though one gust of wind would see her drift apart in all directions. It was an effort to bring her cup to her lips. She lifted her eyes to the room and tried to remind herself of all that she still had in spite of all she had lost. Stephen's absence filled the house, filled her mind, and it was hard to keep moving. It was harder still after finding that he had hidden Maggie's letters from her. Had she really known him as well as she had thought? Had she known him at all? It had been hard enough to feel her role as mother had been built on lies, the idea that her role as wife had been too was too much to bear. In the days since his death, Rose had clung to Maggie to keep her head above water when she felt as though she was drowning. Her grief was powerful and it threatened to pull her beneath its currents on a daily basis. Only the children and Maggie could keep her afloat.

Despite knowing the questions she wanted to ask him would forever go unanswered, Rose felt the weight of all she would never do with Stephen, never experience with him. It wanted to drag her under but she knew she couldn't let it. The children, living in their present, could not yet see all the days that they would miss with their father and so did not experience that loss in advance. Stephen would not see either graduate from university. He would not dance with Emily at her wedding. He would never hold any of their own children. These were a lifetime away for them. That he would not watch their successes, nor console them over their failures, would be heartache that they would experience later down the line. Rose could predict those future moments of grief and they piled up in her heart, sitting heavy on her immediate pain.

It was an echo of the time after Maggie had left, a gaping hole left by one so loved. Rose knew Maggie could see the connection between then and now, and Rose could feel her guilt. Rose felt her own guilt – how she was determined to keep Stephen alive in the children's memories as she had not done with Maggie. She could make a different choice now.

Breaking the silence suddenly, Maggie said to her, 'I've been thinking. We need a break, somewhere different. I was thinking Scotland, to the coast. To Ailsa. I'd like to take you all there. It's beautiful, it's peaceful. It's a wonderful place.'

Rose looked over at her. She wondered about the place that had fixed the broken pieces of Maggie, and who it was who had stopped her from walking into the sea. She wanted to know more about Ailsa, who had put her sister back together and helped send her home.

'What do you think? We could go for a weekend, a week, longer if we wanted. The kids need somewhere they can breathe. We all do.'

'Is there a beach?' Emily piped up, always listening.

'Yes, my lovely, it's really beautiful.'

'Can we go in the sea?' Elliot asked.

Maggie laughed. 'Well, you *could*, but it's still pretty cold this time of year. You might not want to. But you can put your toes in and see!'

Rose fidgeted on the sofa. She was wrapped up in a blanket as since Stephen's death she had struggled to keep warm. Her grief seemed to coat her in ice. She wasn't sleeping and she only ate because she knew she had to. Her days were like wading through treacle, through mud that had been partially hardened by the sun. It slipped itself around you and stuck you to the spot. It wouldn't let you free. She needed to break free.

'Why not?' she said softly. 'Sounds good.'

'Okay. We could go tomorrow even. I'll go and call Ailsa now,' Maggie said, heading off to find her phone.

* * *

Rose stared out of the train window as the ruggedness of the countryside flattened as they headed towards the coast. The journey there had been hard on Maggie, retracing the steps she had taken when on borrowed time, walking, zombie-like, towards an end. Now, returning with her family, albeit not the one she had imagined perhaps, she had to fight hard to keep her emotions in check. Rose had seen the tension in her rise and fall at parts of the journey but now, as they reached their destination, she could see that she was unwinding, relaxing. She was happy.

It was the end of a long day when the train pulled into the station at their destination on the west coast of Scotland. A solitary figure was waiting on the dusk-lit platform, watching the train come in, their eyes scanning the carriages for a familiar face. Maggie was jingling with nerves as she and Rose gathered up their things and woke the sleeping children. One, then the other, had succumbed to the lolling motion of the train as it travelled up the coast and had fallen asleep on each other, exhausted from the journey and the past few days.

They stepped out of the carriage and dropped their bags in a heap around them as the train sidled off, back to the main station. The woman on the platform did not approach them but gave them space to come to her. Time for the children to take in where they had woken up, time for the women to be ready.

Once they had got their bearings, Maggie turned around and walked towards the woman, her face in the shadow from the roof of the small station building. The woman reached out her arms as Maggie approached her and they stepped into a hug. Somehow, despite being the shorter by quite some inches, the woman held a commanding presence. Rose watched and saw her sister relax in a way that she had not yet been able to back at their house.

Maggie was home.

She brought the woman to stand by Rose and the children.

'This is Ailsa, everyone. Ailsa, this is Rose, Emily, Elliot.'

Rose nodded hello, struggling to look Ailsa in the eyes. She did not know how much Ailsa knew about her, but she knew that Ailsa knew everything about Maggie, and Rose felt vulnerable. This woman had opened her house to her and her children, but she didn't know if she would find judgement there. Grief had made her raw. She no longer had the protection that her thick skin previously afforded her.

'Rose, Emily, Elliot. Welcome,' Ailsa said.

Rose relaxed a little more when Ailsa gave her a wide smile as she ushered them all into her car, packing up their bags with a cheerful efficiency before slamming the boot shut.

'Well, lovelies, I hope you like our little town,' she said as she started the car and joined the road which wound its way down towards the sea. 'It is a beautiful place. It has calm in its air. All you have to do is breathe it in.'

She turned to the back seat briefly and smiled at Rose and the children. 'You're all welcome to stay, and to stay for as long as you want to or need to. You'll have to like dogs, though. I presume that Maggie has told you about Alan?' she asked.

'Your dog?' Emily said, her voice suddenly full of energy. 'What colour is he?'

'He's chocolate-brown, my dear, and he loves children!'

'I like dogs. Can we play?' Elliot added.

'Yes, of course, he'll be as happy to meet you as I am.'

Rose's tension eased a little further. Ailsa clearly was not going to be difficult to spend time with, despite knowing all the family's darkest secrets. Maggie was right – she judged no one.

'What's that gorgeous building?' Rose asked, turning on her charm, keen for Ailsa to see her as a good person, a kind one. Not a stealing, cheating liar.

'Och, that's the town hall. A local benefactor built it in the 1800s. It's local stone. It is very lovely. We're very lucky!' Ailsa replied proudly.

Ailsa turned the car around a corner and pulled up at what looked like the edge of a sand dune, the grasses waving in the breeze that swept in from the sea.

'Now then, the most beautiful sight around here is the water. If you look hard enough, you can see all the way to Canada from here!' Ailsa turned and winked at Emily, who stared in amazement at such a wonder.

'Shall I drop you here to see it and go back to get your things in, and you can walk yourselves back when you're ready?' Ailsa looked at Maggie and an understanding passed between them. Rose could guess at what it was.

This was it. The place where Maggie had nearly ended everything. This was what Maggie was nervous about. Rose wondered at first why Ailsa had brought them straight here, then guessed that she thought it best done and out of the way. She seemed very straightforward about it all. Rose watched as Ailsa took Maggie's hand from across the car and gave it a reassuring squeeze.

'Yes – let's,' Maggie said, a little too brightly. 'We can get our first holiday ice cream at the hut,' she gestured to a weather-beaten, brightly painted beach hut that served as a café, 'and then walk down to the beach. Kids? Do you want to? You're not too tired?' Maggie asked.

'They napped on the last leg, I'm sure they'll be fine, won't you?' Rose said.

'Yes!' Elliot jumped in his seat excitedly.

The car pulled away from them, back along the small winding streets that had brought them here. Maggie stood and looked at the ocean, before holding the children's hands, one each side, running gently with them down the sand dunes towards the water. They shrieked with laughter as the sand shifted beneath them, making them stumble as they ran, excited and happy to be free.

Rose held back, surveying the place. She was grateful that

whatever force had moved Maggie from place to place had steered her here. She could see how this was the place that had given Maggie the peace she had feared that she would never find again. Rose felt an optimism creep in. She was scared to acknowledge a future, a happy future, without Stephen, but perhaps this place could heal her and the children in the same way that it had healed Maggie. Perhaps it all really would be all right.

She wanted to believe that it would be, she wanted that to be true. Since Stephen's death, Maggie's behaviour had been more honest, more sincere and Rose's instinct told her to trust her this time in a way that it hadn't done before. Maggie, now knowing that Rose really hadn't lied to her about the letters, seemed more willing to work together with her.

Rose joined them all at the water's edge, putting her feet in the water that once might have taken her sister from her. Maggie stepped back to stand next to Rose, taking her hand in hers and squeezing it affectionately, giving her an honest and open smile.

'I missed you,' she said.

'I missed you too,' Rose replied, as Maggie released her hand and went back to playing with the children.

Rose felt a peace settle over her that she couldn't remember feeling in years. A sense of things being right. This could work. It *would* work. If they stuck together, then surely they could handle the bumps in the road that they knew would come. The children had been through a lot and would need them both on their side.

She looked at Maggie and was sure she felt the same. After so long feeling apart from her or against her, Rose felt their connection return. They were a team again, she felt sure of it. As sure as anyone could ever be. Nothing is ever guaranteed, Rose felt that keenly. The absence of Stephen would stay with her forever, but at least Maggie would understand.

There was laughter from Maggie and the children as she

showed them how to skip stones across the water, the heaviness of the rock somehow jumping along the surface of the sea. It was funny, Rose thought, how sometimes the rock you chose touched the surface and then leapt above it, whereas sometimes it sank without a trace beneath the waves, and until you'd made your choice and taken your throw, you never knew which it was going to be.

ACKNOWLEDGMENTS

This section is both the easiest and the hardest bit of the book to write. Many people have worked with me, helped and supported me in getting this book published and it wouldn't be here without them.

Firstly, to my agent, Marianne Gunn 'O Connor, who saw something in the earlier drafts and took a leap of faith. I will always be grateful for that.

To my lovely editor, Tara Loder, who guided me through the editing process and helped make the book a newer, better version of itself, whilst somehow also bringing it closer to the original idea.

To the wonderful team Boldwood, who brought their ideas and enthusiasm for getting the book out into the world and for making the experience such a lovely one. To my copy editor, Cecily Blench and my proofreader, Rose Fox for keeping me on the straight and narrow. To Aaron Munday for my fantastic cover design.

To the fellow writers who have helped and supported me along the long journey from idea to publication with feedback, advice and plot walks,-Gytha Lodge, Julia Laite, Rana Haddad, Will Dean, Beth Miller, Lee Weatherly and my wonderful Faber Academy group.

To Laura Morley, who encouraged me to start the very first draft and has been nothing short of amazing in her continued support since.

To my wonderful friends, in Cambridge and further afield, the Wonder Women, Clare Cordell, Leila Monks, Adam Garstone and my lovely book group, for listening to highs and lows with a patience, belief and encouragement that kept me going. I am lucky that I cannot list you all but I hope you know who you are.

To the Lucy Cavendish Fiction Prize, who by longlisting the novel in 2020, gave me the confidence to keep going.

To the Cambridge Literary Festival team, for their support, inspiration and encouragement.

To the lovely people of Book Twitter who make up a supportive community that I am proud to be part of.

To my family for believing in me and being on my side at every stage.

And finally, to those who I owe the greatest gratitude, to Malcolm, Beatrice and Madeleine, who have been with me every step of the way. I love you and am grateful to have you.

Thank you.

ABOUT THE AUTHOR

Alison Stockham has worked in TV documentary production for the BBC and Channel 4, and is now the Events Coordinator for the Cambridge Literary Festival. Her debut novel *The Cuckoo Sister* was longlisted for the 2020 Lucy Cavendish Fiction Prize.

Sign up to Alison Stockham's mailing list for news, competitions and updates on future books.

Follow Alison on social media here:

 twitter.com/AlisonStockham

 instagram.com/astockhamauthor

 facebook.com/AlisonStockham-Author

ALSO BY ALISON STOCKHAM

THE

Murder

LIST

THE MURDER LIST IS A NEWSLETTER DEDICATED TO SPINE-CHILLING FICTION AND GRIPPING PAGE-TURNERS!

SIGN UP TO MAKE SURE YOU'RE ON OUR HIT LIST FOR EXCLUSIVE DEALS, AUTHOR CONTENT, AND COMPETITIONS.

SIGN UP TO OUR NEWSLETTER

BIT.LY/THEMURDERLISTNEWS

Boldwood

Boldwood Books is an award-winning fiction publishing company seeking out the best stories from around the world.

Find out more at www.boldwoodbooks.com

Join our reader community for brilliant books, competitions and offers!

Follow us
@BoldwoodBooks
@TheBoldBookClub

Sign up to our weekly deals newsletter

https://bit.ly/BoldwoodBNewsletter